The Lyme Conspiracy

Joseph J. Bradley

Black Rose Writing

www.blackrosewriting.com

ISBN: 978-1-61296-028-9

PUBLISHED BY BLACK ROSE WRITING

www.blackrosewriting.com

Printed in the United States of America

The Lyme Conspiracy is printed in Georgia

Reported Cases of Lyme Disease -- United States, 2009

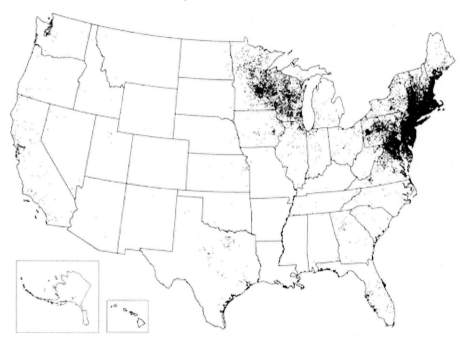

1 dot placed randomly within county of residence for each confirmed case

For Patrick DeFrancesco: a great friend and doctor.

ACKNOWLEDGMENTS

I would like to thank Dr. Dana Wiseman, Dr. Deborah Hoadley, and Dr. Pat DeFrancesco for all the information provided and help in fighting Lyme disease. I would also like to thank Randy Sykes for his contribution in researching Lyme and his continued dedication in the fight against this terrible disease. For encouraging me in my efforts, a big thanks to PHD John, Edie, Bud Peck and Jeff Cook from the only decent bar in our small town of Killingworth: Junes Pub. And finally, my wonderful wife, Yvonne, Miriam Gonzalez, and my children, Ryan and Taylor, thanks for all your love and support.

OTHER NOVELS

The Last Season
Ticket to Paradise
Bottle Park

josephjbradley.com

thelymeconspiracy.com

"True chaos, is when the people we elect to represent and protect us, are in fact killing us."

—*Joseph J. Bradley*

PROLOGUE

Every spring I put on my wool hat and wind breaker and walk down Breen Avenue where my house is located, and I make my way to the sound. It's a good thing that I live so close to the shore, because I don't drive much anymore. People are in such a hurry these days, driving so fast and beeping their horns. Last year I had a young girl cut me off, and then she gave me the finger, as if I was the one that did something wrong. I just waved at her and kept driving along in the slow lane. My vision isn't so good today and I tend to hit the brakes more than I should. My legs aren't as strong as they use to be, but I can make it to the end of the street, no problem. This year isn't any different from all the others and nothing much has changed here, except I'm noticing more rental signs perched up on window sills as I walk down the sidewalk to the end of the street. It seems to be taking me a bit longer this year. Maybe I should have worn my track shoes with the black stripes. I've had them for years and they've always added a bounce to my step.

Crossing the main beach road, Hartung Place, I don't cut straight across like the tourists do, invading people's property, I walk to the boat launch area at the end of the street and enter the beach through there.

Stopping at the beach's fringe, I squint at the bright sun in the morning sky and I watch the gulls scattered along the warming sand. As I stand peering out to the water, I see a few boats bonding with the tide, and behind them, the silhouette of Long Island New York. Soon the summer renters will arrive and cluster the area, and I'll have to put up with the people, and confusion, and loud noises at night. In the fall they'll go away and it will be peaceful again.

Every seventy-five feet or so, there are tall flag poles that run along the length of the beach, and today, old glory is flapping hard in the breeze. I don't remember when they put those poles up, but I'm glad they did. I always feel more comfortable seeing our flag flowing with a breeze. I notice that the old wooden bench isn't occupied, and I'm glad about that. Sometimes it's taken and my visit here is cut short.

As I sit on the oak bench looking out at the water, the warmth of the morning sun feels comforting like an old friend that is always close by when I need him. I don't have many friends these days. Most of them have passed on and all I have left are memories, but they are mostly good ones. It's a strange thing to outlive your friends, and every time I lose one, it's like an amputation. Someone once said that you realize you're getting older when you attend more wakes than weddings. I don't remember who told me that, but I think they had a valid point. I can remember the last wedding I went to, but I don't remember if I gave a gift. I think I have a year to send it along, but the statute of limitations might be up on that. My sister's granddaughter was married in New Haven - I heard she's divorced now. It seems that marriages fall apart a lot more often than they use to. I was married to my Alice for fifty-seven years, and I never once considered calling it quits. She was my best friend, Alice was. Let me tell you, she made the best roast beef ever, and you would never find a lump in her mashed potatoes. I miss her terribly and sometimes my heart aches when I think of her. At times when I'm sleeping, I'll reach over to her side of the bed to feel her warm body, and the reality takes a hold, and sometimes I cry. When I was a young man I used to think that crying was a sign of weakness, but I don't feel that way anymore. At times I feel that my tears are all I have left and they are what keep me connected to my past. Sure I have photo albums, but they are stored away somewhere in the attic. I don't remember where I put them, but they will surface if I need them. One day my great grandchild will blow the dust off them and turn the pages of my life, but will they really know who I was? Can a picture really tell us who a person was, or is that something that has to be told by a close friend or someone that really knew us?

When I was young, I used to be afraid to die, but I don't think like that today. Don't get me wrong, I don't want to suffer, but I'm ready to close the locker door for the last time. Sometimes I wonder if I'll see my Alice again, and all my friends and family that have passed on. I suppose that's a question we can't answer until we're gone, and then we can't tell anyone, because we're gone. I'd like to be the first to share the news; I would tell my daughter if I could. I wish I could spend more time with her, but she's busy with her life and her own family. Sometimes I feel like I'm a burden to her and she may be relieved when I'm gone, but that may just be in my head. I don't think as clearly as I used to and I know I repeat myself a lot, but I can't remember when.

As the birds are migrating north; as they do every spring, I'm sitting here turning back the pages of my life. That's what I have now, my memories. I've heard that when you get older the years pass by more quickly, but I don't believe that. I think the years pass by quickly your whole life. I think they tend to drag on when you're in a slump, and spin a bit faster when you're happy, but it has nothing to do with age.

I wish I could spend more time with my daughter, Linda. I think about when she was a little girl. She was so pure, so clean, and her eyes were always filled with excitement and joy. She grew up too fast. I wish I could have spent more time with her because those years I can never get back. They are the most important and cherished years of my life. I wish I could tell her how much they mean to me and how much I miss them. Sometimes when I think of those days my heart aches.

I never had a son and I don't fret over it. It would have been nice, but it wasn't meant to be. My daughter was enough for me.

She could swing a baseball bat just as good as any of the neighborhood boys, and shine in a dress that same day. She was something special.

I don't really care for Dick, her husband. He is a bridge engineer, but he doesn't have a college degree, so is he really an engineer? My son in law is one of those people that seem to have an answer for everything. Most of the time it's the wrong answer, but I don't tell him that; I just let him believe he's right. One day he'll realize how much he doesn't know, or he won't. I don't know how Linda puts up with him; she must see something in him that I don't.

My granddaughter, Kimberly, is a beautiful young girl. She just turned thirteen and she had her braces removed. She has such a nice smile, but she doesn't show it much these days. She has been sick for quite some time, and until recently, nobody knew what it was that invaded her body, but now I know. She is Linda's only child. Dick always talks about having a son, but it hasn't happened.

This beach, Old Colony Beach, is the best kept secret along the Connecticut shore. At least that's my opinion. It's small, yet wide, about fifty feet. It's nestled in a cove with rock peers at each end, like bookends. Every house along the beach is unique, no two are the same and that's unusual. Behind the capes, colonials and contemporary homes are the great elms and oaks of this old town. Every year they seem to be taller and that's probably because they are. I really love it here and so did Alice. I miss Alice today, and sometimes when I see a lone bird flying above, I think her spirit is in the bird and that she's waiting for me. I know that may sound foolish, but it's all I have to look forward to.

The walk back to the house isn't quite as exhilarating as it was when I started out. I guess it's like the flight coming home from a vacation. It's never as exciting as the flight going out. I can see my house as I approach and it looks the same as it has for twenty-seven years. It's a large colonial built of stucco, and I love it today as much as I did the day we moved in. Dick thinks I should sell it and move into a condo or something smaller. I think he just wants to secure an early inheritance. Well Dick, it's never going to happen. I'll die in this house.

CHAPTER 1
OLD LYME CONNECTICUT

As she opened her eyes, the room was pitch black except for a defiant green light illuminating from the digital clock located on the nightstand next to her bed. Once again, she was up before the sun and the annoying buzzing sound of her alarm clock. The bedroom was like a desolate cave not allowing for disturbances that might prevent her from getting a decent night sleep; most recently, it didn't help. Sweeping the sleep away from her eyes, she saw that it was five-thirty-two in the morning. Also on her nightstand was a glass of water, a cell phone, a gold shield, and a loaded 9MM Smith & Wesson semi-automatic handgun.

Rolling out of bed, she adjusted the blue cotton sweat suit bottoms that bunched up in an uncomfortable manner and she opened the bedroom door to let her cat in. Along with the opening of the door came a ray of light from the night light in the bathroom. She squinted as the cat pranced in acting as if he had been deprived of her company for an eternity.

"Morning, Dave," she said through a scratchy throat that hadn't felt its first cup of coffee. Circling her, he rubbed up against her leg, twice, and then leaped up onto the bed to retain her warmth and scent. The cat was named after the only man she have ever lived with and thought she was in love with. Dave had run off and moved to Florida sixteen months earlier, where he began his new life as a hotel manager. The day after he left entailed a trip to the SPCA to rescue a sleek, white, short haired male kitten, and she decided to name him after the man that abandoned her. After all she was used to the name, and her one way conversations with the cat would be in synch with what she had with the man in the final weeks leading up to his departure.

Her attraction to Dave had been more of an intellectual nature, than a sexual one. The times he did communicate, he was quick witted and funny and that seemed enough to make up for his lack of good looks. When he left, she was upset for about four months, and as she lost herself in her work, his memory dissipated with each passing day.

In the bathroom, she looked into the large rectangular mirror. Her face was average, she thought, with a small bump on the bridge of her nose where she had caught a bat in flight at a softball game when she was ten. Her teeth were sparkling white, but not completely straight with the eye teeth slightly protruding out. She remembered her father telling her that she had the most beautiful eyes of any girl in the entire world and she always found comfort and reassurance in his words. Dave had also reaffirmed this many times, but she knew it was her body he was most impressed with. She pinned her silky light brown hair up and began washing her face.

After finishing up in the bathroom, she pushed her way into the kitchen and made a half pot of coffee. Every other day she tracked a five mile run, but today was her off day for jogging and she wouldn't hit the street. Instead, she clicked on the television and watched the morning news. It was often in the morning that she felt so alone, because she and Dave used to arise together to begin their day with heavy coffee and light conversation.

Soon after Dave left she had come to the realization that she loved men, but she didn't always like them. Most of her dates proved fruitless with young boys disguising themselves as men. All of them wanted the same thing from her, and although she loved sex, it had to be with someone she felt a connection with, and until that person arrived, she was determined to abstain.

The three bedroom ranch she owned was perfect for her with an acre lot of dense woods surrounding the house and a backyard sprawling out to thirty acres of conservation land. In the summer time she could barely see a neighbor from the deck off the back of her house. It wasn't until the leaves fell that she would begin to notice the gray shingles of her neighbor's house peeking though. It was her house, cat, and job that kept her getting up every morning, and most of the time, she thought it was enough.

After eating a light breakfast, she fed Dave and made her way to the gym which was less than two miles away. After finishing a grueling workout on the machines, followed by forty minutes on the stair master, she showered and headed to her office in New London.

Entering through the rear door as she always did, she started down the long dull green hall passing several cops along the way. Some didn't acknowledge her at all, and others just glanced her way with a look of contempt. Unlocking the door to her office and stepping in, she briefly looked at the nameplate perched on her desk that read, Trooper Taylor Marshall. She closed the door behind her, shutting out the negativity in order to focus on her job as a homicide investigator in the major crimes unit for the State of Connecticut.

The office once contained two desks, but now it was only Taylor and her former partner, Trooper Trombley, was now situated at the other end of the office building. The complaint she filed against Trombley for sexual harassment did not sit well with her peers or her supervisors and she had been alienated ever since she came forth. Taylor was told she would be working alone until further notice, and this didn't bother her, but she was concerned if anyone would show up when she needed back-up.

Lunchtime already, she thought as she glanced at her watch. Having been tied to her desk and catching up on paperwork, she felt relieved that she was taking a bite out of the tall pile of manila folders stacked up on her desk. Most of it was preparing for court cases, writing reports, and studying witness interviews.

Taylor began heading down the street to her favorite restaurant, Soup to Nuts. Sitting at a table by the window, her friend Tara sat gazing out at people on the street as they scrambled around to get their fill before going back to their nine to five. The downtown area where her office was located was a two block clump of law offices, accounting firms, small businesses and restaurants. Tara called it a clusterfuck of suits and ties.

"Hey girl," Tara greeted her with a smile and a wave of the hand. An assortment of bracelets wrapped around her wrist sounded out like a set of rusty wind chimes.

"Glad to be out of the dungeon, at least for a half hour," Taylor said as she took a seat across from her.

"I know what you mean," Tara agreed. "It must be in the water or something. My boss has been a real asshole this morning."

"Tara, you work for a senior partner in a law firm. It has nothing to do with the water, more likely the blood."

"You have a point there, detective," she concurred. "Still getting the warm and fuzzies at your office?"

"More like the daggers and arrows," Taylor grimaced.

"I don't get it. What do they expect you to do? The prick verbally harassed you for months and they did nothing when you told them about it," she sighed. "It wasn't until he started playing grab-ass that they transferred his ass out, and now, everybody's pissed at you."

Taylor scooped up the menu from the table. "Welcome to the boys club."

"That's just plain wrong." The waitress came over wearing a bland face and took their order. Taylor wondered how she could make a decent living with such a poor attitude. She remembered working as a waitress when she was in college and she raked in the tips, always offering a smile and being pleasant and positive no matter how awful she felt.

"At least I don't have to work with Trombley anymore, but then again, nobody will work with me. It's like I have AIDS or something," she said as she raised her hands and began shaking them in a self-mocking skit.

4

"Don't sweat it, girl. You just do your thing and let the chips fall where they will and pray those bastards all come down with AIDS," she laughed. Tara had a contagious laugh and a spirit that Taylor found uplifting. They had lunch two or three times a week at the same place, and a couple times a month, drinks at Tommy's Tavern down the street.

Tara was divorced with a five year old son named, Tanner, and she had recently landed a boyfriend named, Reggie, that she tolerated because he was secure and good to her son, but she didn't love him. She wished it was different because he was a good man and a potentially good catch, but there wasn't any chemistry on her part. She knew it was just a matter of time before their relationship would end. The fake headaches and excuses of being exhausted were wearing thin.

Finding men was not a problem for Tara. She was very attractive with smooth brown skin, long black braided hair and a beaming smile. She loved to dance, whether it was at a night club or in her kitchen, she was always dancing. A couple inches taller than Taylor, she stood five feet eight and she was slim, yet curvy. Tara's problem was the men she was generally attracted to, usually turned out to be losers. They were either pretty boys with emotional issues or bad boys without steady employment. Like a large and difficult puzzle, she just couldn't fit all the pieces together.

"You need to get yourself a man," Tara said with her eyes protruding out like some sort of cartoon character.

"Like the one you have?" There was a brief hesitation and they both busted out in laughter.

"Okay, I get the point; changing subject now," Tara said thinly.

"Are we on for Friday night?" Taylor asked.

"Yes. I can taste that Long Island ice tea now," Tara replied, rolling her tongue across her thick lips.

"I may have one of those myself," Taylor said with an escaping grin.

"Now remember, you're an officer of the law and you need

to set a good example for the community and all that."

"Oh I will," Taylor said. "I'm going to have two," they synchronized in laughter.

Lunch was light as usual with many jokes and little drama and that's how Taylor liked it. She looked forward to her time with Tara and they had become good friends in the three years since they met at the gym. Tara was her best friend and she cared deeply for her, and in time, she would prove just how much.

CHAPTER 2

Lieutenant Wayne Preston didn't bother to knock on Taylor's door; he opened it, popping his head in as she sat working behind her desk. "We have a fresh one in Old Lyme," he advised. "Trooper Paul Board is on the scene." He slapped his palm on the door jam. "It looks like an asphyxiation and robbery."

"In Old Lyme?" she asked with a look of surprise.

"That's what I said," he roared, "now get over there right away. Sixty-five Breen Avenue." He shut the door and she immediately opened the desk drawer for her weapon. She had never had a homicide case in Old Lyme and she couldn't recall ever hearing about one. It was a quiet shoreline town with a very low crime rate except for drunk drivers and the occasional domestic disturbance.

When she arrived at the scene the first thing she noticed was how close the houses were together. It was a cute little beach community, she thought, that must have offered countless good memories for many people. *This is going to shake up their sense of security. If there was a disturbance of any real magnitude, the people that lived in the house next door would surely have heard something.* Sixty-five Breen Ave. was one of the nicer houses in the neighborhood and quite a bit larger than most of the others. It made sense to her that this particular house would be the target particular house would be the target of a robbery.

Trooper Board was standing on the front porch watching as she pulled up. They vaguely knew each other, yet word had spread to the resident trooper that Taylor was trouble and should be avoided at all cost.

"Hello Trooper Board," she greeted him as she opened the car trunk for her crime scene kit.

"Hey," he said with little enthusiasm, remembering what a trooper friend had told him about her making up some story of a sexual assault by a fellow officer.

"What have you got here?" She slammed the trunk shut.

"An eighty-four year old male found in the bedroom. A Mr. Harold Brown; he lives alone and it looks like a robbery gone bad," he added. "It appears as though he was strangled and the house was ransacked."

Taylor spied the area and saw several neighbors across the street in a huddle and talking in low voices. "Who reported it?"

He gestured toward a middle-aged woman wearing a yellow sweater. "The lady in yellow," he pointed, "she lives next door and when she hadn't seen him for a couple days she became worried because he lives alone," he said with a slight stutter. "She knew where he kept a spare key, so I went in and found him on the bedroom floor."

Taylor examined the trooper for a brief moment. He seemed a bit edgy, she thought. "Has anyone else gone into the house other than you?"

"No."

"Good job. Can you speak to the neighbors and find out if anyone heard or saw anything out of the ordinary?"

"Sure," he said under his breath and started toward a clump of people as she went inside. Upon entering the house, the first thing she noticed were the books. They were located everywhere, on the floor, the shelves and piled high on small end tables in the living room. It was apparent that the perpetrator was looking for something as he had rifled through the bookshelves leaving a scattered mess in his wake.

It was immediately apparent to Taylor that the victim was an academic of sorts. She quickly scanned a small corner bookshelf and read the title of one of the larger leather bound books, Advanced Biochemistry. She thought that he may have been a scientist or professor. Making sure she didn't touch anything, Taylor headed toward the bedroom on the first floor where she assumed she would find the body. At his age she figured he wouldn't sleep in a second floor bedroom because the trips up and down the stairs could be treacherous.

The body was positioned on the floor face down and turned to the left. The victim was wearing pajamas which indicated he was killed at night or early morning. Most educated elderly men are up, out of their pajamas and dressed, unless they are Hugh Hefner, she thought.

Other than the open drawers and closet being ransacked, she didn't see any signs of a struggle that would indicate he had a fighting chance with the perpetrator. Slipping on her latex gloves, she knelt down next to the body and pealed back the collar of his pajama shirt. She noted into her hand held mini-recorder that he had a half inch wide contusion around his entire neck area. By the degree of Livor Mortis, Taylor figured he had been dead between twenty-four and forty-eight hours. Extracting a metal tool that looked like a scalpel with a small hook on the end, she scraped under his finger nails allowing the remnants to fall into a small paper bag. Like many homicide detectives, Taylor used paper bags for evidence that might otherwise stick to a plastic evidence bag, therefore, making it more difficult to extract later on. By the marks on the base of his skull, it appeared to her that the perpetrator attacked him from behind with some sort of rope or cord, pulling it tight around his neck causing asphyxiation. Taylor searched the bedroom for anything that might have been the murder weapon, possibly a belt or necktie, but she came up with nothing. All items that may have been used were neatly hanging in the closet and she took all of them into evidence to be tested at the lab.

Taylor spent a couple hours inside the house trying to get a feel for who the man was and who might be responsible for such a senseless crime. *If the motive was robbery, why did they have to kill him? They could have knocked him out or simply tied him up and made off with his belongings.* She learned that he was a scientist with a PHD in chemistry and biology. He had graduated from Yale University in 1945, the year the Second World War ended. There were photographs of his family hung on walls and perched up on tables covering most rooms in the house. From the display of pictures, Taylor figured he has a daughter, granddaughter and a wife that is deceased. In his study, she noticed that the tower for his computer was missing; the CRT and keypad were sitting on the desk, but the hard drive was gone. *Why would a thief bother to take such a bulky item during a burglary?*

Another thing that troubled Taylor was an empty bottle of Rolling Rock beer that she located in the kitchen trash can. Inside his refrigerator was a single brand of Michelob beer and no other. *Where did the bottle of Rolling Rock come from?*

Before calling for the photo and print squads, Taylor noted down his number so she could do a phone record check and find out who he had been in contact with leading up to his death. After that she would speak with the neighbors and learn about his habits, any regular visitors that came by and any laborers he may have hired to work on his property. Once she was finished interviewing, she would compare notes with trooper Board. It was going to be a long couple of days.

As she walked out the front door, Taylor immediately noticed the media gathering across the street donning their attitudes and oversized cameras. Board, along with two other Troopers, was doing a good job keeping them at bay, but it wasn't going to be long before they would be releasing breaking news stories of the murder on television. Taylor wanted to keep the murder quiet until the family was notified. The last thing she wanted was his family to see it on the news while sitting in front of the tube and munching on popcorn.

Trooper Board was fending off Fox news reporters as Taylor approached.

"Detective, is it true there is fowl play in the death of Dr. Brown?" A good looking reporter asked as she thrusted her microphone forward, like a saber in a duel.

"No comment at this time," Taylor responded dismissively.

"Has the victim been positively identified as Dr. Brown?"

Taylor looked at her coldly. "No comment." She pulled Trooper Board aside. "I have called for photos and prints; they should be here any minute. Keep the vampires under control, and if you need any help, call it in to Lieutenant Preston. I need to contact the family and have someone ID the body. I think I'm finished here, so I'm heading over there now," she said, "I'll follow up interviewing the neighbors later on."

"Are they local?"

"Yes, they live in Killingworth. I found the information in his address book."

"Good luck with that," he said with a look that indicated he was glad it wasn't he who had to deliver the devastating news.

"Yeah, thanks. Anything good come from the neighbors?" she asked as she turned toward her car.

"Nothing, nobody heard or saw anything out of the ordinary."

"Alright, thanks for your help. I'll be in touch and we can compare notes." After taking one last look at the house and the press that was now growing like a pack of hungry wolves; Taylor got in her car and drove away.

As Taylor pulled up in front of the house, she saw a man splitting wood at the end of the driveway. He was dressed in a flannel shirt and blue jeans and he was holding a sledge-hammer that seemed to be too heavy for his chunky out of shape frame. She watched him work as she got out of her car and headed up his driveway; he placed the wedge on a log and tapped it a few times until it lodged into the center and then he came down hard with the hammer a few times until it split in half. Once she was half way up his driveway, he stopped and confronted her, as if she was selling something or was part of some religious cult.

"What can I do for you?" he hollered.

She didn't answer until she got closer. "Mr. Kasinski?"

"Yeah, that's right."

"I'm Detective Marshall with the state police." She reached out and handed him her card and shook his hand with the other. He didn't bother to take his leather work glove off.

After scanning the card he looked at her with curiosity. "What can I do for you?" he asked again, this time in a lower tone.

"Is your wife at home?"

"No, she's out, why?"

"Will she be back soon?"

"Yes, any minute," he said with a concerning look. "What's the problem?"

"Mr. Kasinski, her father is Dr. Harold Brown, right?"

"Yes. Is he alright?" He really didn't care, but tried to seem concerned.

"Where does her father live?"

"In Old Lyme, what's going on here?"

"Is his address 65 Breen Avenue?"

"Yes!" His agitation was apparent and increasing by the second.

"I'm afraid Dr. Brown is dead."

He felt instant relief. The house in Old Lyme is paid for and has to be worth over a half million, he thought. "Dead," he asked with a raised eyebrow. "How?"

"We really can't say until he's examined by a medical examiner."

He glanced at the car pulling up the street and turning into his driveway. "Here they are now," he said. "They're coming back from swim therapy for my daughter." He started toward the car as it came to a halt and he helped his daughter out of the car. She appeared to be a teenager and it became evident that she was disabled. Dick whispered into his wife's ear and Taylor noticed her change of expression; even from a distance she could see the concern on her face.

"Honey, help Kimberly into the house," she said and walked directly toward Taylor. Dick was practically holding up his daughter as she ambled to the door. She was a pretty young girl with a braided ponytail and thick glasses. A gray cotton sweat suit covered her one piece bathing suit and she wore casual slippers.

"Is my father alright?" she asked as she approached Taylor.

"Hello, Mrs. Kasinski. I'm afraid your father has passed away." Taylor reached out and touched her shoulder. The look on her face invaded Taylor's shell and settled in her heart. "I'm so sorry."

Her grief was cancerous. "Oh my God," she said appearing as though her legs might give way.

"Can we sit for a moment?" Taylor asked.

She didn't answer as she started toward the front steps, nearly collapsing, Taylor took her arm and guided her to the steps and took a seat next to her. "Where is he?" The crumbling words found her lips.

"He's at home right now. They will be taking him to the morgue to be examined." Taylor placed her hand over hers. "I'll need someone to identify the body."

Tears still had not found her and Taylor thought it was because the reality hadn't settled in yet and she knew that sometimes it took days or even weeks depending on the person, but when it hit, it came hard. "How did he die?" Her voice was scattered.

"We're not sure, but it looks like he may have been murdered." Taylor didn't want her to hear it from the media first.

"Murdered?" A spike of adrenalin forged through her. "What do you mean murdered?"

"It appears as though he may have been strangled during a burglary." Taylor caressed her back.

"Oh my God, Pop," she moaned.

Taylor thought she saw the woman age right in front of her. "Do you know anyone that might want to hurt your father?"

"No. He's eighty-four years old; he doesn't even go out that often."

"Are you up for coming in to identify the remains or should I ask your husband?"

"No," she spoke up. "I'll go, just give me some time with my family first."

"Of course," Taylor said. "I'll wait out here, take your time." That would allow some additional time for the body to be taken to the morgue, she thought.

As Taylor stood up and strolled back toward the driveway, her thoughts began to drift back to a time in her life that was so long ago, yet so very clear in her mind. The year was 1991 and she had just graduated from Northeastern University with a degree in Criminology. Summer had arrived and she was excited about beginning graduate school in the fall. Her only brother was in dental school at Georgetown and was working through the summer to get an early start of a long and prosperous career staring into people's mouths. Taylor had known what she wanted to do with her life since middle school, and there was nothing that would stand in the way of her becoming a police officer.

When she received the call that her parents had been in a car accident, she didn't know how bad it was until she arrived at the hospital. The hospital administrator wouldn't provide any details on the phone, and looking back, she now understood why. The information they offer regarding accident victims to family members is limited to avoid additional accidents as they drive to the hospital. Not long after Taylor entered the hospital, she learned that both her parents had been killed in a head on collision with a tractor trailer truck. The truck driver had fallen asleep at the wheel and veered into their lane colliding head on into their Ford Taurus, killing them both instantly. The sudden and tragic loss of both her parents had knocked her into a state of depression that lasted nearly three years. Taylor never went back to finish graduate school until six years later after she was already wearing the wide-brim hat of a Connecticut State Trooper.

Her brother had finished school and eventually started a practice in San Diego California. He told Taylor that people in California seemed to care more about their teeth than people in

Mississippi and they had more of them, so that's where he decided to settle down. Her brother, Carl, was the only family she had except a few distant aunts, uncles, and cousins, she never really knew. Taylor missed her older brother terribly and wished he had settled closer to her. The best she could do was to phone him once a week and get together with him once or twice a year. Carl had started a family and had a wife and a two year old girl, so most of their reunions meant her flying out to see him and his family. They seldom discussed the summer of 1991.

CHAPTER 3

The firing range was fairly quiet as Taylor stood alone with only one other person in the hall; a scruffy- looking middle aged man with a keg for a belly and a week old beard. She usually arrived early in the morning when the indoor range first opened its doors for business, and that way she would be assured to get a lane right away. State Police Officers had a special deal with the range owners; they could go for free and the tab was discounted and picked up by the state of Connecticut. Once a month Taylor would pop off a hundred rounds at, "On Target" shooting range with her service weapon, and occasionally she would practice with her Colt Python 357 magnum revolver. Positioned in the Weaver Stance with her left foot forward and the gun in her right hand supported with her left, Taylor exhaled and slowly squeezed the trigger. She did this until her clip was empty and finished by extracting the empty clip and placing it on the counter. Pushing the button that activated the auto-target retriever, she watched as the silhouette came into focus. She smiled as it rolled in about ten feet away and she could see her results. The paper bad guy that was pointing a gun at her had several holes in his head and the center of his chest. He was dead. She snapped the target off the holder, policed up her spent cartridges and cleared out of the room content with her shot groupings.

On her way to the office, Taylor stopped for a take-out coffee. She was dressed in her usual pant suit attire. Today it was a navy blue suit with a white button down shirt and black shoes. When working, she usually pinned her hair up, if she didn't, it would hang down to the center of her back.

As she walked into the office, Preston immediately intercepted her. "In my office," he commanded as he pointed down the hall.

"I'll be there in a minute," she responded with confidence. He didn't like that she didn't jump at his command. After stopping in her office and finishing the last of her coffee, she walked down the hall to Preston's office.

"Close the door," he ordered, "and take a seat."

She sat down and crossed her legs, looking him in the eye without speaking.

"Why did you leave the scene of the crime in the Brown case before the print and photo guys arrived?"

This is what this is all about? He really needs to find something to keep him busy. "I had to notify the next of kin before they learned about it from the media."

"Protocol is that the primary investigator is to secure the crime scene until all matters are concluded. This means prints, photos and body removal," he snarled. "You are the primary investigator."

"Look, I had three troopers securing the scene and they weren't letting anyone into that house except necessary crime scene personnel."

"Yeah, well it wouldn't be the first time that method has been breached," he snarled, "going forward you are not to leave the scene until the crime scene is completely processed. Am I clear?"

"And what about the family?" she asked contemptuously.

"You call me and I'll send someone to notify the family," he roared. "Do you read me, trooper?"

"Yes."

"Now, where are we in this investigation?"

"It looks like burglary gone array. The victim is an eighty-four year old male found strangled on the bedroom floor. It appears some type of cord was used and I think the perpetrator snuck up from behind."

"Any witnesses?"

"No."

"None of his neighbors noticed or heard anything?"

"No," she repeated again while quelling an itch behind her right ear with a quick scratch.

"Is there a possible murder weapon?" he asked roughly.

"No." *Is this guy deaf? I just said some type of cord was used and if there was a weapon I would know what type was used.*

"Great. We have an old man murdered in a quiet tourist beach community and we have nothing," he let out a twenty knot sigh.

"We're waiting on the lab results," she said. "I'm going to call over there this morning and see what they have. I'm also going to interview his neighbors again to see what they don't know they might know."

"Alright, there are a million eyes on this. We can't afford to let this one slip away. This guy was a well known and regarded scientist, you know?"

"Yes." *I'm going to learn more about Dr. Brown.*

"Get hopping." He pointed toward the door with the end of his nose. She walked out without saying another word. Preston made her skin crawl and she hated interacting with him and avoided him whenever possible.

The trip to the morgue had not been a very pleasant experience for Taylor and much less so for the daughter of the victim. Mrs. Kasinski had positively identified her father as Dr. Harold Brown, retired scientist. They didn't speak much about her father's past, but what she did find out was that he had worked for the federal government and retired twelve years earlier. She was his only child and he had a sister that lived in Hawaii that was a retired songwriter. Mrs. Kasinski agreed to meet Taylor at the house so she could help to determine what items may have been stolen. They were to meet at ten in the morning the next day.

"Taylor Marshall," she answered after her cell rang twice.

"We have prints," Marcus said. "They're ready for

processing."

"Great," Taylor said as she pulled the phone tighter to her ear. "Where did you lift them from?"

"We got them off the beer bottle," the lab technician responded with enthusiasm.

"Nice job Marcus. I'll be right down."

A half hour later, Taylor was in the lab waiting for Marcus to return from his break. She stood outside the laboratory peering in through the window. The door was locked and the room appeared empty and she was curious where all the lab technicians had gone. She had read that there were state employee layoffs and she wondered if the lab technicians had been affected, or maybe they were just short that particular morning.

"Good morning," Marcus greeted her as he appeared out of nowhere. Taylor was a bit startled and she quickly spun around.

"It's like a morgue down here," she said. "Where is everyone?"

"Just me this morning," he sniggered. "Ben is on jury duty and Karen called out sick."

"Okay, let's get the ball rolling." She gestured toward the lab door.

Marcus pulled the key out that was attached to a flexible cord; stretching it out he opened the lab door. He had to bend over a tad to perform the task because he stood six feet six inches tall. His long white lab jacket fell below his knees and Taylor wondered if he had to special order it at the big and tall store. The brightness of the jacket made his brown skin appear even darker. "I already scanned the prints into the computer and ran them for a match before I left for break. Let's see what, if anything comes up," he said, "I eliminated the victim's prints from the process, so there should only be prints that are suspect."

Taylor followed him to the computer and when he ran the mouse across the pad, the screen saver faded and a profile appeared on the screen. "Alexander Xavier Windows," she muttered, "white male, age thirty."

"It looks like he's spent much of his thirty years behind bars," Marcus said as he scrolled down.

"Yes it does," she said as she took control of the mouse; double clicking on his photo to enlarge it and get a better look at his profile. Scrolling down further, she began to peruse his criminal history. "It doesn't add up," she said. "All of his convictions were for burglary, uttering and theft." She moved down the page. "All of his crimes were of a non-violent nature."

"Well, maybe he finally graduated to the major leagues."

"Maybe," she said, "but it really doesn't fit his profile." Clicking the mouse she moved to the next page. "It looks like he was released from prison eight months ago."

"Yeah, he was convicted for conspiracy in his involvement in stealing government bonds."

"He only did five years for that," she said.

They kept reading until Marcus broke the silence. "That explains why. The inside person, Kate Nottingham, was the main culprit. She was a federal employee, he just helped her plan and execute."

"Hence the conspiracy charges," she said.

"Yup."

"According to his parole records he lives in Norwich."

"Not very far to travel for an arrest," Marcus said with a smile.

"No it isn't," she said through a grin. "Good work Marcus."

"Then how about dinner Saturday night?" he asked as his smile faded.

"Come on Marcus, we've been through this a hundred times. You're way too tall for me and too nice a guy. I'd just end up corrupting you."

"Please, corrupt me, corrupt me," he pleaded.

She laughed and hit the print button and walked over to the singing printer. "I do have a friend that may interest you," she said.

"Tara, right?" he followed.

"That's right. She's a sweetheart."

"Baby you know I'm only interested in vanilla."

"Maybe you should give chocolate a try for a change."

"Nah, I'll stick with what works for me."

"Well, this vanilla is sour right now," she said as she started toward the door. "Thanks again, Marcus."

"Anytime," he said as she walked out. He thought about what had just transpired and he knew he wasn't being completely honest. It wasn't so much that he prefers Caucasian women; he had a thing for Taylor.

It took quite a bit of convincing to get the judge to issue a warrant based on a finger print lifted off a bottle found in Dr. Brown's kitchen trashcan. He had many questions he wanted answered before issuing the writ. Was there any chance that the victim knew Mr. Windows and possibly invited him over for a beer? Was there another family member, house cleaning person, or maybe a maintenance man that invited Windows in for a beer?" He also brought up the possibility that the empty bottle was tossed into his yard by the suspect and the victim picked it up, disposing it in his trashcan.

Taylor had a bit of work to do in order to address the judges concerns, so she spent a couple hours with Linda Kasinski at her father's house. As far as his daughter knew he had never been in contact with Mr. Windows and he didn't use a cleaning service and hadn't recently hired anyone to do any work around the house. A neighborhood teenage boy did his yard work and seldom came in the house and he was checked out by Taylor and cleared. Linda went through the house recollecting some personal items of her father's that she remembered and Taylor took note of the missing items.

Linda told her a story of a man that spent his life dedicated to his work and family: a man of high integrity and character. He was a generous person that gave quite a bit of his earnings to charity and he often did volunteer work and published articles in researching cures for various diseases. After finishing his doctorate, he was recruited by the federal government where he spent his entire career conducting animal disease research. His wife, Alice, had passed away four years earlier and he was still having a hard time adapting to the loss. Taylor could tell by the way she spoke of her father that he was very dear to her and she was heart-broken over his passing and particularly in the manner in which he died.

With the information Taylor gathered from Linda, she went back to the judge the next day and convinced him to issue a warrant to search Alexander Window's apartment, personal belongings, and automobile. After a meeting with Preston, he insisted on choosing the team that was going to execute the warrant. He wanted two of his cronies in on the raid, so they could report back to him every detail of the operation. Preston was typically limited to his office, so he depended on several of his spies to keep him abreast of everything that was going on in the field.

A total of four troopers sat in a car preparing to hit the beat up duplex that he had registered as his place of abode with his parole officer. They were advised that Windows had been abiding by the conditions of his parole including: passing his drug tests, staying out of bars, avoiding the company of known felons and being gainfully employed as a dishwasher at a local Italian restaurant. According to his parole officer, he was a model parolee.

The crony in charge was Sergeant Cisner and he had his head so far up Preston's ass that all one could see was the soles of his shoes. He insisted that Taylor take the back of the house as he and the two other male troopers hit the front. Taylor didn't argue, even though it was her case she didn't want to put up a stink and have to endure listening to Preston blabber on about policy and chain of command. They exited the car and quickly shuffled up the street to the right side of the house where Windows lived. Taylor worked her way around to the rear of the dwelling and got into position. The team members all carried hand held radios tuned to a remote frequency that was exclusive for their mission. The plan was that they would hit the house from the front, not allowing Windows anytime to arm himself or destroy pertinent evidence. After crashing through the front door they would secure Windows and conduct the search. The team knew he was home because his automobile was parked on the street about twenty yards south of the rental property he lived in. Also, prior to moving into position, Cisner called his house and Windows picked up the phone; after hanging up Cisner gave the order to move out.

Taylor stood by the back door scaling the shingles of the house with her service weapon drawn and in the ready. Even though Windows didn't have a violent history, she knew he was now going to be in a desperate situation and might be capable of anything. She pictured the old man lying on the floor with dark strangulation marks around his neck and she wondered what could have gone so wrong that Windows resorted to murder. Listening to the whisper on the hand set, "let's roll" a loud bang followed and she heard the commotion inside the house. A few seconds later, the back door flung open and a blurry figure came bolting out. In a split second, Taylor saw that it was not one of the team and she reacted without hesitation. As Windows jumped off the stair landing, she was right behind him taking a three step plunge. Diving forward, she tackled his legs trapping his feet by pulling them in tight, like a pro football player. Windows came crashing down face first onto the overgrown lawn: surprised that someone had come out of nowhere to take him down. He began to squirm, trying and get away from her grasp, but she held on, crawling up his body like she was climbing a tree. Once she reached his upper torso, she stuck the barrel of her gun to the back of his head. "It ends now, Windows!" At that very moment, Windows body went limp, like an instantly deflated balloon. As she holstered her piece and reached to the small of her back to grab her handcuffs, the other troopers came running out to assist her. Taylor snapped the cuffs on, assuring them she had it under control. Even though none of the other officers commended her on the action, she knew she had done her job and felt really good about it.

In the bottom bedroom drawer hidden under a sweatshirt was a visa card with the name Harold Brown inscribed on the front. Also found in the inside pocket of a suit jacket hanging in the closet was a ruby ring that was similar to a ring Linda Kasinski had described to Taylor. Windows had his Miranda rights read to him and he was placed under arrest. As Taylor pushed him into the back seat of the cruiser, he began yelling obscenities at her, stating he was innocent and that they planted the items. Ignoring him, she closed the car door, happy that she had closed the case almost as quickly.

CHAPTER 4

When the phone rang, Taylor was sitting at her desk devising a strategy for her upcoming interview with suspect, Alexander Windows. He had been booked and processed and he immediately contacted a lawyer. Taylor had been waiting for the chance to interview him because it was a slam dunk case having his prints found at the crime scene and the victim's belongings recovered from his residence. Preston gave her a length of rope to work the case and he was hoping she would hang herself with it. She was determined not to do that.

"Detective Marshall," she answered.

"Hello Detective. My name is Gary Mitchell and I represent the New Haven Register. How are you today?"

"I'm fine, Mr. Mitchell, how can I help you?" The last thing she needed was a vulture bothering her and it was obvious in her tone as it traveled through the wire.

"It's my understanding that you are the lead investigator in the death of Dr. Harold Brown, is that correct?"

"Yes."

"I'm calling because Dr. Brown had contacted me six days ago asking me to meet with him and that would have been two days ago," he hesitated, allowing her to calculate the timeframe, "he never showed up at the designated meeting place because he was already dead a day."

He had Taylor's attention; she reached for her pad and pen. "What was his reason for wanting to meet with you?"

"He said that he had something very urgent that he wanted to speak with me about and he went on to say that I was the right person to expose the truth to the world."

"Please continue," Taylor said.

"I asked him to elaborate and he wouldn't go into detail. He just said it involved a travesty at the hands of the federal government."

"That was it, nothing else was said?" Taylor began gently tapping her pen on the clean pad.

"Only that we agreed to meet two days ago at 6:30 PM at Cherrystone's restaurant in Old Lyme."

"I wonder why he chose you?" she asked.

"That's what I'm wondering, because he said I was the person that should expose the truth to the world, whatever truth he was referring to."

"What exactly do you do at The Register, Mr. Mitchell?"

"Investigative reporting."

"And you think his contacting you has something to do with my case?"

"I don't know, however it is ironic that Dr. Brown called me out of the blue asking to meet him to expose something that has to do with the government and three days later he's murdered, don't you think?"

"Yes, it may also just be a coincidence. We have a suspect in the murder and a very solid case, I might add," she said. "Let me take your contact information and if something comes up I'll be in touch."

"Please do."

After Taylor took down his information, she finished noting down a few things for her interview with Windows and she headed out the door for a lunch date with Tara.

Tara had not arrived yet and Taylor sat thinking about the call she got from Mitchell. She thought it was strange that Dr. Brown had worked for the government his entire life, and now after all these years, he decided to become a whistle blower. When she had time, she thought that she would do some research into what he had actually done for Uncle Sam.

"Here's the superstar," Tara said as she approached and slid into the booth across from Taylor. "I'm impressed, it didn't take you long to find the bad guy that murdered that poor old man, did it?"

"It's not a done deal yet," Taylor said with humility, "Besides I had some help."

"Yeah right, who would help your sexual harassment complaining ass?"

Taylor laughed. "You are really on top of things pertaining to my life aren't you?"

"Who's got your back, sugar?"

"You do," she said without hesitation through a fixed facial profile.

"What can you tell me? Give me something juicy." Tara had an exciting look on her face, like a child sitting by the campfire waiting for a scary story.

"Come on, you know I can't talk about the case. Once he's prosecuted I'll tell you everything. Well, almost everything," she smiled. "So what's going on in your life?"

"I broke up with Reggie."

"You did not." Taylor was glad to hear the news because she knew it was a dead end for Tara.

"Yes I did," she gushed.

"How did he take it?"

"Not good. He pretty much begged me to reconsider, and when that didn't work, he got pissed off and threatened me."

"Threatened you, how?"

"He just said I'd be sorry, that's all."

"Be careful with this guy," she warned as she reached for the menu.

"I'll kick his ass if he comes around bothering me. I grew up in the streets." She made two fists and then turned them into a gang sign with her thumbs and index fingers extended.

Taylor laughed. "You're crazy."

"Like a rabid dog, I am." She showed her large teeth and growled before turning it into a smile.

The server came and took their order. They both had grilled chicken salads not realizing the threats Reggie had aimed at

Tara were very real.

Preston ordered Taylor to allow Sergeant Cisner to sit in on the interview with Windows and his attorney, making sure his man was there to report back to him everything that occurred. Windows sat hunched back in his chair like he didn't have a care in the world; wearing a light blue jump suit that was temporarily issued by the county. His brown hair was gel combed back and touching the sides and back of his collar. He had a tattoo on the left side of his neck with an Asian character written on it. Taylor wondered what it meant. Probably world peace or something of the sort, she thought. Window's eyes displayed nothing but contempt for the officers that sat across the table from him. Taylor noticed this when she pushed him into the cruiser after the arrest and she figured he was a person that blames the police, the judges, and society for all the problems he had endured during his lifetime.

His attorney, Jim Hatch, sat to his right and he was dressed in a light brown two piece suit with a yellow tie. His blond hair was thinning at the top and he wore a thin, neatly trimmed, mustache. Hatch had a short stack of paper in front of him, with his gold pen lightly gripped in his hand, he was prepared to take notes.

Taylor had come equipped with a recorder and she placed it on the table. "Are you ready?" she asked looking deep into the eyes of the killer.

Windows nodded his head and his attorney said yes. "This is Trooper Taylor Marshall and Sergeant Michael Cisner of the Connecticut State Police and we are interviewing Alexander Windows, and his council, Jim Hatch, is present." She looked back at Windows. "Mr. Windows, where were you on the night of April seventeenth two-thousand and one?"

He leaned his head in and Hatch whispered in his ear. "I was at home."

"Were you alone or was there anyone else with you?"

"I was alone."

"What time did you arrive home and when did you leave the

house?"

"I got home just after work and I stayed in all night until I got up for work the next day."

"What were you doing?"

"I was watching TV."

"What was on; what did you watch?"

He leaned his head in again. "I don't remember."

"Is it your testimony that you never left the house all night?"

"Yes."

"Mr. Windows, do you drink beer?"

Hatch whispered in his ear. "Yes."

"What brand?"

"Whatever's on sale." He smiled.

"Have you ever had a Rolling Rock beer?"

All questions were now answered after listening to his attorney. "Yes."

"How is it that your finger prints were lifted off a Rolling Rock bottle found in the victim, Dr. Brown's trashcan?"

This time he didn't listen to his attorney. "Because you fucking cops planted it there!" he shouted. Hatch grabbed his arm and spoke into his ear and he seemed to calm down.

"Do you know or have you ever met, Dr. Harold Brown?"

"No," he defiantly responded as he rolled his eyes.

"How did Dr. Brown's belongings end up in your apartment?"

"I don't know. You tell me?" He shot his head forward and his eyes burned into hers.

"Why did you run when we came to your house with a search warrant?"

The instructions from his attorney went on a bit longer this time. "I was scared and didn't know what was happening or who it was smashing in my door."

Taylor was curious as to what had happened to Dr. Brown's computer tower, but she declined to ask him about it. She was still checking pawn shops and her underground informants and didn't want to tip him off. She thought there were still a few things that didn't quite add up yet. *Why did he feel the need to kill the old man? Where was the tower? Why did he leave prints on the beer bottle, but no place else? Why is it that he had four Rolling Rock beers in his refrigerator when they served the warrant? Why was there only one Rolling Rock empty bottle found in Dr. Browns trashcan? Maybe the beer brands were a coincidence and maybe he killed Brown because he put up a struggle. The credit card and ring were both found in Windows apartment. He must be responsible for the murder.* Once the interview was concluded, Taylor left the room no better off than when she entered. There wasn't going to be a confession in this case and it was going to go to trial.

CHAPTER 5

In the shadows, he stood waiting for his target to emerge from the Majestic Theater in New York City. He was a man with many names and many faces and they changed on a regular basis according to his mission. Today his name is Ben. He had no close friends or family and didn't care about anyone but himself, and if this wasn't the case, he probably would have been killed or captured a long time ago. Ben didn't kill for revenge or causes and he didn't kill for pleasure; he killed for money, and he only had one client. At first Ben had concern for his targets and why they were on contract for execution and at times he questioned if they really deserved to die. Maybe in the beginning, he had a conscience and felt a need to justify their death, but after the first half dozen hits, he rationalized that the people he terminated were bad people and the world was much better off without them sharing the air.

Dressed in a dark sweat suit with a black knit cap covering his head and wearing dark sunglasses was enough to conceal his true identity. Holding onto a small radio that he put up to his ear whenever someone was nearby, helped him blend in with many New Yorkers that hung out on the street. Ben kept the volume low as he listened to Chopin's nocturnes at a minimal decibel because classical was the music that put him in a place that provided peace of mind and this is what he listened to most of the time. Ben knew he didn't choose his line of work, it chose him. When he wasn't researching and studying his next target, he was doing extensive physical training or expanded his knowledge of the world. Ben spoke five languages fluently and was conversationally qualified in two others and he considered himself a student of history. The many books he had read on great warrior leaders had numbered in the hundreds. Alexander the Great, Napoleon, Genghis Khan, Julius Caesar and Patton were some of his favorites. Ben was a fitness fanatic and he kept himself in top condition through daily vigorous training that sometimes lasted up to four hours. An expert in the martial arts and many weapons, Ben was comfortable in most situations no matter what part of the world he was located in. Ben was a perfect weapon; the perfect assassin.

A couple came strolling toward him playfully holding hands and acting in love; he had heard them approaching from nearly a block away. They were discussing their upcoming wedding and making tentative plans. The man seemed to be a timid fellow dressed as a preppie and walking with a light, unconfident step. Ben thought they would probably be married for a long time. As they got closer, he placed his radio close to his ear and bent his head forward as if he was caught up in some sort of musical trance.

Ben wasn't sure if he would ever get married and he had never even had a serious relationship. Occasionally during a work lull he would venture to the south of France or Brazil and find a woman for a night or even a long weekend if he felt inclined to do so, but he never saw a woman more than once. Ben didn't have any trouble finding women because they were naturally attracted to his look and style. He was a man that carried himself with confidence and precision and it flowed from his pours; most women found him very interesting and sexy. There was something mysterious about him, and at a glance, many people wanted to know who he was and where he was going, like a James Bond character. What they didn't know is that Ben made James Bond look like a florist.

The only liquid Ben put into his body was water, nothing else. It had to be distilled or at least a reputable brand of bottled water. His diet was as good as Jack Lalanne's, and this contributed to his lean and muscular build. Ben stood taller than the average man and the way he carried himself made him appear even taller. His body was riddled with scars from various battles he fought in the military and fights he had on the street as he learned to make his way through the world.

One of Ben's greatest attributes was his ability to remain patient. He would wait for days or sometimes weeks to strike his target. Even though he could take the person out anytime, the timing had to be perfect or he might be noticed. Ben was confident he wouldn't get caught alive, but he needed more than that, he wanted to be like a ghost. The police were not a real threat to Ben because he was too proficient, and they were usually dumb and arrogant, he thought. On countless occasions, he stood in the shadows or sat in the brush as the police drove by or walked past just a few feet away without noticing him. He was an expert at concealment.

Spending most of his time alone was his way and he seldom felt the need for company. Raised by an older couple, Ben was adopted as a four year old and he had never felt a mother's love as an infant. His adopted parents had no other children and they lived in a secluded wooded area in upstate New York. They were good people and tried to do the right thing, but they never gave Ben the love he needed to understand basic human emotions such as remorse, pity or mercy. The deep resentment they sequestered by not being able to have children of their own often found its way to Ben's world.

Growing up, Ben spent much of his time outdoors, tracking, hunting, and fishing, and being raised in this manner helped pave the way into the U.S. Navy and graduating at the top of his class as a Navy SEAL. One thing he was grateful for was that both his adopted parents were educated people and they pushed him hard to do well in school. It paid off when he was accepted to Yale University where he finished in the top ten percent of his class and this also contributed to his acceptance into the SEALS. It was at Yale where his character began to shape itself as he became a member of a secret society at the prestigious university and he remained committed to the Skull and Bones until the middle of his junior year in college when he was approached by, Ken Kraus, a senior at Yale. Ken had been selected as the recruiting spokesperson for the Rosicrucian illuminati, a secret order within the skull and bones. They had been watching Ben for over two years and thought him to be perfect for their small group at Yale. They liked the fact that Ben kept to himself and none of his activities involved a team. At night he trained at a local martial arts school in New Haven where he earned a black belt in Hapkido and he was also a member of the fencing team and chess club; all being solo activities. Ben believed in himself and couldn't rely on a team member to help him out when the going got tough. The fact that Ben picked up on new languages easily was also a deciding factor in their decision to approach him. It took some convincing by Kraus, but Ben was curious about the illuminati and was eventually inducted into the society. Throughout his entire adult life, Ben considered the brotherhood of the Rosicrucian illuminati like a family. He had parents that he visited from time to time, but they didn't understand who he was, what he was capable of, or what was important to him. The time he spent with them was generic and usually in a vacuum. Ben's character was directly influenced by his brothers in the secret society, and the brotherhood stretched out to all corners of the globe and they were very powerful men. The brotherhood consisted of politicians, corporate CEO's, military generals, government employees, and assassins.

As he hid waiting, his mind drifted to a place in time when he had received his first assignment. Ben had killed before, but it was war and that was different. In time he would learn to believe that it was always war, even during peacetime, and he would justify his actions by thinking this way. It was a typical rainy day in London as he waited under an umbrella near Albert memorial in Hyde Park. The huge gold structure was magnificent and he was in awe of its beauty. His assignments were always hand delivered, and never by the same person or anyone he had ever seen before. In many cases, the couriers were in disguise, but if he had to find them, he knew he probably could.

This must be him now, Ben thought, as the old man in a London fog overcoat and wearing a dark hat that looked like the hat Gilligan wore on the Desert Island approached. This guy is good, he thought, and the walking cane added a special touch. Who would ever suspect this guy? The exchange was made in a matter of seconds and the man vanished into the park leaving in the opposite direction that he had arrived.

Back in his hotel room he opened the package and it contained three photographs of the target and a short summary of his background including: his name, most recent address and current habits. Before he completed his mission, Ben needed to learn more about the man he was about to kill. After scrolling through newspaper articles in a London library, he was comfortable with the task he was about to undertake. The target was a Syrian man that was in the importing business and he had been suspected of harboring Islamic extremists that were responsible for several bombings in Europe.

After watching the man for several days and determining the best course of action, he was ready to complete his assignment. His training and experience had taught him to never use a gun when terminating a target unless it was absolutely necessary, however this being his first civilian kill, he resorted to the use of a small caliber handgun. A knife would be up close and personal and he wasn't ready for that yet.

As his target left the office building where his company was located, Ben waited near his car in a parking garage. Kneeling down behind a truck, Ben's heart began to pace faster as the man moved closer. Just as he placed his ass on the seat of the car and was about to close the door shut, he saw the shadow and felt the fear that so many of his terror victims had felt in the past as they drew their last breath. Ben stopped the car door with his left hand and placed the barrel of his gun against the side of the man's head with his right; delivering two bullets into the man's brain. The gun had a silencer attached and the garage was empty at the late hour, so Ben was confident he was not heard or seen as he disappeared into the shadows.

Many things had changed since that night in London. Now, Ben didn't bother to research his targets, he was comfortable believing that the people he killed deserved it and were a threat to the good citizens of the world. Ben seldom used a gun when taking out a target because leaving a bullet behind and the sound of the projectile caused an unnecessary risk, however; he usually had one within an arm's reach as a back-up.

The man he was about to relieve of his life was a tricky character and was harder to get close to than most targets. Vinny "the pigeon" Vanucci always had soldiers nearby wherever he ventured. Even as he escorted his mistress to a play, they were nearby, armed with pistols, and keeping a close eye on him. Vanucci had two soldiers protecting him and Ben had been watching their every move for nearly two weeks and noting their weaknesses. His conclusion was that they weren't very alert and were out of shape.

Vanucci, a mob boss with a ruthless and unforgiving reputation grew up in the Bronx, where as a teenager he took care of the pigeons that gathered on the rooftop of the old building where he lived with his parents and three brothers. This was how he earned the nick-name, Vinny the pigeon. Two of his brothers were also made members of the family and the third brother was dead; he had taken three bullets to the back of the head. Vinny was the brother that killed his way to the top and he left a pile of bodies in his wake, and for this, he was feared by everyone that knew him and many that didn't.

Ben looked at his watch and it was now time to move into position because the play would be getting out in approximately two minutes. Just after the play started, he had asked an usher what time it was going to wrap up, figuring a theater employee would know exactly what time it would conclude.

As the crowd began to flow out of the building, Ben stood hidden around the corner of a tall brick building across the street that housed a large book publishing company. He stooped down and did a one second peek around the corner and he observed his target walking side by side with the tall blond with the big hair and they were heading his way. He had watched them enter the theater a couple hours earlier and he knew where they had parked their car. There were several other people scattered about and scrambling toward their cars in a hurry. Vanucci's bodyguards had split up, with one of them holding the car keys and walking several yards in front of Vanucci and the other, fifteen yards behind, picking up the rear. Ben knew he had to move with stealth and accuracy, and that there would only be one shot. If he failed, it would be very difficult to get another chance at his target because he would be on full alert and guarded like Fort Knox. Ben had never failed before and this would not be the first.

When the first soldier passed by, he hardly paid any attention to the punk with the radio up to his ear. Ben started around the corner just as Vanucci approached about ten feet away. As he quickly walked passed Vanucci, he was positioned to the left of the couple and his target was to his immediate right and was holding his girlfriend's arm with his left hand. Vanucci saw Ben and thought he was walking a bit too close for his comfort, but thought nothing of it. When Ben passed by the couple he accidentally bumped into Vanucci, "excuse me" he said as he collided into him and kept walking by. Vanucci's girlfriend stopped as the big man halted in his tracks and began coughing and holding onto his throat like a person choking on a piece of meat.

"Baby, are you okay?" she asked. A second later she saw the blood leaking out from between his fingers. Looking into his eyes she saw the horror as his eyes bulged from the sockets. She screamed a high and deafening pitch as he fell to his knees. Both of his bodyguards were now alert and came running over. When they saw the blood flowing out of his neck like a punctured garden hose, they knew he had been attacked and immediately began to scan the area, but it was too late. The man that bumped into Vacucci had disappeared into the night, like a phantom.

Ben had used a thin razor sharp blade that he held hidden along his inner-wrist with the point of the weapon pointing toward his elbow. Once he was a step away from Vanucci his strike was a quick, smooth, motion that hit his target exactly where he intended, slicing through the carotid artery on the right side of the neck. He was so fast and precise, no one knew what had occurred, except Vanucci. Ben felt no pity or remorse for the man he just snuffed out, because he knew that his employer would only order the extermination for those that gnawed at the core of society. It was just another completed mission and now he would move on to the next. The offshore bank accounts he had in the Cayman Islands and Switzerland had grown significantly over the years and he seldom had a chance to enjoy the fruits of his labor; one day he would.

CHAPTER 6

The gym was busy at 10:30 AM on Saturday as Taylor was encouraging Tara to push out one more set of free standing squats and she was cursing her under her breath with each upward motion. "Come on girl, are you trying to kill me or what?" she complained.

"You want buns of steel, right?" Taylor slapped her hand hard against her hip.

"Yeah I do, but isn't there a pill I can take or something? This shit sucks!"

"If there was, I'd have a cabinet full of them," Taylor said.

Tara finished her last one, grunted and took a seat on a bench. "Reggie has been calling and it's getting old, really fast."

"What does he want?" Taylor asked as she began banging out crunches.

"He keeps leaving messages saying he loves me and he can't live without me. A couple times he was balling his eyes out so hard I had to wipe down my answering machine."

Taylor laughed. "It doesn't sound like he's wrapped too tight."

"No, he isn't!"

Taylor's crunching motions began moving side to side. "How long were you seeing him?"

"Just over four months," Tara replied as she reluctantly joined her friend on the floor.

"Hardly enough time to fall apart over someone," she said. "I'd say Reggie is obsessed with you."

"Ya think?" Tara said facetiously "The other day he delivered two dozen long stems to my office. You should have seen how envious the other girls were," she grinned. "The card read: I can't live without you."

"Maybe you should consider getting a restraining order on him," Taylor suggested.

"No, he isn't threatening me."

"Not yet," Taylor said.

"I'll just keep on monitoring my calls and ignoring him. Eventually he'll go away."

Reggie sat behind a bottle of Jim Beam whiskey, turning over one card at a time onto his kitchen table until he reached the end of the deck, and then he started all over again. His mind was focused on one thing only, and that was getting Tara back. Confused at why she dumped him, he thought about all the positive steps he had taken in his life in the past eleven months. Until now, he hadn't picked up a drink or taken any drugs and he had followed the teachings of Jesus. Reggie had been going to regular AA meetings and he had totally resigned himself to his higher power. He no longer had control over his life, God did. *Where have I failed her? I was good to her son and I treated her like a queen. How could she not see that I'm a good man and that I can offer her and Tanner a good life?* Reaching for the bottle, he tipped it back for several seconds. It burned his throat as it went down. It burned so nice.

After nearly a year of being sober, his drinking had resumed, and it started two days after Tara had given him the bad news. Reggie knew he shouldn't drink and he sat remembering what his life was like before he jumped on the Devine wagon. Diane, his former girlfriend had taken him to court for stalking and physically abusing her. Because it was his first offense the judge gave him probation and ordered him to attend a thirty day rehabilitation clinic in Upstate New York. Before that, his life had been a disaster with one bad drinking episode after another. Although he was able to avoid felony charges, Reggie had been arrested for driving under the influence of alcohol on two occasions, and there were a series of misdemeanors that were all substance abuse related.

40

At the age of eight his mother abandoned the family leaving him and his two siblings alone with his father. A year later, Reggie's father had enough and dropped the kids in his estranged wife's parent's lap and headed west. Reggie never recovered from the abandonment he felt by his mother, and then, when his father did the same, he completely withdrew throughout his adolescence. His grandparents did the best they could, but it was never enough for Reggie and he always wondered if they were going to dump him off on social services or some distant aunt or cousin.

It was at the age of fourteen when he picked up his first drink and the marijuana followed shortly thereafter. As the years passed on, this was the only time he felt content and stress free so he continued to drink and smoke his way through life. After being pushed through high school, Reggie landed a job with a flooring company, and although laying tile was hard on the knees, he made pretty good money and he stuck with it. At the day's end, he had a pocket full of drinking cash, and what was better than that? When Reggie was drunk he felt invincible and he often led people to believe he was more successful than he really was, and occasionally; he even fooled himself. Occasionally, Reggie would remain sober for a couple of months, and during this time, he would realize his drinking was leading him on a path to nowhere and that he needed to quit, but it never lasted.

Flipping over the ace of spades, he slammed it hard onto the table. *She hasn't seen the last of me. I'm not going to let her get away so easily, that bitch. Either she'll be mine or she won't be with anyone. She owes me that much and more and I'm going to collect.* Grabbing the bottle around the neck, he turned it up-side-down until it was empty, and then he pitched it against the kitchen wall and it shattered into a hundred pieces.

The telephone records of Doctor Brown had arrived Monday morning and Taylor was at her desk looking through them with a cup of coffee at an arm's reach. It was now ten in the morning and she was sore from a grueling hour of torture at the gym. A trainer, that looks like Arnold Schwarzenegger on Steroids, had beaten her up with a series of core-strengthening exercises. He had offered her a free training session with an agenda that it might win him a date. Taylor accepted the offer for the workout but declined the date. She wasn't interested in the body building type, but she was always up for a physical challenge, and that was the extent of it. Her ass was solid and shaped as a heart, and to keep it that way required serious work, pain, and sweat.

Doctor Brown's phone records indicated he had made several calls in the few days leading up to his death. He had called his daughter's house twice, a call to the New Haven Register and a call to a Mr. George Lynch of Greenport Long Island. As Taylor sat sipping her coffee, she thought about her conversation with Gary Mitchell from the New Haven Register. Placing down her empty cup, she began to do some research on Mr. Mitchell through the internet. After thirty minutes of research, she stopped searching, thinking she had enough information for now. Mitchell had an interesting background, she thought. He had attended Connecticut College, and right after graduation, he joined the Peace Corps where he was assigned to Croatia for three years. After returning to the States, he began his career with a small shoreline newspaper and eventually moved on to become a reporter with the New Haven register where he's been employed for the past seven years. Taylor dug out his information, picked up the phone and called him; she wanted to meet with Mr. Mitchell in person.

Gary had chosen a quiet diner on route 1 in Branford that was owned and operated by a Greek family he had become friendly with. He used to eat there at least once a week when he lived in the town several years earlier and he always ordered the same thing, a grilled chicken Gyro and a side of macaroni and cheese. The table he had chosen was located in the rear of the establishment and was surrounded by over-sized plants. Ivy vines flowed down the walls from large pots that hung from the ceiling and they seemed to have grown ten- fold since he was last there. It was almost as if the stories that resonated from the booths and tables provided them energy to grow. Gary thought he picked a good place for them to talk in private and enjoy cleaner air at the same time. As Taylor walked in and began scanning the restaurant, Gary figured it was her because she carried herself with the confidence of a cop.

"Mr. Mitchell," she asked approaching with a smile.

He stood up, immediately noticing her stunning blue eyes. "Yes, and you must be Detective Marshall," he said as he extended his hand.

"I am." His hand seemed soft, yet strong.

"Nice to meet you, please sit." He gestured toward the chair next to him and she sat down. Taylor was surprised by his appearance, not expecting him to be so handsome. He was tall with neatly trimmed black hair and dark green eyes. Well dressed, he wore a sport jacket over a collared shirt and pleated dress pants.

"Thank you," she said. "I've been thinking about our last conversation and I wanted to follow up with you on a few matters."

"I'm at your disposal," he said.

"I checked the phone record of Dr. Brown and verified he did call you three days prior to his death. I really couldn't quite figure out why he called you, so I did a little checking on your background."

"I hope I'm not a suspect," he said through a wide smile. They both knew that wasn't the case.

"Not yet," she said with less of a smile. "Tell me about what you've been reporting on recently."

Pushing himself up straight, he crossed his leg and seemed to get comfortable. Taylor sat straight up with her legs together and her posture correct. He thought she looked like a true lady with an elegance rarely seen in a police officer. Not that he didn't like or respect the police, they were just a different breed that marched to the beat of their own drum. "I've been digging into local government corruption."

"I see," she said as she took out a pocket-sized notebook and a pen." Can you be more specific?"

He was wondering if she ever read the newspapers. "Okay, Hartford is the insurance capital of the world, right?"

She nodded her head.

"Also, Yale medical and many of the large pharmaceutical companies are in the Connecticut area."

"Go on." She was thinking of how enormous Pfizer in New London was.

"They have some of the most powerful lobbyists in the world and I've been investigating the link between the governor's healthcare legislation regarding coverage for Lyme disease patient's in our state and the lobbyists that are in bed with her."

"Alright, I've read something about that. Please continue." She knew more than she led on, but she wanted to hear it from him.

"This disease is a fast growing chronic illness that is affecting thousands of people in our state and maybe over a million nationwide," he said gloomily, "I believe it's an epidemic and spreading just as fast as AIDS."

"Really," she responded in a manner that led him to believe she was unconvinced.

"Yes, really," he said. "The difference is that Lyme disease is a very tricky disease and hard to diagnose. If you take an AIDS test and you are infected, eventually it will show its ugly face. Sixty to seventy percent of the people that have Lyme disease test negative. Many doctors refuse to treat them with antibiotics even though they have telltale Lyme disease symptoms."

"I thought Lyme disease could be treated and cured with simple antibiotics," she said.

"In many cases, yes," he said. "If the patient is given a heavy dose for a period of thirty days or more, chances are they may be cured and become symptom free."

The waiter came over and took their order and Gary ordered the same thing he always did. He recommended the grilled chicken gyro to Taylor and she decided to try it. "The problem is that when a patient test's negative, most doctors won't prescribe antibiotics, and if they do, it will probably be a light dose for ten days. This usually will not kill the disease and it may eventually become a chronic illness."

"I understand," she said, "but from what I understand it's not a fatal disease. I know people that have arthritis issues from Lyme, but a disease such as AIDS kills people."

"This is where part of the problem lies." He leaned forward with a serious look on his face. "Lyme disease does kill people. It mimics other diseases and most people in the medical community have their head in the sand regarding this issue. The disease mimics: Multiple Sclerosis, Lupus, Chronic Fatigue Syndrome, Parkinson's, Alzheimer's, Rheumatoid Arthritis, Fibromyalgia, and many other diseases."

"Really." Her level of interest seemed to rise which fueled his flame even more.

"That's right. It's a very complicated and illusive disease and it can be very deadly. Granted, most Lyme patients won't die, but many wish they would," he said bitterly. "Once it takes hold of your body, it will completely destroy your life as you know it. I interviewed the parents of an eleven year old boy that went undiagnosed for five years and now he's blind. This disease puts people in wheelchairs and the pain is often unbearable. In many cases it invades the central nervous system, and when it does, it sometimes leaves patient's shaking uncontrollably. People have committed suicide just to relieve the pain and mental anxiety it causes."

"I never realized Lyme disease was this serious," she said thoughtfully.

"Most people don't, until they have it," he said. "In many serious cases it attacks the internal organs and causes a lingering and painful death. It's not just here in Connecticut, it's everywhere," he said shaking his head. "Lyme disease is a world-wide problem.

"And your story is about local government's neglect in passing laws that take Lyme disease serious?"

"That's part of it. I think the problem is a compilation of issues. I truly believe the insurance and pharmaceutical companies have the Governor in their pocket. Look, they don't want to admit that Lyme disease is a chronic illness. It would cost the insurance companies millions in healthcare claims. Most insurance companies will not cover long term treatment for Lyme disease. As long as there are no laws on the books that dictate they must cover Lyme disease, they will continue to deny patient care."

"That sounds crazy to me," she said in an exasperated tone. Their drinks arrived and Gary immediately took a long sip to sooth his dry throat.

"Another issue is that there is very little money allocated to research this disease. The first case of Lyme was reported in nineteen seventy-five. Why isn't there a cure or vaccine? I'll tell you why, because nobody takes it seriously enough to properly fund it, and I'm not even sure the medical community wants a cure," he said."

"Why is that?" she asked.

"Look, Lyme mimics so many diseases, and if a cure was discovered, how much money would be lost in the sale of prescription drugs and endless doctors visits? It keeps the pharmaceutical and medical industries fat with a continuous cash flow."

"Sounds like you've been doing your homework, Mr. Mitchell."

"Please, call me Gary."

"So has your news coverage made any difference, Gary?"

"Not yet, but I think it will. I've been doing a lot of digging into the relationships between our fine Governor and the lobbyists' for the insurance and pharmaceutical companies and I think there may be some corruption involved."

"I think I may know why Dr. Brown called you," she said.

He was a bio-scientist for the government and was preparing to reveal some information on disease research and he might have thought you were the right person to contact because of your investigation into possible local government corruption."

The reporter sat looking at Taylor in silence and it began to make sense to him. "That's probably it," he finally said. "That's why he chose me."

"Yes."

"What are you going to do now?" he asked.

"I need to look a little deeper into what Dr. Brown was working on when he was a government employee."

"I'd be interested to learn more about that. After all, I am a reporter," he said through a grin.

Taylor didn't trust reporters and knew she should keep her cards close to her chest, but something about Gary seemed different to her; he seemed genuine. "I'll keep you in the loop," she said.

The food arrived and they ate while enjoying a cordial conversation, mostly about work and family. Gary liked that the conversation slipped away from a professional one to a more personal level. Taylor normally wouldn't do this, but she liked him and found him to be pleasant to talk with and she thought he was very attractive. After lunch he insisted on picking up the tab and they shook hands, traded smiles, and turned in their own direction.

CHAPTER 7

The small room that was occupied by Windows, didn't have any windows. There wasn't a kitchen or television and it didn't have a shower. All he had was a book that the guard let him borrow from, John Martins, an inmate in the next cell who went by the name, Shrimp. He had earned his nick-name because he weighed three hundred and sixty-five pounds, and that was only because he was on a diet.

Windows thumbed through a book as he sat on his hard bunk. The cover was blood red and it was thicker than most books he had held. He hadn't read very many books in his life and he doubted whether he would finish this one. Rich Man, Poor Man, was the title and he liked it because he thought it to be fitting to his life story. Windows always wanted to be rich, but was always poor and the more he aspired to be rich, the more time he spent in prison.

Stonington correctional facility was a holding pen for suspects waiting for trial and home to felons convicted of various offenses ranging from assault and battery to drug dealing. Most convicts with sentences of ten years or more were usually sent to Somers prison located near the Massachusetts state border. Stonington, being a small facility, carried a reputation of being controlled by the guards where many larger prisons are run by the inmates. Captain Oswego, the officer that ran the day shift ruled with an iron fist and nothing went down in the facility without his approval or there was hell to pay. Occasionally an inmate would rebel and stir up the pot and he would experience the wrath of Captain Oswego. A few years earlier a young man incarcerated for motor vehicle theft tried to start a booking operation in cell block C without the consent of Oswego and he was beaten half to death and thrown off the tier.

"When's supper?" Shrimp groaned. "The gates of hell should be opening by now, I'm starving." Just after he spoke, a buzzer sounded and the cell doors automatically slid open and came to a dead halt with a loud crash. "Now that's what I'm talking about."

Windows had noticed Shrimp when he first arrived and thought he could do without a few meals. Windows got up and stepped to the entrance of his cell, stopping just short of the threshold. He stuck his head out peeking to the left and right watching as inmates filed out, standing at attention in front of their cells. A mountain of a guard, without a neck, appeared and barked out an order that Windows was unable to understand, so he followed the others and turned to the right. The entire tier block moved together like a poorly coordinated band in a parade and began filing out until the block was empty.

After moving through the chow line, Windows scanned the mess hall in search of his only acquaintance, Shrimp. They had been separated during the merging of tiers, because Shrimp pushed his way toward the front of the line in order to get the crusty layer of the macaroni and cheese that came off the top of the large baking pan, otherwise he'd have to settle for the creamy middle part of the serving. Windows spotted him sitting alone at the end of a long table and wolfing down his chow like it was his last meal. With tray in hand he headed over and took a seat across from Shrimp.

"Mac and cheese is my favorite," Shrimp said through a full mouth causing a projectile to fly out and land somewhere on Windows' tray.

Windows was hungry and the food didn't look or smell too bad, so he dove in. "Not bad," he muttered as he impaled his plastic fork into the mound of pasta. To his surprise, Shrimp abruptly stood up with his tray and walked away and a large man with a tattoo riddled body moved in where Shrimp had been and he stood glaring down at Windows with eyes that lacked any notable sign of life. Finally, he slowly took a seat and began eating, never taking his eyes off Windows.

"How's it going?" Windows greeted, thinking the guy needed a heavier dose of medication.

He stopped eating and continued to stare Windows down. "Do you know who I am?" he groaned.

"No, I don't."

"They call me Fixer," he said between clenched teeth. "Do you know why they call me Fixer?"

"Because you fix things," Windows coyly replied.

"That's right. I fix things."

"That's a good thing to know how to do. You'll never have to worry about finding a job if you know how to fix things."

"Shut the fuck up!" he hissed.

Windows did as he was told. His hunger was dissipating and he was avoiding eye contact with the man called Fixer. The man's arms were nearly the size of Window's legs and he was built with solid muscle. Windows wondered how many people he had killed in his lifetime, because the story his eyes told indicated more than one.

"I read about you in the paper," he said. "Big man you are whacking out an old guy while he sat having tea in his living room."

"I didn't do it," Windows pleaded. "I'm innocent,"

"Oh yeah, well I'm not," he fired back. "There are a lot of people in here that have grandfathers like the old man you *did*, including me."

Windows began to feel light headed and he had stopped eating altogether. "Like I said, I didn't kill him," he faintly responded.

"Let me give you some advice. If you want to remain healthy while you're in here, you're going to need protection, and that will cost you."

"I don't have any money."

"Get some."

"How?" Windows had a picture in his head of a huge dude wearing a cowboy hat bending him over his cell bunk hooting and hollering while humping and slapping him on the ass.

"That's your problem," he grumbled. "You have fair warning." Fixer got up and moved to a table with several other inmates that were all staring at Windows as he sat alone absorbing what had just occurred. He knew Fixer was a bad ass, but what he didn't know was that he worked for Captain Oswego and that Oswego was gunning for Windows for killing the old man. Fixer was just looking for a payday before Windows paid the ultimate price.

The mail had arrived like clockwork and Taylor shuffled to her mailbox dressed in a red and white sweat suit. She thumbed through the short stack of letters that consisted mostly of her monthly bills. One of the letters stood out and she waited until she was back in the house before opening it. When she first saw it, she had a good idea what it was and it was confirmed as she tore it open at her kitchen table. A hearing date had been set for her sexual harassment hearing. Trooper Robert Trombley was listed as the defendant and Taylor the plaintiff. The more she thought about it, the less she wanted to continue going forward with the complaint. She knew he was probably very scared and paying for his mistakes every day as he thought about the possible consequences he faced. Taylor was not a vindictive person, but she needed to let Trombley and Preston know that this type of behavior cannot be tolerated or go unpunished.

Tossing the notice down, she started to think about Gary Mitchell and how much she was attracted to him. It wasn't just that he was extremely handsome and sexy; he had a way about him that she found exciting. It was more than his intellect and his cultural experiences that gave her a tingle, she summed it up as him having a high level of compassion and integrity and she was hoping to see him again and soon.

The clock read 11:00 AM and she thought that it was late enough to make the call. It was Saturday morning and she hoped she would catch Linda at home.

The phone rang three times before Dick answered. "Hello."

"Good morning. May I please speak with Linda?"

"Whose calling?" he questioned in a roar.

"This is Detective Marshall with the state police."

He didn't say another word and the next voice she heard was Linda Kasinski's. "Hello."

"Hello Linda, this is Taylor Marshall. How are you?"

"I'm alright, considering."

"I'm sorry to disturb you on the weekend but I have a quick question."

"Yes,"

"I pulled the phone records of your father in the days leading up to his death and I noticed that he made a couple calls. One was to a reporter named Gary Mitchell at the New Haven Register. Do you know why he would call a reporter?"

Without hesitation she answered. "No."

"Are you sure? Is there anything he may have said in passing or any indication that would lead you to believe he would have a reason to call there?"

"I can't think of anything."

"Mr. Mitchell has been covering Lyme disease and various issues regarding local government and the lack of funding and research. Does that make any sense to you?"

There was an unsettling quiet on the line. "Linda."

"My God," she said. "I know who that reporter is. My daughter, Kimberly has been diagnosed with chronic Lyme disease."

Taylor sat absorbing what she had just heard. She remembered watching Dick and Linda helping their teenage daughter out of the car, nearly carrying her up the driveway to the house.

"Your daughter has Lyme disease?"

"Yes and that would most likely be the reason Pop called the Register. He was very upset that Kimberly went undiagnosed for so many years. The doctors she saw were reluctant to prescribe any medication because she tested negative for Lyme, and by the time we found a doctor to properly treat her, it was too late."

"I see. That's probably it. I'm sorry about Kimberly and I wish her the best."

"Thank you."

"The second call of interest was made to a George Lynch of Greenport Long Island. Does that name ring a bell?"

"Uncle George," she said. "Well, he's not a real uncle, but we always call him that. He was one of Pop's best friends. They worked together for years."

"Where did they work together?"

"They worked for the federal government, on the island."

"Long Island?"

"No, Plum Island."

Taylor thought for a moment and it all began to make sense. "Plum Island Animal Disease Research Center?" she asked.

"Yes."

"How long did your father work on Plum Island?"

"Ever since I can remember; we used to live on Long Island and he'd take the boat over every day with Uncle George."

"I see," Taylor said. "Uncle George is also a scientist?"

"Yes, they both have PhDs."

"I think that's all for now. I appreciate your help, I'll be in touch."

"Goodbye."

"Bye for now," Taylor said and she gently placed down the receiver. She was going to pay a visit to Dr. Lynch in Long Island and she would call Gary Mitchell on Monday and ask him to come along.

CHAPTER 8

The ferry from New London, Connecticut sailed at ten in the morning and was scheduled to arrive at Orient Point, Long Island in an hour and twenty minutes. Gary sat in a booth across from Taylor and he could barely keep his eyes off of her. From the first moment he laid eyes on her, he knew he wanted her. She had the face of the girl next door and the body of a playmate centerfold. What intrigued him was that Taylor had a certain kind of innocence about her, yet at the same time, a tough and confident demeanor. It was a combination seldom found in a woman and it made him think of his days in the Peace Corps while assigned in Croatia.

A Bosnian woman about the same age as Taylor was dying on the floor in front of him and he felt totally helpless as her body was being drained of blood and life. When he was first escorted to the room where she lay surrounded by her family, he observed a unique character in her that he would later notice in Taylor. Although she had been raped and stabbed, she still maintained a certain strength that defied self pity and she harbored her resolve a naive hope for her people. Her name was Samira, and in the short time he knew her, he had found love for her as he tried his best to comfort her in a time of chaos and death. Her large brown eyes had shed no tears and her mouth spoke no condemnations as she suffered a painful demise.

Samira had committed no crime nor had she taken to violence against the Serbs that were attempting to methodically exterminate her people. She was simply a victim of politics and war crimes like everyone else she knew and loved.

The year was nineteen ninety-three and Gary had been in

country for seven months. The Serbian army led by Radovan Karadzic had been ordered into Sarajevo to wipe out all Bosnian Muslims and Gary found himself knee deep in blood. This tragic episode in his life would shape him into the man he would ultimately become and he would spend his days fighting for the average person that had become victims of injustice and political agendas, just as Samira had.

"How's the coffee?" she asked.

He snapped out of his past and came back to life. "It's not bad for boat coffee," he responded as he reached for his cup that was wrapped in cardboard.

"I read about your case," he said.

Taylor didn't know how to respond to a man she was just getting to know, so she didn't.

"I just want you to know that I think you're doing the right thing," he said with sincerity. "There is absolutely no excuse for that kind of behavior anywhere in this God's world."

"I think we still have a long way to go," she said.

"I think you're right. And it has to start with someone like you speaking out against it. I don't know exactly what happened, but I'm pretty good at reading people and I can see that you're a professional person with high integrity."

For Taylor this was a great compliment and it produced a smile on her face. "Thanks, Gary." She took a sip of her coffee and scanned the cabin. There were quite a lot of people stuffed into the boat for a Tuesday morning, she thought. Some seemed to be taking an early vacation and others were sailing off to work. "He was my partner for seven months and he never even knew who I was as a person. To him I was just a piece of meat," she grimaced. "Whenever we had a conversation it would always end up about something sexual, and even though I ignored it, he didn't get the hint. I had complained a couple times to my boss and he shrugged it off as a burden that women troopers had to deal with in our line of work." She glanced at a man in a suit that was looking her way and he quickly fixed his eyes back on his newspaper. "It wasn't until he grabbed my breast and tried to kiss me at a barracks Christmas party that I made a formal complaint." She took a draw from her coffee. "I just couldn't take it anymore and I knew this was the only way I could get him out of my car," she said as she peered out the window watching the sun's reflection off the water. "I like working homicide, and I wasn't about to ask out because some asshole can't keep his hands and thoughts to himself, so I lodged a complaint."

"You had no choice, Taylor." A comfortable silence followed and they sat looking into each other's eyes. "I would imagine it's not the most pleasant working environment now."

"No, it's not. Hardly anyone will look at me, never mind speak to me."

"You know what?" Gary raised his cup. "To hell with them,"

"To hell with them," Taylor repeated and they touched cups and drank together.

Ben sat with his newspaper covering most of his face. His short blond hair was slicked back with gel and his thick dark glasses made it appear as though he would be blind without them. Wearing a typical dark blue pinstriped suit helped him blend into any crowd appearing as a business man. He wore a gold wedding band on his finger and a Movado watch that looked natural on him. Ben avoided anything other than short conversations and polite gestures with the people he came in contact with and he was practically unnoticeable in his subtle demeanor. Folding his paper, he stood up at the same time and moved to the food and beverage area, taking in a quick glance at Taylor and Gary as they sat talking in a booth across the deck. His dark medium sized sedan sat parked on the lower deck, not far from Taylor's car, because he wasn't about to lose sight of her and her friend. Ben had watched them closely and he could tell by their interactions they were not old friends, and he could also sense there was a mutual physical attraction between them. He bought a bottle of water and moved closer to the hatchway as the boat was nearing its destination. Looking out the window he thought about the beauty the water offered his eyes and how one day he would live in peace near the ocean.

As the cars slowly departed the vessel, Ben was four cars in line behind Taylor and Gary. He wanted to keep his distance, because she was a police officer and might be a bit keener than your average citizen. As the cars thinned out and turned in different directions, he would try and keep one or two vehicles in between them, avoiding any suspicion.

When they arrived at the address of Dr. Lynch, Taylor was in awe of their property in Greenport. The two story house was a frosty gray cedar dwelling with white shutters and a large country wrap-around porch. From three sides of the house there was a fantastic view of the sound and she thought that Dr. Lynch had done alright for himself in order to have such a nice place. A woman's head peeked through a window on the first floor as they pulled up to the circular driveway, and as they parked, the front door opened and she came out.

"Hello," Taylor said as the woman approached.

"Good morning," she responded.

"Hi," Gary said with a smile.

Taylor immediately took her hand. "Mrs. Lynch, I'm detective Marshall and this is Gary Mitchell with the New Haven Register. Thanks for having us out here."

"Well, my husband may not be quite as welcoming as I am," she said with an apprehensive smile. "Please call me, Yvonne," she said as she led them around the side of the house. "He's having a hard time with the death of Harold. They were best friends for nearly sixty years, you know."

"I'll try and keep that in mind as we speak," Taylor said.

"He's around back having his tea on the porch." Taylor thought her to be a young eighty year old woman with eyes that displayed strength. She was attractive and kept her gray hair neatly pinned up in a bun that rested at the top of her head. Her skin was sun beaten with a few dark spots and lines that had weathered the winds off the sound for many years. Not much shorter than Taylor, she was thin and wore faded blue jeans that were somewhat baggy around the thighs and a white button-down sweater with a thick collar. They followed her around the house to where Dr. Lynch sat on an aging rocking chair that was once pure white, now a faded gray.

"It's a beautiful morning," Taylor said as she viewed the sound.

"Maybe for some," he said without looking at her.

"I'm detective Marshall. We spoke on the phone."

"I know who you are," he said woodenly.

She didn't bother to offer her hand as she noticed both his hands were firmly clutched onto the arms of the chair. He sat motionless like a granite statue with only his lips moving. "This is Gary Mitchell; he's a reporter for the New Haven Register."

"Hello, Dr. Lynch."

"I don't much care for reporters." He reached for a cup of tea that sat on a small table to his left and raised it to his mouth.

"Can I get you something to drink?" Mrs. Lynch asked.

"Water would be nice," Taylor said.

"I'm fine," Gary said.

"Certainly," she said before disappearing into the house.

"Dr. Lynch, I'm very sorry about the loss of your friend and I can assure you that I'm doing everything I can to find out what happened and why."

"Whoever is responsible will probably get out in ten years anyway. That's all they get for murder these days. I read the paper."

"Let's hope this case will be different," she said. "As I said on the phone, the reason we are here is that Dr. Brown had called you prior to his death and we were hoping you could tell us what he called for and what was said."

"Every year in the late spring we go fishing for stripers. That's why he called."

Taylor looked out at the dock with a fishing boat attached to it. "That's your boat?"

"I paid for it."

"Dr. Lynch, can you tell us what type of work you and Dr.

Brown did on Plum Island?"

"We were scientists for the federal government."

"Yes, I know that. What I'm asking is, what exactly did you do for the government?"

For the first time, he looked at Taylor. "I can't talk about that."

Mrs. Lynch came out with a glass of ice water and handed it to Taylor. "Here you are, dear."

"Thank you."

She went back into the house, but kept an ears distance away.

"Why can't you talk about that?"

"It's classified, that's why," he said in an elevated voice.

After a long sip of cold water Taylor walked over and sat in the empty chair next to him and she placed her glass on the table next to his tea. "Dr. Lynch, are you sure Dr. Brown didn't talk about anything other than your plans to go fishing?"

He hesitated as he reached for his cup. "Yes," he said without looking at her.

"I guess there isn't much you can tell us about anything, is there?" she asked with a look of disappointment.

"I'm afraid you've wasted a boat trip."

She looked at Gary. "It wasn't a wasted trip at all," she said through a smile.

Gary smiled back at her and turned to the old man in the chair. "Dr. Lynch, did you know that Dr. Brown's granddaughter has Lyme disease?"

He glanced at Gary. "So, who doesn't around here?"

"Yes, you have a point there," he agreed. "I've been reporting on Lyme disease and the issues associated with the disease and our local government's failure to respond appropriately to this epidemic." Lynch didn't respond. "Dr. Brown had called me just prior to his death and asked to meet with me. Apparently he had information he wanted to expose to the press regarding his work with the government. We were never able to meet."

"I know nothing about that. I can't help you," he said defiantly."

"Is it that you can't help us, or that you won't help us?"

"Both!" He sat looking out to the water.

Taylor looked at Gary and then shifted her eyes in the direction they came. He nodded and she stood up. "Thanks for your time Dr. Lynch."

Lynch glanced at her and grunted.

She briefly looked down at the old man in the dark brown corduroy pants with a seal brown sweatshirt that read Brown University across the front in cardinal red and white letters.

"Goodbye."

Gary just nodded his head without speaking and they started off the porch.

"Detective Marshall," Lynch called out.

She turned around.

"How do you know you have the right man?"

She didn't respond, but right then she knew he was keeping something from her and that he was afraid.

As they boarded the ferry back to New London, Ben wasn't on the boat, he stayed behind.

CHAPTER 9

Windows turned the page and was starting a new chapter in his story. He was nearly half way through the book and he was proud of himself that he made it this far. He figured it was because there wasn't much else to do, and he was intrigued by the character, Tom Jordache, and the rebellious way he led his life.

"Hey," Shrimp wisped from the next cell.

"Yeah," Windows rested the book on his lap.

"Word is that you're marked," Shrimp said. "Anyway, that's the skinny."

Windows thought for a moment as he felt an uneasy feeling growing in his abdomen. "Who?"

"Not sure, but you better keep your back to the wall," he warned.

"Thanks." Windows thought about what Fixer had said, but he wasn't able to get a hold of any cash. He had made a couple calls that turned out to be fruitless and he was running out of options. Windows folded his book and tossed it on the bed; concentration would be a difficult task *now*. His mind began to drift and he thought about how Tom Jordache would handle this situation. Tom would beat the crap out of anyone that tried to make a move on him, however, Windows knew he wasn't a fighter and he immediately snapped out of his fantasy.

Sitting with his knees pulled tight to his chest, he thought about how he got into the predicament he was in. *My entire life has been spent taking from people. I have never given anyone anything; all I do is take things from people. I have never built anything; all I do is tear things down. I guess I'm finally paying my dues. The big guy is calling in his marker. What am I going to do?*

The tension in the mess hall was so thick Windows thought he could cut through it with a knife. Inmates either didn't look at him at all, or they took sneaky glances in deceptive intervals. Picking at his plate, Windows had little appetite as he sat alone in the far corner of the mess hall. Fixer approached without taking a seat and asked one question, "Do you have the money?" Neither of them liked the answer, but it was the reality of the situation.

The rest of the day came with jumping nerves and nausea as Windows ran through all the different possible scenarios on how he was going to be hit. When shower time arrived, he was going to decline, but was told he had no choice in the matter. The guard informed him that inmate hygiene was a policy, not an option. He pleaded his case to the corrections officer telling him the entire story and how he knew he was a marked man that needed protection. The guard agreed to let him shower after the other inmates were finished, but that he would have to make it quick. What Windows didn't know was that this particular guard was the brother in law of Captain Oswego.

The shower room was empty as Windows carefully shuffled in with his soap and towel. "Hurry up!" the guard ordered and he turned and walked out. Quickly removing his clothes, Windows turned on the shower and tested it until it was the right temperature. Climbing under the shower, he sighed as he felt the hot water pounding against his weary face. He had made it another day and that's how he was going to live for now, day by day. Taking his soap, he began to wash his head and face and as he began to rinse off, he felt the presence of another person. While turning to face the intruder, Windows felt hands grabbing his ankles and the knotted sheet being wrapped around his neck. There were two, maybe three men attacking him, and he began to struggle, but was pulled off his feet, landing hard on the tile floor. One attacker was holding his legs as another was strangling him from behind, and he felt the hardening blows to his midsection by a third person. The make-shift rope was pulling tightly against his throat and he lost all avenues of air. He tried to scream, but nothing escaped his body except the urine that flowed uncontrollably out of him. Gasping for air, there was none. Praying for help, there was none. Finally he stopped breathing and his body went limp. Quickly the three men went to work by lifting him up and tying the end of the sheet to the shower head to make it appear as a suicide. Once they were finished, they ran out of the shower room knowing they had done well and Fixer would be happy. Windows was left naked and motionless hanging by the neck in the shower room.

In his small corner office, Gary sat at his desk thumbing through campaign contribution records for Governor Bell. Several contributions that caught his attention were all from the healthcare industry including: two fortune 100 insurance companies, one fortune 500 insurance company and two large pharmaceutical companies. Millions of dollars in PAC contributions had been donated to Bell's campaign and the donations were ongoing. He began to research the lobby firms that worked for the five companies lobbying with the Governor's office, and one particular stood out. Garret and Molina Associates was employed by the largest Health Insurance Company and one of the pharmaceutical companies on his list. The lobbying firm had been investigated in the past by the FBI for unethical practices, but was never prosecuted. Gary decided to dig a little deeper into the relationship between the Governor and Garret and Molina Associates.

The ferry ride to Orient Point kept forging its way into the forefront of Gary's thoughts. He couldn't get his mind off of Taylor and he couldn't ever remember feeling this way before. There had been many girlfriends, and he had been engaged once, but he never had an attraction to any of them as strongly as this. Taylor had given him a card with her cell phone number on it and he was twirling it between his fingers thinking of how he should address her.

He dialed and after four rings she picked up. "Hello."

"Hi Taylor, this is Gary."

"Hello, Gary."

"How are you?"

"I'm fine, and you?" she asked.

"I'm well. Listen, I know you were a little disappointed the other day with the information you obtained from Dr. Lynch, or, lack thereof; so I was wondering if I might cheer you up with some dinner at my favorite restaurant tomorrow night?"

She was surprised, yet delighted he was asking. "Sure, that would be great."

"Would you like me to pick you up?"

"That depends."

"On what?" He was wondering if she was concerned about him knowing where she lived.

"On where you're favorite restaurant is located."

"New Haven."

"Then I'd better meet you there."

"I don't mind the drive, really." He thought he would prefer the time spent with her, even in the car.

"Are you sure?"

"I've never been surer of anything."

"All right then. What time?"

"Does seven work for you?"

"Perfect. The address is 244 Rockledge Lane, Waterford."

"Alright, I'll pick you up at seven tomorrow," he said as he scribbled on a pad.

"See you then. Goodbye," she said.

"Bye." He placed the phone down brandishing a wide smile.

Corrections officer Peter Florian was new to the job and was kept in the dark, like most new guards were, as to what was happening behind the scenes at the facility. While conducting a routine building check, he turned the corner of the shower room and saw Windows body dangling from the shower head. In a panic, he darted over; picking up the dead weight and untying the makeshift noose from around his neck. Florian never had the occasion to perform Cardiac Pulmonary Resuscitation (CPR) and this was going to put him to the test. Laying the body down, he went to work in the manner that he had been recently trained. Everything was fresh in his mind as he tilted the head back, pinched the nose and began blowing and compressing the chest. "Come on!" he yelled at Windows, like a kid in little league cheering on a teammate. As he continued his life saving efforts, he noticed a twitch and then some remote responsiveness. "Yes!" he shouted as Windows was slowly being brought back to life, for now.

Tre Scalini restaurant was located at the very end of Wooster Street and was a bit secluded from the other eating establishments on the street. As always on the weekends it was booked solid and Gary was glad he had made reservations. They sat against a wall in the center of the room with a flickering candle between them.

"So Windows tried to kill himself in the shower room," she said shaking her head.

"Really," Gary said. "How did he do that; by jamming an oversized bar of soap up his ass?"

Taylor busted out laughing. "Gary, that's awful," she said still chuckling.

"Yes, well it's hard for me to find compassion for Mr. Windows."

"I know," she agreed. "He hanged himself and was very fortunate that a guard found him in time."

"Apparently he's not going to see it that way; he was planning on the big sleep and had his eternal rest interrupted."

"That's a funny way to put it, the big sleep," she said.

"I can be funny, you know?"

"I can see that."

"So what do you think of the comment Dr. Lynch made before we left? What was it, how do you know you have the right guy?"

"It makes me feel like he knows more than he's telling us," she said.

"I have to agree with you." The waiter came over and took their drink order. Gary asked Taylor if she preferred wine and she said she did, so he ordered a bottle of merlot.

"May I ask you something personal," he asked.

"Yes."

"Do you find your dates to be intimidated because you're a police officer; you know, having a gun and all?"

"Sometimes I do, if they aren't police officers themselves."

"So you've dated many cops?"

"I haven't been dating a lot of anyone these days."

"Neither have I, so we can have our own little lonely hearts club." He raised his glass of water and she did the same and they toasted.

"So your pretty passionate about this Lyme disease thing, aren't you?" Taylor asked.

"Yes, I am," he said. "I recently attended a Lyme disease support group and I couldn't believe how sick many of the people are. One woman told me she is so miserable and depressed that she often thinks about suicide and she never had a history of depression or chronic illness prior to contracting Lyme."

"That's pretty sad."

"So many of the people I spoke with had been diagnosed with other diseases like MS, Chronic Fatigue Syndrome, Lou Gehrig's, Fibromyalgia and others. Many of them tested positive for Lyme disease after they took an extensive blood test not covered by insurance, but by the time they started on antibiotics, it was too late. The problem is that insurance companies' will only cover basic blood screening and that usually will not reveal the disease. There is no documented cause for diseases like Fibromyalgia, why not Lyme disease? The symptoms are the same and many of these patient's eventually test positive for Lyme disease.

"That's unbelievable," Taylor said.

"Do you know that around seventy percent of people that have Lyme disease test negative? Most doctors ignore the symptoms and insist the patient doesn't have Lyme disease. They have no clue what they're doing, and because of their ignorance, the patient suffers."

"I didn't know that." The waiter arrived with the wine and began pouring.

"The thing is that many people with advanced Lyme are suffering so bad they would rather be dead. Some things are worse than death and this may one of them," he said as he took a large gulp from his glass and sat back. "The pharmaceutical companies are making a mint off the antibiotics and antidepressants Lyme patients are taking. Many of these people are on antibiotics their entire life."

Taylor picked up her glass. "There is no cure."

"There's no cure for chronic Lyme disease," he said. "And the problem is that anyone can be bitten by a tick." He took another sip of wine. "A patient's symptoms may subside, but it lays dormant and can flair back up any time the immune system is compromised.

"I think it's a noble cause, what you're doing." She raised her glass and they toasted.

"Thanks."

The remainder of their dinner was light conversation as they were getting to know each other. With every word spoken they liked each other more. After dinner they took a walk down Wooster Street and Gary held her hand for the first time. Taylor was excited about the prospect of finding a new love and he was already falling for her. Gary was hoping she would ask him in when he pulled up in front of her house, but she didn't. A gentle kiss inside the car ended the night.

CHAPTER 10

When Taylor received the call she was at home and just getting out of the shower. Windows had left an urgent message with the office administrator asking that Taylor call him back immediately. After returning his call, Taylor could tell by the shakiness of his voice that it was urgent and she agreed to pay him a visit the next morning.

Sitting with cuffed hands and ankle shackles, Windows appeared edgy as she opened the door and entered the private visiting room. "Hello Alex." The room was a dull gray with a small table and two chairs.

"You gotta get me out of here," he demanded in a stormy gush.

"Calm down and tell me what's going on," she replied steadily.

"Look, if I don't get transferred out of here, I'm a dead man."

"From what I've heard that's exactly what you want," she said as she took a chair across from him.

"What?" he said with a blank face. "What are you talking about?"

"My report read that you hung yourself in the shower room."

He nervously looked left and right and leaned in toward her. "I didn't hang myself, they tried to kill me."

"Who?"

"I don't know who, a few guys- inmates."

"Why did they do that?"

"I guess because they don't like people that kill old men."

He put his hands over his head. "Or someone they think killed an old man."

"And you think I can help you, how?" she asked metallically.

"I need you to ask a judge to put me into protective custody and get me out of here," he said with a nervous twitch. "Transfer me to another facility."

Taylor tilted in her seat. "Why would I do that?" she said callously.

"Because if you do, I'll confess to the murder."

"You'll sign a full confession if I can get you transferred?"

"Yes," he spouted without hesitation.

"So you're now admitting that you killed Dr. Brown?"

He hesitated. "Yes."

"Let me see what I can do." She got up and moved to the door.

"Please hurry. I don't have much time," he pleaded.

"I'll be in touch." She walked out and he sat alone tapping his fingers on the table.

As the sun began to rise, Ben slipped into the water to avoid detection. In the darkness, he was safe and unseen as he blended into a bush near the shore. His wetsuit was snug to his frame and his BC had one full tank attached with three thousand pounds of air. Covered by an overgrown tree, he lay in the water thinking about hell week during his SEAL training. He had gone sixty hours without sleep and many trainees were dropping like flies. Some of the toughest men he had ever known were brought to tears as they rang the bell that ended their dream of becoming a Navy SEAL. On the first day training began there were one hundred and seventy-six recruits competing to become one of the finest fighting machines in the world, and at the completion of hell week there were only thirty-one remaining, and Ben was one of them.

In the distance, he saw a large sailboat floating by and he submerged himself, so only his mask and the top of his head were visible. It brought him back to the long, miserable days of being wet and sandy. That's what the instructors would yell at SEAL recruits in training, as they lay on the beach exhausted after three hours of paddling against the tide in their inflatable raft, followed by a three mile run on the beach with the dead weight of a telephone pole on their shoulders. "Wet and sandy," the instructor would yell. Ben and his fellow trainees responded by jumping into the frigid pacific, and as the waves slammed into their faces, they closed their eyes and mouths to avoid the stinging sand. Just prior to succumbing to hypothermia, the instructor would order them out and command pushups to get their blood circulating, and then the grueling process would continue all over again.

The water Ben lay submerged in was like a vacation in the Caribbean compared to hell week, he thought. Ben watched as his target boarded his twenty-six foot fishing boat and began his short sail out to his usual fishing spot a couple hundred yards near shore. Completely still except for the air slowly entering and leaving his body, the assassin waited until the boat was in place and the anchor dispatched. Watching his target cast a line, he waited until he appeared settled in his seat before disappearing into the water. Equipped with a close circuit breathing unit, there were no bubbles floating to the surface, as he approached ten feet under the water undetected. Once Ben was below the vessel, he placed his vest and breathing unit on the mucky floor of the sound. He didn't bother to bring a weight belt because he wasn't going to dive deeper than thirty feet and the weight of his gear would be enough to keep him submerged.

Ben had spent several days watching his target and he noted the man's daily schedule. He knew what time he woke up in the morning, and how long it took him to clean up and have breakfast. The target had gone fishing at the same time every morning and he usually came back with one or two strippers. Every morning he dropped anchor in the same general area and sat in the same place with a thermos of coffee at his side. This job would be a piece of cake.

Ben was supposed to be on vacation in Spain by now and

this was an unexpected and urgent assignment. His contact had sent a message stating this job was critical and had to be closed out immediately and that it was to appear as an accident. He didn't like to work in this manner, but this was an unusual circumstance according to his contact. Ben had come to the United States to take out Vanucci in New York and then he would vanish to blend in with unknown faces in a desolate corner of the world for a couple of weeks before heading off to Barcelona. His contact had ruined his entire plan by requesting that he terminate Harold Brown while he was still in the tri-state area. Ben didn't argue because he knew Brown would be an easy target and he figured he'd earn another quick payday while he was in the area. A few days later he received a new target and this caused much concern because he was increasing the percentage of being caught and this was unacceptable. His contact indicated that this was critical to the security of the U.S. Government and Ben was also advised this job was related to the termination of Harold Brown. Reluctantly, he agreed to do it even though he wasn't feeling great about the target, an old man on a fishing boat. Ben was a patriot through and through and he knew there was a good reason these men were flagged for extinction, so he never asked why.

His outfit was light now, wearing only a wetsuit, mask and snorkel, he ascended toward the bottom of the boat. Once he reached his destination, he carefully ran his fingers along the bottom until he found the edge of the starboard side of the boat. Slowly, he elevated his head out of the water staying close to the side of the boat as he took in the fresh sea air.

As he quietly treaded water, he thought about hell week once again and how they had lost so many recruits that couldn't tread water as long as necessary to pass the course. Some nearly drowning in their attempt to carry the heavy weights and remain above water level.

Peeking his head up, just enough to spy his target on the port side, he saw that Lynch was oblivious to his surroundings. Carefully and with smooth precision, Ben elevated his body onto the stern of the boat, and once his feet made contact with the floor, he attacked in a flash of a second.

As the target sat with pole in hand, he didn't even know what hit him. One second he was trolling a line and the next he was tackled off the side of the boat and held under water by a strong and blurry figure. Ben had leaped forward clutching onto the target, knocking him overboard in an instant. Once they hit the water, Ben pulled him under the surface, spinning him around, pinning his forearm around the throat from behind and holding him under until the thrashing stopped. After the target went limp, Ben ascended just enough to take in air and scan the area. The coast was clear and he dropped back down to the floor of the sound and re-engaged his equipment. As he placed his regulator into his mouth, he took one last look at his target floating lifeless along with the current, and without hesitation, he swam to shore.

CHAPTER 11

As Taylor walked into the building and toward her office she was inadvertently intercepted by Lieutenant Preston. "Come to my office," he commanded with a stern face.

"What is it?" She asked in frustration because his continuous drama was getting very tiresome. Preston didn't bother answering as she followed him to his office and he closed the door and adjusted the blinds so they opened up allowing a clear view into his office. Taylor knew it was a slap in the face to her, but she brushed it off like a piece of unnoticeable lint on her shoulder.

"Now, that Mr. Windows has confessed, this case is buttoned up until the trial." He didn't bother sitting down and neither did she. "Has he been moved yet?"

"He's being moved today."

"Good."

"Maybe good, maybe not," she defiantly said.

His eyebrows tilted. "What do you mean?"

"I'm not sure he did it."

"What the hell are you talking about?" His voice bounced off the walls. "We have his prints in the victim's house and Dr. Brown's credit card and other belongings found in his apartment. Not to mention a full confession."

"I'm not sure he is responsible for the murder," she said. "Look, the only prints lifted from Dr. Brown's house were taken off an empty Rolling Rock beer bottle. There wasn't any other Rolling Rock beer in the house, only Michelob. When we searched Windows' apartment he had one type of beer in his fridge, Rolling Rock." She crossed her arms. "What are the chances that the exact type of beer Windows drinks was found with his prints on it in the victim's house? No other prints lifted, just the bottle."

"Who gives a damn about a beer bottle?" he asked briskly. "He confessed to the crime."

"Yes, he confessed to save his ass. Someone tried to kill him and he's desperate to get transferred to a safer facility," she said. "Look Lieutenant, that bottle could easily have been planted and while they were dropping off the bottle they could have grabbed the ring and credit card and planted them in Windows apartment."

"Who?" he roared, "you keep saying, *they*, who the hell are they?"

"I'm not sure, whomever wanted to make it look like Windows was the perp."

"You're living in some sort of a cartoon. I think you need to see Dr. Marvin," he said as he cowardly shifted his eyes away.

Taylor just looked at him, insulted by the suggestion that she see a Psychologist. She decided not to justify his comment with a response. "Look at Windows' history. He has never committed a violent crime, and all of a sudden, he goes and commits a murder. It doesn't add up."

"I'll tell you what adds up and doesn't add up around here, Trooper," he said behind a firm chin. "This case is shut down and you are to move onto the Hermanette case." He walked to the door and opened it. "Get out!"

Taylor stood staring at her boss for a moment before exiting the room. She wondered if he had always been an asshole or if it came with his wide-brim trooper's hat.

Roy Hermanette had been stabbed through the heart and died before the ambulance arrived at his apartment located in the heart of Norwich. Taylor always got a kick out of the sign that read "Norwich the Rose of New England," every time she entered the city limits. She thought it to be more fitting to read "Norwich the weed of New England." Many of her cases were a product of a Norwich resident and this one was no different.

Roy's wife, Elsa, admitted on the scene that she had killed him in self defense. The pair had emigrated from Nicaragua and spoke very little English; therefore, a translator was needed to be brought in for Elsa. His wife of seven years cried that she had been beaten and raped on many occasions, and that this time, he intended to finish her off. Roy was found on the bedroom floor with two deep stab wounds through the chest. Elsa was taken to the hospital where a rape kit was initiated and the results showed she had intercourse within two hours leading up to the incident. A large bruise on her right cheek had become swollen and turned a dark blue color and it was accompanied by a few bruises on her thighs and arms.

Roy had worked for the same flooring company for four years laying rug and tile and Taylor thought that would be a good place to start right after she interviewed Elsa. All the evidence pointed to a clear case of domestic abuse and self defense. The two initial investigators had been reassigned and put on a juicier case and Preston thought this would be the perfect case to assign Taylor. Roy's family was adamant that Roy didn't abuse Elsa and that she made the whole story up. In Preston's eyes, it was a dead end case that nobody cared about, and he figured he'd go through the motions of looking into it in order to appease Roy's family. Taylor knew the two month old case was just another form of punishment for her filing the sexual harassment complaint against her ex-partner, Trombley. And to add insult to injury, Trombley was one of the homicide investigators Preston pulled off the Hermanette case.

The next morning at Elsa's apartment, Taylor sat across from her with a state interpreter that spoke fluent Spanish. The kitchen floor looked as if it hadn't been washed in a year and dishes were piled high in the sink. No charges had been filed against Elsa pending the results of the investigation and she felt confident that she would be exonerated.

"Mrs. Hermanette, please tell me what happened the night you killed your husband?"

The interpreter repeated what Taylor asked. She was a

Hispanic woman in her mid forties with short black hair, a black skirt and white blouse and several extra pounds below the waste.

"He beat me and raped me and he was about to kill me, so I defended myself with a kitchen knife," she said as if it had been rehearsed over a hundred times. The interpreter did her job, speaking very clear English

"Please tell me exactly what happened from the beginning," Taylor asked.

"He came home from a bar and asked where his dinner was. I told him there was no dinner because I didn't know what time he would come home." She rubbed her nose. "Then he slapped me with the back of his hand."

"Where did he hit you?"

"In the face," she said with a smug look.

"Yes," Taylor said, "but where in the face?"

"In the mouth," she responded and reached for her pack of generic cigarettes.

"I see. What happened next?"

"Then he said I wasn't a good cook anyway, so all that was left was sex," she said as she lit up. "I told him no, that I didn't want to do it and he punched me in the eye." She pointed to her right eye.

Taylor wrote down what she was saying because she had refused to be taped. "What did he do next?"

"He went to the cabinet and poured a drink of tequila and that's when I put a kitchen knife in my pocket."

"Why didn't you just leave, run away?"

"He would have stopped me and I was afraid he'd kill me," she said with smoke billowing out of her nose and mouth."

"So you took a knife for self defense?"

"Yes."

"When you took the knife; were you intending on using it?"

"Yes, I mean no," she flipped, "Only if my life was in jeopardy."

"I see," Taylor said as she worked her pen. "Go on."

"He drank down some tequila and leaped at me, grabbing me by the hair and dragging me upstairs," she said with no emotion. Taylor found her detachment troubling.

"What happened next?"

"He attacked me and tore off my clothes. I kept telling him to stop, but he wouldn't." The interpreter sat still with only her mouth in motion, like a puppet.

"Is that when he raped you?"

"Yes."

"What happened next?"

"He was mad because I didn't participate and he ordered me to go onto my knees, you know and please him."

Taylor didn't say anything; she just sat looking at her. "I refused so he kicked and punched me."

"Where did he kick and punch you?"

She didn't like that Taylor was being so specific. "He kicked me in the leg, here." She pointed. "And he punched me in the head, here."

Taylor took notes. "Go on."

"He was out of his mind and screaming that I was a no good bitch and I didn't deserve to live," she said with little emotion as she stubbed out her cigarette. "He said he was going to kill me and he came at me and that's when I cut him."

"You mean you stabbed him?" Taylor asked.

"Yes."

"How many times did you stab him?"

"Twice," she said woodenly.

"What did he do after you stabbed him the first time?"

"He kept coming at me."

"You still felt that you couldn't escape even after you put a large knife through his chest?"

Her eyes widened. "No!"

"What did he do after you stabbed him the second time?"

"He stopped attacking me and fell on the floor." She reached for another butt.

The interpreter revealed more facial emotion than Elsa as

she listened. "Where was he when you stabbed him, exactly?"

"He was to the right side of the bed."

"You mean the right side if you're looking at the bed or laying in it?"

"If you're looking at it," she gasped.

"What did you do next?"

She broke out in a coughing fit. Taylor wasn't surprised by the way she chain smoked. "I called the police."

"What phone did you use?"

"The bedroom."

"Why didn't you use the phone downstairs? You had just been attacked and raped and the man responsible was still in the room. Why wouldn't you get out of the room right away and call from a safe area?"

"The bedroom phone was closer and he wasn't moving." She scratched her head and rolled her eyes toward the ceiling. Taylor thought her attractiveness was negated by her demeanor.

"I see." Taylor watched her as she got up from the table and poured a glass of water. She didn't ask them if they wanted anything. Looking around the room, Taylor would have refused anyway.

"You had stated that he had abused you many times before. Why did you stay with him?"

"Because I loved him," she said unconvincingly.

"Have you ever called the police and made a report after his past abuse?"

"No"

"Why not?"

"Because, I loved him," she said again, but louder.

Taylor's eyes met the interpreter's and it was as if they had a meeting of the mind. Something was wrong with this woman and they both knew it. *Why didn't the initial investigators see it?*

"I think that will be all for now, Mrs. Hermanette," Taylor took to her feet and the interpreter did the same. Without hesitation, Elsa marched to the door and opened it, not making eye contact with either of them. "I'll be in touch if I have any more questions," Taylor said as she passed through the threshold.

Taylor sat in her office looking at the crime scene photos. She tried to put herself in Elsa's shoes. *If I loved my husband and I had recently stabbed him to death, wouldn't I become upset if I had to relive it as I told someone the bloody details?"* Scanning through the pictures, she noticed a spatter of blood on the bed. The major quantity of blood was on the floor by the right side of the bed where the body was found, however it puzzled her that there was no blood spattered on the wall or nightstand; it was only on the bed. She studied the photos taken of Elsa after the incident and most of the bruises were minor, except for the right eye that was swollen shut and shiny black. She put the folder away and headed for Roy's place of employment.

After speaking with Roy's boss, Mr. Sampson, Taylor learned that Roy was a dependable worker that seldom missed work or came in late. Sampson went on to say that he was a quiet and well liked employee that never gave him a problem the entire time he worked there. Taylor asked Sampson who Roy was the closest with at the company and he told her it was Jose Calento.

To Taylor's surprise, Calento spoke pretty good English as she spoke with him while he ate lunch outside the commercial building he was laying carpet in.

"Did you know that Roy was abusing his wife?"

"No, that's bullshit!" he said in an angry tone. "Roy was gentle as a florist, he would never do that."

"A florist," she mimicked. "He was a pretty big guy, right."

"Yeah, like a gentle giant," he said as he tore a huge wedge off his tuna sandwich.

"He did have a drinking problem, though. Maybe when he drank too much tequila he flew off the handle."

Jose stopped chewing. "Drinking problem, what are you

talking about?" The confused look on his face was obvious.

"Elsa said he went to the bar after work on a regular basis."

"Elsa's a liar!" he said through clenched teeth. "Roy didn't drink much at all, and he never drank tequila. If anything, he'd have a beer or two, that's all."

Taylor examined the man as he took another bite. "Roy never drank tequila?" She asked.

"Hell no, Roy didn't even like the smell of it."

"How often did he go to the bar after work?"

He reached for a bottle of Gatorade. "Once or twice a month," he said before tipping back his cold drink.

"Once or twice a month; that's all?" she asked.

"Look, I was his best friend. Roy didn't speak much English, so he would only communicate with me, and we became amigos." He took another bite from his sandwich. "Elsa is a lying bitch! She murdered Roy. It wasn't self defense like the papers say." He put down his food. "He loved her, you know?"

"How often did you see Roy drunk?"

"Never, he always kept his head about him, you know?"

"Did he ever talk to you about his relationship with Elsa?"

"No. Not really. He did say that his wife had more mood swings than he had ever seen in a woman." He finished the last of his sandwich. "He didn't talk about her much," he said as he stood up. "I have to get back now."

"One more thing," Taylor said. "Did Roy always swing a hammer with his left hand?"

"Left hand," he said with a bewildered look. "Roy was right handed."

CHAPTER 12

The large bucket of balls was nearly empty and Gary was glad because he was getting tired and his shot placements were declining. Placing his driver back in his bag, he pulled out his nine iron to finish off the remaining balls. It was a sunny Saturday morning and the range was beginning to fill up, mostly with hackers, so his timing was perfect, he thought. After dropping his last range ball a hundred and twenty yards out, he packed it in and headed to the city library.

In the library, Gary sat behind a computer scrolling through newspaper articles on Plum Island and he was surprised at the limited information on the Island and the federal facility that occupied it. As he found anything of interest, he took notes and moved on. Once his time at the machine was finished, he began searching though books and magazines looking for anything that might stand out. Pulling a few books from the shelves, he took a chair and began speed reading, stopping only to take notes. In the end, what he realized is that there was not a whole lot of available information on the animal disease research center.

Pulling back his sleeve, Gary looked at his watch and he realized he had been there for over three hours. He picked up the four books he had been scanning though and replaced two of them back on the shelf and headed to the front desk to check out the remaining two.

As Gary walked out the front door, a man with round, gold, glasses and slick black hair walked over to where Gary had just been. He was wearing a gray button down sweater and brown corduroy pants and he would appear to most people as a nerd.

Stopping exactly where Gary had placed the two books, he reached out sliding a book into the palms of his hands. The title he was looking at read, The Belarus Secret. He quickly concealed the book under his sweater and walked out the door. He felt a little guilty as he made his way down the sidewalk. Ben wasn't a thief of items, only lives.

When her cell phone rang, Taylor was walking off a five mile run. The white sweat suit she wore was damp and clinging to the skin around her upper torso. Pulling the phone from her pocket she saw that it was Tara and she pushed the green button bringing it to life. "Hello, Tara."

"Hi," she replied in a less than enthusiastic tone. Taylor knew something was wrong because Tara was always upbeat and full of life.

"Are you okay, you sound a little down?"

"Reggie was just here and he's out of his mind."

"What happened?" Tara could sense the concern in her voice.

"He just won't let go. I think he's totally obsessed with me." Her voice was splitting as she tried to maintain her composure. She didn't want to appear weak to her trooper friend. "He said he couldn't live without me and that he wouldn't."

Taylor thought there was something else that she wasn't revealing. "What else happened, Tara?"

"When I told him I wasn't interested in him and that I didn't want to see him again, he grabbed me by the throat and began choking me," she cried.

"Did you call the police?"

"No, I called you."

"How did you get him to leave?"

There was a short lull before she responded. "I fell to the floor nearly unconscious and he let go and stormed out," she busted out in a loud lingering cry. "He said if he couldn't have me, nobody would."

"Oh my God, Tara," she wisped. "Call the police; you need to get a restraining order on him. I'll be right over."

82

When Taylor arrived at the house the local police were already there. She identified herself as a state trooper and proceeded to console her friend. She made sure all the proper information was given to the officers and that they understood how serious this was. A report for assault and battery was taken and Tara was advised she would need to go to court on Monday to follow up in order to have a thirty day restraining order put into effect. Once Reggie was served there would be a court date to determine if the order would stand and be continued for a longer period of time. After the police left, Taylor stayed with Tara assuring her everything would be alright. Although she did a great job convincing Tara, she knew it may not be entirely true because in many cases a restraining order didn't prevent the offender from confronting the victim again.

Mrs. Lynch sat in her kitchen behind a cup of green tea. Her tears had dried since the death of her husband and she had begun to settle into the loneliness that followed the funeral and all the support family and friends had offered her in her time of despair. They had moved on to reclaim their own lives and she lingered around her house and yard with the memories of the man she loved for the better part of her life.

A letter from Linda Kasinski had arrived and she slid a long, narrow, letter opener into the envelope cutting it open. Linda had been like a niece to her and they always stayed in touch with an occasional phone call and letter. Linda had taken the ferry to Greenport to attend the service for Dr. Lynch and afterward she and her aunt Yvonne had a long conversation regarding the circumstances surrounding the death of her uncle and father.

Inside the envelope was a short letter that read:

Dear Aunt Yvonne,

I hope you are doing well in coping with the loss of Uncle George. He was a fine man and I will miss him terribly. If there is anything I can do, please do not hesitate to call. I would like to bring Kimberly out when you are feeling up to having visitors. Please let me know when we can arrange this. I have enclosed an article that you may find interesting. It was written by the reporter that came to your house along with Trooper Marshall to interview Uncle George a few weeks ago.

Take care.
Love Linda

The article was printed in the New Haven Register and was titled, IDSA Panel Conflict Probed. It was written by Gary Mitchell and it went on to read: In 1980 the United States federal government declared that government institutions and universities could patent and profit from organisms, and in some cases, dangerous pathogens. Many of these bio-scientists and professors had stopped sharing information on certain organism research in order to protect future funding and profits. One of the main organisms being researched is Borrelia Burgdorferi, the spirochete bacteria in Lyme disease. Prior to this new law being passed, scientists were open in the sharing of information for the betterment of science and the community in which it served. After the new law was put into affect, the very same people that previously protected public health interest such as the, CDC, NIH and Universities now became partners with large pharmaceutical companies and their motivations completely changed. For these doctors and re-search scientists it was now about research agendas, federal and private research funding and less about public interest. The industry that once had oversight and checks and balances has now become riddled with conflicts of interest in medical care.

A panel of fourteen doctors that make up the (IDSA) Infectious Disease Society of America had recently published their Lyme disease diagnosis and treatment guidelines. The importance of these guidelines cannot be understated in that these guidelines set a standard in the treatment of Lyme disease patients and are used to investigate doctors and their treatment practices. In many cases the IDSA Lyme disease treatment guidelines have caused doctors to be investigated and some have lost their license to practice medicine. Many of the investigations are brought on by complaints to state medical boards by insurance companies trying to get rid of doctors that cost them a significant amount of money. Also, the guidelines are used in court cases relating to insurance companies that cut off patient treatments.

The IDSA Lyme disease diagnosis and treatment guidelines state that Lyme disease is easy to treat and cure and that two weeks of antibiotic treatment is sufficient in most cases. It reads that chronic Lyme disease doesn't exist, and if patients still suffer after two weeks of treatment they have something other than Lyme disease, and it may be psychological.

Many opponents of the IDSA guidelines state that the guidelines are designed to restrict the treatment of Lyme disease. The question is why? Many suggest that the concept of managed care by the insurance companies play a significant role in guidelines set forth. If insurance companies and HMOs can get researchers and universities to define diseases and write guidelines for diseases a certain way it would help decrease the escalation of medical costs.

Many opponents of the IDSA panel state that the doctors were subjective in their research on Lyme disease and only chose publications that fit their agendas. Many published articles considered were written by researchers at the universities where they were employed.

The Connecticut Attorney General has begun an investigation into conflicts of interest by the panel of fourteen doctors that authored the Lyme disease guidelines for the IDSA. Half of the doctors in the panel or their universities hold patents related to the Lyme bacteria or its co-infections. Four of the fourteen doctors on the panel have received funding from Lyme test kit manufacturers. Another four doctors on the panel have been paid by insurance companies to write Lyme disease policy guidelines and have testified as experts in legal cases for said companies. And to conclude, nine doctors on the panel or their universities have received large sums of money from Lyme disease vaccine manufacturers.

The question is: should doctors who serve on the IDSA panel be allowed to have any ties what so ever to any manufacturers that have a stake in the Lyme disease guidelines outcome? Based on the guidelines written by this panel of doctors, many Lyme disease patients are denied treatment by reluctant doctors, ignorant doctors, and insurance companies. It is clear that the authors of these guidelines have a direct financial interest in writing these subjective Lyme disease guidelines. Shouldn't these doctors not only be subjected to investigations of conflict of interest, but medical malpractice as well?

As she placed the article on the table she thought about Kimberly and her battle with Lyme disease. Pleased with the article and Gary Mitchell's relentless pursuit of the truth, Yvonne picked up the phone and called him. She didn't believe her husband drowned in a boating accident, not for one second.

CHAPTER 13

The sky opened up and rain poured down, like a waterfall from the heavens. Taylor had just returned from attending an unusually long Christian service at a congregational church located in a neighboring town. Since moving into Waterford, she had not been able to find a place of worship that suited her needs. Not caring what denomination it was, Taylor just wanted a Christian service with a humble priest whose only agenda was to preach an interesting and genuine sermon. After sitting for nearly two hours she decided it was not what she was looking for, an hour a week would be sufficient.

Sitting on her tan leather couch, she looked around her place and thought it was time to consider redecorating because she hadn't replaced any furniture for nearly ten years. Buying new things seldom crossed her mind. Most of her paycheck went into the bank and it was beginning to show some real progress; she was a good saver.

Opening a folder on the Hermanette case, she scanned the list of clients she had obtained from Elsa. Since moving to Connecticut, Elsa started a house cleaning business and the current list amounted to seven customers. She was never able to get the business to take off because she wasn't bonded or insured, and that made many people nervous. Customers came and went according to economic conditions and other factors such as an overall unhappiness with Elsa's cleaning capability. Most of her new clients came as referrals from people she was currently working for, and also responses to small ads she posted in the local reminder. Taylor decided to call all seven customers and see what she could dig up on Elsa.

The first four people she connected with had good things to say about Elsa, but they didn't give her extraordinarily high reviews. It was the fifth call and the last on the list she was able to connect with that raised her antenna. Mrs. Heffernan could not praise Elsa enough, as she went on about how reliable she was and how well she cleaned the house. She went on to say that she liked Elsa so much she recommended her to State Senator Warren Gibbles wife. Mrs. Heffernan stated that she and her husband were friendly with the Gibbles and that her husband had been the senator's roommate in college and they remained the closest of friends ever since. At a fundraising party, the senator's wife had mentioned that her house cleaner was moving and she was looking for a replacement and Mrs. Heffernan said she took the liberty to recommend Elsa, and from what she told Taylor on the phone, Elsa was still the senator's house cleaner. Taylor wondered why Elsa had kept the senator's name off her list of current clients. She decided she would do a little sniffing around and see what came up.

Monday morning brought the sun and the large puddles that flooded the streets were drying out. The first stop was a visit to Senator Gibbles house located near the corner of Main and Nile Street in Niantic. The old shoreline town was rowed with old colonials with well manicured lawns and flower gardens. The visit with Mrs. Gibbles was short lived with the stuffy woman quickly confirming that Elsa was indeed their house cleaner and she was due to arrive Thursday for her weekly cleaning.

Taylor decided to take a walk up the street to get a cup of coffee at a place she noticed as she drove into town. As she rounded the corner, she observed many people coming and going from the quant coffeehouse and a few people sat outside where they had stationed three, small, round tables. After a short wait, Taylor approached the counter and ordered a medium cup of Columbian coffee from an unusually tall teenage boy. He took her money without a smile and she went for the low fat cream located at a counter in the corner. After the line cleared out she approached the counter again, but this time she had a photograph of Elsa. The lanky boy came strutting over like Lurch from the Adam's family show.

"Hello, I was wondering if you have seen this woman in here?" Taylor asked with a smile hoping it might be contagious.

The boy glanced at the picture as if he couldn't be bothered. "No," he said with a fixed face.

"Are you sure?" She held it a little closer and he barely looked at it. "Yeah," he said dryly.

Taylor noticed a chubby worker standing behind the tall boy; he shot a quick glance at the photo and went about his business. She decided to take a seat and rest for a few minutes before heading back to her car. After five minutes, Taylor got up and headed outside with a half full cup clutched to her left hand. As she started down the street, the chubby boy that was behind the counter approached her from behind.

"I saw the picture of the woman," he said. "She has been in here a few times."

Taylor turned around, pleased to hear the boy's statement. "Has she really?"

"Are you a cop or something?" he asked with a look of intrigue.

"Something like that." She smiled and he did the same. "When did you last see her?"

"She has been in here with *that* jerk a few times."

"What jerk is that?"

"Senator Gibbles," he said bitterly. "Not only is he the cheapest customer I have ever seen, he's got an attitude like he's better than everyone."

He had Taylor's full attention now. "You saw him in here with this woman?" She produced the photograph again and showed it to him.

"Yes. They sit together and have coffee once in a while," he said while quickly glancing back toward the shop. "The guy never tips, not even a dime."

"What time of day have you seen them together?"

"Usually in the afternoon, around two or three."

"Do you remember the last time they were in here together?"

"I'm not sure, maybe a couple weeks ago." He was getting antsy and Taylor knew he had to get back. "I have to go."

"Thank you," Taylor said and she walked back to her car feeling exhilarated.

That evening Taylor took a long walk around her neighborhood and her thoughts went from the murder of Dr. Brown, to Gary, and eventually to Elsa. *Why would the senator have coffee with his house cleaner on a few occasions unless there was some sort of friendship between them?* She knew the reputation of Senator Gibbles behind the scene and it was one of an arrogant and pompous nature. Elsa, although detached and cold, was an attractive woman with a certain sensuality men might find attractive. *Is it possible that they have a sexual relationship?* She decided it was worth looking into and she was resigned to do just that.

The hotel gym was empty when Ben walked in. He was known as Mr. Hodge by the clerks at the front desk. Ben became adept at learning to change his name and remaining consistent with each new identity. He had slipped six years earlier in Prague by using the name of his former false identity when checking into a hotel and that was the first and last time that happened. Whenever he assumed a new identity he would hold the passport close, studying the photograph while reciting the name over and over again until it became natural. Ben would become the new man in every sense of his being. The way he talked, and walked, and what he wore, was all part of the creation of his newborn character, and with each new identity came a unique disguise that was never used twice. Every job he engaged in meant a new look and bogus occupation, and with that, came the death of another human being. Ben equated it to what a Hollywood actor might go through, as they become absorbed into a new character in a movie. He had created a new character and identity on thirty-three separate occasions, and he thought that he might call it quits at number forty and retire.

His workout would last three hours, starting with a half hour of stretching and meditation and moving into a series of calisthenics including: sixty pull-ups, two hundred push-ups, and four hundred abdominal exercises. Once he was warmed up, he worked three body parts on the free weights and nautilus machines. Ben would finish his workout with a hard cardio-vascular regimen that he changed every time. Today he would do a six mile run, but the last time he had swam two miles, and on other occasions, he pounded a heavy bag for six three minute rounds or spun on a stationary bike for an hour.

Ben tried to avoid thinking about the tasks he was assigned, and why he completed them, because he knew if he began to include emotions into the equation it would be counter-productive and may possibly jeopardize his missions. At times Ben had thought about his days as a Navy SEAL and when it was that he became so callous regarding humanity. He tried to pinpoint exactly when he lost his sense of empathy, pity and remorse, and he narrowed it down to a mission in South America when he discovered his best friend's tortured and disemboweled remains tossed off the side of the road like an animal carcass. Travis had been double crossed by a politician that had gained his confidence and ultimately caught him off guard. After learning who was responsible for his friend's murder, Ben retaliated by killing the two men in the same manner, by tearing open their abdomen, and the politician that gave the order was found hanging from a bridge. His death was reported as a suicide. Back then it was rage that drove Ben, but today it was so very different, today it was money.

CHAPTER 14

It was a beautiful June morning and Yvonne Lynch was waiting outside for Taylor and Gary as they pulled up to her house on the Island. Gary had briefed Taylor on the ride over regarding the conversation he had on the phone with Mrs. Lynch and they both agreed that it sounded urgent.

This time on the ferry ride over they sat a little closer and their eyes engaged considerably longer than the first time they took the ferry to meet Dr. Lynch. The peculiar way the beaming sun reflected off Taylor's eyes created a stunning sparkle that stayed with Gary the entire way to their destination.

Once again, Mrs. Lynch was waiting to greet the pair as they exited their car and started up the driveway. She invited them inside where they took comfort in the living room that offered a magnificent view of the open sound. The room was clean and nicely decorated with modern furniture and a few signed and numbered prints hanging on the walls, mostly consisting of landscapes.

"I was just about to make some tea, would you like some?" She looked at Gary first and then motioned to Taylor.

"Yes, please," Gary said.

Taylor noticed something different about her since the last visit; her smile was not as lingering and her eyes seemed to have dulled. "Yes, that would be nice," Taylor responded.

"Please make yourself comfortable while I heat up the kettle." She walked out and Taylor stood up and began prowling the room. She moved toward an adjoining room that was partitioned with two large white columns holding up a circular archway. The library walls were covered with tall, white, book cases with hand crafted cabinets and crown molding. A black leather couch was flanked by two matching leather high-back chairs with reading lamps on emerald glass end tables. One shelf was dedicated to science, chemistry, and physics and the rest were an assortment of novels and political non-fiction works. She began browsing through the books, thinking she should start reading more.

"This is where my husband spent much of his time." Her voice broke the silence and Taylor turned and smiled at the depleted woman.

"It's a beautiful room." She started back through the archway and joined Gary and Mrs. Lynch in the living room. "Mrs. Lynch, I'd like to offer my sincere condolences on the loss of your husband." She reached out and took a hold of her hand.

"Thank you, dear." Her hand was soft and warm. A mother's hand, Taylor thought. Gary had told her how sorry he was over the phone, and she heard him. "Please, call me Yvonne." She looked from one to the other and it sank in. "It was my grandmother's name." She gestured toward a photograph standing upright on an end table. "She was born in a small village in British Columbia and we buried her there almost thirty years ago." A whistle sounded from the kitchen. "I'll be right back." She hurried out of the room to quell the alarming noise.

"Such an interesting woman," Taylor said.

Gary smiled at her. "Almost as interesting as you," he said.

"Are you flirting with me again?"

"Absolutely." His perfectly straight white teeth seemed to brighten up the room. How she loved his smile.

"Good." She gleamed.

Yvonne came in with a tray of tea and some fresh corn muffins. Gary had savored the aroma since he first entered the house and it reminded him of his kitchen as a child. They accepted their tea and Gary helped himself to a muffin. Taylor declined.

"Now, let's get down to business." Her face hardened. "My

husband was a scientist that worked for the federal government for over forty-five years. When he started, he was so excited about the prospect of conducting research that could determine the causes of diseases and help find cures and vaccines that would save people's lives. That was so many years ago, and how young and naïve we were." She frowned. "Just before he died, George indicated to me how distraught he had become with the way his work had turned into anything other than what he had hoped and dreamed it would be." She took a sip from her cup. "You see, it was as though he knew something was going to happen and he opened up to me; he was afraid." She placed her cup down in order to focus. "In all the years we had been together, he never spoke of his work on the Island."

Gary took out a pocket recorder and held it up. Yvonne nodded her head in approval. "What did he tell you?" he asked.

My husband and Harold were both recruited out of college by the government. George actually started about six months after Harold and they had grown to become life-long friends. When Harold was killed, a part of George seemed to die along with him. He didn't talk about it, but I could see it in his eyes. You know the men of that generation seldom spoke what was on their minds, it would be a sign of weakness, you know." She shook her head. "Back in the mid-fifties our government brought in scientists from Germany. Apparently they were the world-wide experts in biological warfare, and it wasn't until later that we found out that many had been Nazi's during the war. One of them was, Erich Traub, and there have since been books written on his shenanigans," she offered with a hint of disgust. "Neither George or Harold worked side by side with this German scientist, but after some time it became clear to them what he was up to."

"And what was that?" Gary asked.

"He was an expert in biological warfare agents and was researching different pathogens that could be used to kill and disable the enemies of the United States." There was little movement from either guest and their eyes were fixed on

Yvonne. "George had indicated they were working on many different bacteria agents such as Anthrax, Smallpox, West Nile, and Lyme disease." She cleared her throat. "This hit Harold especially hard because he was Jewish.

"Borrelia burgdorferi," Gary said.

"Yes, the Lyme disease spirochete," she added. "You see, George believed that Harold was killed because he was going to expose our government's involvement in the spreading of this disease."

"Wait a minute," Taylor interrupted. "Are you saying that your husband thought our government may be responsible for the death of Dr. Brown?"

"I'm afraid so. He didn't believe it was intentional that the disease was spread throughout our population, however he was certain they were negligent in their experiments."

"Go on," Gary said.

"One of the workers on the island, a custodian I believe, watched as a small airplane dropped something into the air over the island. It wasn't until later that it was determined it had been thousands of ticks that had been infected with the Lyme bacteria."

"Why would they do that, exactly?" Taylor asked.

"Ticks, along with mosquitoes are the best creatures to spread a disease throughout a population. They are natural blood suckers that attach to warm blooded creatures and they are much so small and harder to detect than a leach for instance. Ticks are also extremely resilient and can live in all kinds of temperatures," she said. "Did you know you can freeze a tick and when you thaw it out it can come back to life?"

"No." Gary said.

"Have you ever tried to kill a tick?" Yvonne asked.

"Yes, Gary responded. "It's very hard."

"Yes. They are the perfect carrier to spread a disease."

"But why spread them on the island? Why not just test them in a lab?" Taylor asked.

"They did test them in labs. They thought it was the best

95

way to determine the effectiveness of the carrier by spreading them throughout an open population and then calculating how long it would take for the animals on the island to become infected."

Taylor folded her arms across her chest as if she felt a chill. "Wouldn't that be dangerous for the workers on the island?"

"No," Yvonne declared. "George said no one was allowed to leave the facility. A bus drove them to the front entrance and a bus drove them back to the port. They were not allowed anywhere near a vegetated area."

Gary squeezed the sides of his chin causing his face to crinkle up. "That explains why the first case of Lyme disease occurred in Connecticut. The infected animals somehow got off the island to infect the general population."

"Actually, Mr. Mitchell, the first case was not in Lyme Connecticut, it was right here in Montauk Long Island," she said with raised eyebrows; her expression reminded him of his high school science teacher. "In 1970 people began coming down with swollen joints and they called it, Montauk knee," she said. "These were our first cases of Lyme disease in the United States, they just didn't know it. Plum Island is located two miles from Long Island and ten miles from Old Lyme, so that would make sense because it's closer."

"Right, closer for the animals to migrate to," Gary said. "If a tick attached to a bird and it migrated off the Island and landed in Long Island or Connecticut that could explain how the disease began infecting people."

"Yes, that's one possible way," Yvonne agreed.

"This is unbelievable!" Gary looked at Taylor.

"Too bad we can't prove it," Taylor said. "We can't prove any of it."

"Yes." Yvonne peered out the window at the calming water. "My husband did not drown in a fishing accident," she said hauntingly. "He may have been old, but he was an excellent swimmer and he never fell off boats," she said earnestly. "Like Harold, my husband was murdered."

"You really believe that, don't you?" Taylor asked.

"Yes I do," she said. "You see, when Harold learned that Kimberly, his granddaughter, had been misdiagnosed after several years of suffering from Lyme disease, he was pushed to the brink. He called George and said he was going to blow the whistle on the federal government for their involvement in the spreading of the disease." She picked up her cup and tilted it back, it was no longer hot. "George tried to talk him out of it, but his mind was made up."

"That's when he called me," Gary said.

Yvonne nodded her head. "Whoever killed Harold must have known he called George or thought that George was a threat because they were friends and worked together on the Island," she said bitterly. "They killed my husband."

"This is mind blowing," Gary said. "If this is the case, then our government is responsible for spreading one of the worse diseases in recent history, and to cover up their negligence, they are killing scientists to keep it from being exposed."

"This certainly appears to be the case," Yvonne said. "After Harold was killed, George was withdrawn and out of sorts. He didn't say it, but I think he knew he was at risk."

"Is there any documentation or any kind of proof that your husband had to substantiate any of this?" Taylor asked.

"I'm afraid not." Her jaw hardened. "I've gone through his things and have found nothing pertaining to this."

Gary stood up and began pacing in tight circles. "We need to do some digging and find out who else was on that Island that may have seen something."

Both women looked at Gary appreciating his enthusiasm, but they were not as optimistic. Taylor figured that too much time had passed and finding a person with valuable information about what types of experiments took place on Plum Island would be nearly impossible, and if they did locate someone, chances are they wouldn't divulge a word.

The pair thanked Yvonne and assured her they were determined to find out the truth and expose those responsible.

Although she appreciated their tenacity, Yvonne knew they were dealing with something so much bigger than they, something that couldn't be penetrated.

On the boat ride back to Connecticut the mood was somber. They stood on the aft holding onto the rail and looking out at the glossy water in a mesmerized state. Taylor reached over and placed her hand on top of Gary's and he leaned in and gave her a soft kiss. She felt him tighten his grip on her hand. "Look, there!" he said while pointing.

Less than fifty yards away, the heads of four white tailed deer bobbed above the water and were swimming across the sound at a remarkable pace. They glanced at each other without speaking, clearly knowing what the other was thinking. In silence they watched the family of deer swim across the sound until they faded out of site.

CHAPTER 15

The air conditioning was blowing at the lowest fan level and the car vents were aimed upward as Taylor sat in her car about two hundred feet from the Gibbles residence. With a clear view of the front door, she waited for Elsa to finish her house cleaning duties and exit the property. She had been waiting for an hour when she observed Elsa arrive in her minivan and enter the house with her cleaning apparel. Taylor glanced at the dashboard clock; it was a few minutes after three in the afternoon. She had arrived around eleven in the morning and was getting antsy. Every half hour or so, she would pull up her legs and stretch them across the passenger seat before placing them back to the natural position.

A few minutes later, the door swung open and Elsa appeared. After loading up her van, she got in and drove up the street in the opposite direction that Taylor was parked. Pulling out behind Elsa, Taylor kept a comfortable distance as she followed her past the coffee shop where she had uncovered the information that brought her to where she was today. Elsa drove out of town and merged onto the highway heading south and Taylor was curious because Elsa lived north and she wondered if she had another house to clean this late in the day. Following at a speed of eight-two miles per hour, Taylor hoped she didn't get pulled over because a half day of surveillance might be wasted. The right signal on Elsa's car came to life and she pulled onto the off ramp in Old Saybrook and headed onto route 1 south. Less than a mile up the road, her right blinker illuminated and Taylor slowed down as Elsa pulled into the Country Motel and parked in the rear next to a black BMW.

Stopping short and watching as Elsa knocked on a motel room door, Taylor had a feeling she knew who was on the other side. The door opened and Elsa slipped in carrying a small bag and closed the door behind her, and a couple seconds later, the thick curtains were pulled shut not allowing in any daylight or views from the outside world. Taylor accelerated slowly past room number forty-seven; parking a distance away but close enough to keep a watchful eye. Popping open her glove compartment, she extracted her camera with the zoom lens; making sure it had good batteries and was loaded with film. For the second time that day she sat in wait, hoping Elsa was faster at sex then she was at cleaning.

Just before five, the door opened and Elsa came out wearing different clothes than when she went in and Taylor figured she must have showered and changed out of her work clothes in the room. The question was: what was she doing for the other hour and a half? Zooming in close, Taylor snapped pictures of her with the room number in the background. The camera had time logging capabilities, so she could prove the date and time that each photo was taken. As Elsa made her way from the motel to the car, Taylor had snapped eleven pictures. Now she had to wait to see who was going to surface once Elsa was gone. The only other car close to the room was the black BMW and she had run the plate as she waited, and it had come back registered to Senator Gibbles. Taylor was certain that the person in room number forty-seven was the owner of that car; a married man and a politician.

As the door slowly opened, Taylor picked up the camera and began shooting as she observed Senator Gibbles poking his head out from the motel room, making sure the coast was clear before exiting. Again, she made sure she captured the room number in the photos of him as he closed the door and dashed to his car for a quick and sneaky getaway. Taylor was pleased with her photography skills as she had taken thirteen pictures of the cheating senator. Now she had to figure out how she was going to approach him on this. If she wasn't careful, it would give Preston ammunition to go after her, and she knew he was waiting for any little excuse to try and nail her to the cross.

Taylor decided not to question Elsa about her affair with Senator Gibbles. First, she wanted to speak with the senator, because she didn't want Elsa to get to him beforehand and synchronize a plan. When she called the senator's office, Taylor advised his secretary that it was regarding his recent stay at the Country Motel, and a minute later, he was on the other end of the line. Taylor didn't get into anything specific on the phone, she just asked for a meeting and he agreed.

The playground at Harkness Park was busy for a weekday, Taylor thought as she pulled up and parked her car. She got out and walked toward the large swing set, realizing the absence of fathers as she got closer. As young moms played with their preschoolers, she studied with envy the bond between mother and child. A feeling of loneliness overcame her and she stopped for a moment to settle her emotions. Although her work kept her busy, she often fantasized about having a family of her own; a husband that adored her and a couple of kids that looked up to her as if she were their whole world. She resigned herself to keep believing that is was eventually going to happen for her, and her thoughts suddenly drifted to Gary. Every time she saw him she fell a little deeper into his eyes, and when they touched, their bond became stronger with each embrace.

The sound of a car coming closer sliced through her thoughts and she turned to see a black BMW crawl to a stop and park beside her car. Dressed in a fine suit, Senator Gibbles got out and started toward her in a fast pace. As he approached, she pictured him and Elsa together in the dusty motel room grappling in lustful deceit.

"I hope this is important," he said before he reached her.

"I think it is, Senator."

"Well, get on with it then." There were no kind gestures or greetings between them.

"Let me be frank with you, Senator. I'm investigating the death of Roy Hermanette and I have reason to believe there may be foul play involved."

"What has that got to do with me?" he belched out.

Taylor reached into her pocket and took out four photographs and handed them to him. "I know about your affair with, Elsa Hermanette."

He glanced at the pictures and his expression declined, like a boxer absorbing a hard body shot.

"Alright, we were in a room together, so what!" He slid the pictures into his pocket.

"I have several copies, Senator," she said. "To be honest with you, I don't care who you roll around with. What I do care about is a dead man who had a knife plunged through his heart."

His jaw set. "I know nothing about that."

"How long have you two been seeing each other, and don't lie to me Senator, because I'll find out exactly how long."

He didn't like the way she spoke to him and he was thinking of who he knew in the state police that could lay a hurting on her. "About eight or nine months," he said in a descending tone.

"What is the extent of your relationship; are you in love?"

He hesitated. "Love, no." He scanned the park. "We have some fun together, that's all."

"I have a feeling she won't see it that way, will she Senator?"

"Probably not, you know how women are."

Taylor resented the comment. "No I don't, enlighten me, Senator."

"It started as a fling and she agreed that was as far as it would go, but then she started questioning our future together. I told her I wasn't planning on leaving my wife and I reminded her that she had a husband."

"How did she respond to that?"

"She said she could care less about her husband - that he was a peasant."

"Do you think she killed him?" Her eyes bore into his.

"I don't know. I doubt it."

Taylor watched a mother lifting her toddler and placing him on a swing. "I don't believe you," she said.

"Well too God damned bad," he retorted.

"Senator, make no mistake. If I don't get full cooperation from you, your wife will wake up tomorrow to her morning coffee and her newspaper and these photographs will be on the front page. Am I making myself clear?"

He took a big swallow. "You would do that?"

"You bet your cheating ass I would."

He stood looking at her as if she was his executioner. "Over here," he said and he walked to a park bench and took a seat. She sat next to him, but a few feet apart, he gave her the willies. "After a few months she began to become controlling, asking me about my sex life with my wife and what our future together held. It came to the point where I was going to call the whole thing off, just end it."

"Why didn't you?"

"She threatened to expose our relationship."

"So you just played along despite her intentions?"

"Look, she's a beautiful woman." He looked at Taylor in a peculiar way and she tilted away. "My wife and I don't have, let's just say our sex life is less than exciting, if you know what I mean.

"What did she say about her husband and their relationship?"

"She said she didn't care about him and that she was going to leave him."

"That's all, she didn't say anything else?"

"Not really." His eyes shifted and he cleared his throat.

He's lying. "What did she say after she killed him?"

"She said he was abusing her and that he was going to kill her and she defended herself." Again, he cleared his throat.

Almost word for word as her statement. "You know what, Senator. I'm finished playing games with you."

"What are you talking about?" he asked coyly.

"It's clear to me that you're lying. You can say goodbye to your political career and your wife. I'm placing a noose around your neck. Enjoy the rest of your last day!" She said coldly and turned to walk away.

"Wait!" he quivered. "What do you want from me?"

"I want the truth! You're lying to me, and it's clear as day," she belted out as she sat back down. "I have a dead man on my hands, and from what I've learned, he was a good man." There was a brief hesitation as she looked deep into his eyes. "Do you want his blood on your hands for the rest of your life?"

"Wait a minute! I had nothing to do with that man's death."

"That's not the way I see it. You're having an affair with his wife. You both come up with a plan to get rid of him, and by the way, collecting on his two-hundred thousand in life insurance is a nice bonus," she added. "So you helped her in the planning and execution of his murder to get him out of the way and cash in on the insurance."

"That's a lie!"

"Let's see what the media does with this story. This will make national news and you'll be a famous man, or should I say infamous?"

"You bitch!" he roared.

"Goodbye, Senator." She snapped to her feet like a marine being confronted by a superior officer.

"Alright!" he said. "I didn't know she was planning to kill him."

Taylor stopped and faced him. "Go on."

"I thought she was going to divorce him, that's all."

"I'm listening, Senator."

"Then she told me that the only way we could be together and happy was to get rid of him and the money would help us to start our new life together."

"She told you this, *when*?"

"After the incident; we met at the hotel and she told me then."

"Why, why would she tell you this?"

"Because she wanted me to know how serious she was about our relationship, how much she wanted us to be together."

"She's in love with you?"

"Yes, I don't know," he spluttered. "The power, I think she's in love with my status."

"So, Elsa told you she planned and murdered her husband?"

"Yes."

"Aren't you a little afraid of her? If she did this to him, why wouldn't she do it to you, if she was uncertain about your future together?"

"I told her I was planning on divorcing my wife."

104

"And are you?"

"Yes, I told Elsa I would after the election."

"What did she tell you about the murder, how did it happen?"

His face declined as if the nerves had died. "She waited until he fell asleep."

"She stabbed her husband while he slept?"

"Yes," he said guiltily.

Taylor had to sit, so she stepped back to the bench. "Were you really going to leave your wife for Elsa?"

"I don't know," he cried. "I was just buying time until after the election. I needed time to think things through." He wiped the tears from his cheeks. "I've been forthright with you. Please keep me out of this."

"I'll do what I can," she said metallically.

"What does that mean?" he asked.

"It means, if I can get her to confess, I'll keep you out of it the best I can, but you should have come forth after she told you that she murdered him."

He hesitated for a few seconds, just looking at her with glossy eyes. "What if she doesn't confess?"

"Then you'll have to testify in court."

"I'll be ruined!"

"You'll have a clear conscious, Senator." She got up. "Thank you for opening up and being truthful."

"Please try and keep me out of this," he pleaded.

She looked at the deflated man without responding and simply nodded her head and walked toward her car. Once she was back at her car, Taylor got in and stopped for a moment to look at the senator as he sat slumped on the park bench. She pulled out her pocket recorder and pushed the button, turning it off.

CHAPTER 16

Taylor hadn't said anything to Gibbles, but she figured the only way they were going to nail Elsa was to have him wear a wire. She wanted to speak with Preston and the district attorney first; after all, he was a state senator. At first she received thundering resistance from Preston and then she played him the tape. After he scolded her for illegally taping a high level politician, she assured him it was for his purposes only, so that he would hear the truth for himself. Even though Preston despised her for her action against Trooper Trombley, he admired her for her cunning ability to out-smart a perpetrator. Together they took it to the district attorney, absent the tape. Taylor revealed what she had heard from Gibbles and the DA agreed to bring the senator in and try and convince him to wear a wire.

After a long and drawn out battle with Gibbles, Taylor and the DA played on his emotions regarding the brutal death of Hermanette, and he agreed to wear a wire. They devised a plan that would get Elsa to open up and admit to killing her husband and that plan entailed the senator making promises of marriage and a happily ever after.

Three days later, Taylor arrested Elsa for the murder of Roy Hermanette. As she escorted her out of her apartment in handcuffs, Elsa didn't say a word; she just burned holes into Taylor's eyes with a satanic glare. Two days later, the story of the senator's affair hit the news media and it was the beginning of the end of his career and marriage. Although he was distraught over his consequences, deep inside he felt good that he had done the right thing. The leak of the affair had not come from Taylor, she kept her word.

Armed with her best weapon (her recorder) Taylor waited inside a secluded visiting room at the Vernon Correctional facility where Windows had been transferred. The private room she waited in was for attorneys and police officers to meet in private with inmates regarding criminal justice matters. The place Windows now called home was a facility that was used for high profile cases such as mob informants, convicted police officers, and anyone that needed to be protected. Although Windows was safer at Vernon than he was at Stonington, there was less interaction and freedom and it became boring very fast.

Taylor had made the drive without the knowledge of Preston. He had made it perfectly clear that the Brown case was closed and the right man was locked up and awaiting trial. What he didn't know was that Taylor had uncovered new information about the death of a former government biological scientist, George Lynch, and that opened up some serious questions regarding the guilt of Alexander Windows.

Windows was escorted in with his shackles and smug look intact. He took a seat across from Taylor without speaking and his eyes were situated on hers.

"How are you making out in here, Alex?" The tape was rolling.

"It sucks, but at least the vultures aren't pecking at my neck." He spoke out of one side of his mouth and he needed a shave.

"This is what you wanted, and here you are, *safe*."

"Am I supposed to thank you or something?" He snarled.

"No, but you could start by ending the lies."

He straightened up in his seat. "What do you mean?"

"You've been throwing so much crap at me, I'm nearly buried," she said.

"How so?" he asked as he bore into the table with his overgrown nail.

"You didn't kill Dr. Brown, did you?" He didn't respond. "You came up with a tall tale just so you could get the hell out of

Stonington, didn't you?"

"What do you care?" he asked. "Your case is all wrapped up nice and neat."

"I care, Alex, because if you didn't do it then there's a killer running around out there and I need to find him." She crossed her arms. "Besides, I'm not one that likes to see an innocent man go to jail for a crime he didn't commit."

"Isn't that special; a cop that cares." His words were like small daggers, but she deflected them without concern.

"Look, we aren't going to move you back to Stonington, even if you recant your confession," she said. "It's only you and me here." She stood up and pulled her chair closer to him with a closer view of his overgrown sideburns.

"Alex, tell me the truth. Did you kill Dr. Brown or not?"

"No!" he shouted. "Do I look like the type of person that kills old people?"

"No, you don't."

"I'm a thief. That's all I've ever been," he said in a declining voice.

"So you confessed to the murder of Dr. Brown, why?"

"To get the hell out of Stonington; they were going to kill me in there. I had to say whatever it took to save my ass, that's why."

"Alex, is it your testimony that you have never been on Dr. Brown's property and that you never had contact with him?"

"Yeah, I wouldn't have known the guy if he sat on my lap, and I've never stepped foot on his property."

"Alright, Alex." She stood up. "Thanks for your candor. I'll be in touch." She motioned to the guard that stood on the opposite side of the heavy metal door and he turned his key.

In Preston's office, a tape rolled for the second time in five days. The first time wrapped up the Hermanette case and Taylor was hoping that this time she would convince Preston to re-open the Brown case. She had started with the statement taken by Yvonne Lynch and then she played the Windows tape. After the second statement ended, she pushed the button and it stopped rolling. Preston sat for a moment, absorbing what he had just heard and then he rose to his feet and paced the room, stopping at the window and looking out to the street.

"This old lady has quite an imagination," he said watching the street traffic.

"I think she may have something," Taylor rebutted. "What are the chances that two very best friends that worked together at Plum Island for over four decades both end up dead in a matter of a few weeks?"

"Coincidence, that's all I see." He turned around and walked back to his desk.

Taylor noticed he was calmer than usual and she attributed it to the Hermanette closure. "You heard Windows' statement," she said. "I don't believe he did it, and if he didn't, a killer is still out there. Don't you think we owe it to ourselves and Dr Brown's family to at least look into it?"

"You really believe Windows?" He took a seat back in his chair.

"Yes I do," she said with sincerity.

He examined her for a moment. "And you believe that there is some kind of a federal spook running around killing people to cover up a government conspiracy about Lyme disease?"

"I don't know for sure, but I think the person responsible for killing Dr. Brown is still out there and we should catch him."

"Alright, I'll tell you what." He straightened up and folded his hands like a man in the front pew of a church. "I don't have any hot cases right now, so I'll allow you to look into it, however, you have two weeks."

"How about three?"

"Don't push it, Trooper."

"Alright, two weeks," she agreed.

"You better get busy," he said as he looked toward the door.

"Thanks, Lieutenant." She got up and walked out with a hidden smile.

CHAPTER 17

If it weren't for the endless, lingering, smoke in the air, the night would be perfect, Taylor thought. They had arrived at the casino early and noticed that the band, America, was playing at the Wolves Den lounge. If they had arrived ten minutes later, it would have been too late for them to find seats at the bar. As the bar filled up, so did the smokers and this was the price they had to pay for a free show. The band was playing, the drinks were flowing and the buzz was growing. Taylor was sipping red wine and Gary was on beer. Neither of them were big drinkers, but the drinks seemed to fall back smoothly on this particular night. Gary was resigned to keeping the conversation about anything other than work, because he wanted this night to be special, a night Taylor would remember.

"This band is amazing," she said. "I can't believe they don't charge a cover for them."

"They sound just like the record, don't they?" he said as his palms collided.

"They do, and the amazing thing is that the record was made twenty years ago."

Gary laughed. "I still say the best music was recorded in the seventies."

"I'll drink to that," Taylor said as she raised her glass and they toasted with, Sister Golden Hair, playing in the background.

As their eyes met they became stuck and neither of them had the willpower to disengage. "You are the most beautiful and interesting woman I have ever known." His words came to her like an unexpected gift and she felt a warm wave beginning to stir inside. Gary leaned in and softly kissed her and she accepted it openly as she ran her fingers along his bicep area. His arms were chiseled and strong and his physical condition excited her.

When the music ended, Gary took her by the hand and led her to a craps table. He didn't jump right in and start playing; he stood watching as the hungry gamblers lay down their cash and rolled the dice.

"Aren't you going to play?" she asked.

He glanced at her, and the way the light caught her eyes and shiny hair nearly made his knees weak. She was wearing a red dress, with a diamond necklace and earrings and her hair was perfectly pinned up exposing her neck. She had such a soft and creamy neck and he wanted to gorge himself into it.

"No, not yet," he said. "I want to see how the luck is running for the players."

"I see."

"If the house is killing the table then I can bet with the house, and if the players are winning, I will go with them."

"I didn't know you had that option," she said naively.

Her innocence intrigued him. "Yes, we do. Another option is to find another table with good karma."

"Do you believe in karma?" she asked.

"Are you kidding? I live by it."

Her smile widened. "Me too, and I'm not feeling it on this table," she said.

Gary chuckled, kissed her, and took her by the hand leading her to another table. After five minutes they were in agreement that the second table was the one. Taylor was reluctant to play, but Gary convinced her to join in and he put up the money. After a half hour on the table, they were both thrilled with their decision as the chips piled up in front of them. They were betting against the house and the house was taking a beating. When the time came for Taylor to roll the dice, she went on a winning streak for nine rolls, and the table roared with excitement as she continued to toss two little squares across the table. After an hour, the luck of the table began to change and Gary could smell it. "I think it's time for us to cash in," he said.

"Sounds good," she agreed and they collected their chips and said their goodbyes to the happy gamblers they would never see again.

At the cash out window, Taylor was excited as the winning bills were spread out, one at a time in front of her.

"Six hundred and sixty bucks!" she said with a beaming smile.

"Not bad for a beginner," he said. His take was just over nine hundred and after collecting his due, Taylor stopped and pulled him aside and began kissing him. Her advance was unexpected and exciting to him. She opened his hand and placed her winnings in it.

"What's this?" he asked.

"It's yours," she said. "You gave me the money to play."

"No way." He handed it back. "It doesn't work like that; you won the money and it's yours to keep."

"I don't feel right about it," she confessed.

He hesitated not wanting to discount her feelings. "Alright, I'll tell you what." He took a hundred dollar bill from the fold and handed her the remaining bills. "This is what I gave you to start with and I'm taking it back, the rest is yours. I think that's fair, don't you?"

She grinned and it bloomed into a full blown smile. "Okay." She took the money and they moved toward the exit, stopping for ice cream on the way.

When his car pulled up in front of her house it was well after midnight and the moon was full in the sky. Gary leaned in for a long kiss and she began to become more aggressive with her tongue. "This has been one of the best nights of my life," she said.

"It has been for me as well."

"I don't want it to end."

"Nor do I," he said.

"Would you like to come in?"

"Sure," he said and he pulled the keys from the ignition.

Inside the house, soft, sexy, music was playing and Gary thought it to be Barry White. Taylor had opened a bottle of Merlot and they sat on the couch inches apart.

"Cheers," Taylor said as she raised her glass.

"I can't remember the last time I toasted so many times in a single night," he said. "Cheers."

They drank. "It has been one hell of a celebration," she gushed.

"Yeah, it has," he agreed. "What the hell are we celebrating?" They snared a glance and they both began laughing.

When the laughter settled, Taylor spoke. "We're celebrating *us.*"

Without removing his eyes from hers he placed down his glass and he found her lips and they engaged in a long, soft, kiss. When it was time to come up for air, he moved down to her neck area, pelting her with a series of soft pecks all over her neck and chin area. Taylor began to breathe heavier and her heartbeat became rapid. Her tingling began moving south and she knew she had to have him. She broke free of his grasp and stood up and Gary knew it wasn't for rejection. In his entire life he couldn't recall ever wanting a woman so desperately. He craved her so much he felt a hunger in his center that seemed to radiate throughout his entire body. Taylor began to take off her dress and he wanted so badly to see her naked flesh, but not yet.

"Wait," he whispered as he stood up. "I want you so much, but not now." He took her hands, stopping her from undressing. "I don't want this to be a short lived romance," he said, "I want this to be long term, and I want us to know each other better." He leaned in and kissed her.

Taylor didn't know what to say. She had never had a man decline her sexually before. "I understand," she said as she sat back down.

"I'm not sure you do," he said as he took a seat next to her. "Almost every time I jumped into bed with a woman within the first few dates, it was a short lived relationship. I don't want that with you." What he also wanted to say, but didn't, was that he was falling in love with her. "Our time for making love will come, and when it does, it will be perfect." He took her hand and squeezed it firmly.

"Where did you come from?" she asked with a grin. "Gary Mitchell, I don't believe I have ever met such an interesting man before."

"Just interesting?" he asked with puppy dog eyes. "Not sexy?"

"Yes, very sexy."

"Are we good here?" he asked.

She kissed him. "We are much more than good."

Gary stayed for three more hours and they talked and laughed and kissed as he held her close. After he left, they both thought about each other and could hardly wait until the next time they would be together. They were equally falling for each other. There was no imbalance in their feelings, but neither of them knew that for sure.

CHAPTER 18

When it came to investigative reporting, Gary left no stone unturned. He earned a reputation of a relentless and often annoying reporter that most politicians tried diligently to avoid. Although most deflected him onto their aids and assistants, Gary usually found a way to get in front of them, and he always asked the hard questions. The main reason he ducked the blows of repercussion from his superiors at the Register was that he always did his homework, and in the end, he exposed the truth.

Governor Bell knew Gary was on the warpath and she was beginning to feel a thorn poking into her side. She had recently run into the owner of the Register, Thomas Deutsch, at a party and she mentioned Gary's name and how he was beginning to stir up some unnecessary dust. She also stated that she thought a different line of work may be more suitable for him. Deutsch knew exactly where she was going with her statement and he didn't respond, he just grinned, nodded his head and moved toward the hors d'oeuvres table. He and Gary were friends and he believed his top reporter was onto something and he wasn't about to terminate him because the Governor didn't like the way he conducted his investigation into a possible Lyme disease corruption case.

Gary began digging into campaign contributions to the governor's office and fundraising activities over the past couple of years. He spent many hours reading and taking notes of public files and what he found was beginning to put a bounce in his step. Even though there is a limit to the amount of contributions a corporation can donate to a political campaign, he learned that millions of dollars in excess of the limit were being donated to Governor Bell's campaign. Major pharmaceutical and insurance companies had found loopholes in the law by donating the maximum of five thousand dollars per individual employee in PAC contributions. Gary began to add up the amount of money the Governor was getting from four of the biggest companies in Connecticut by using PAC funds and he was astonished that it added up to millions of dollars.

The next thing he began to do was to find the common link between the Governor and these companies and what he found was they all pointed to Barret & Melino Associates lobbying firm.

After digging into the infamous lobbying firm, Gary began to research terminated employees that had left the company in the past five years, particularly lobbyists and their aids. After a deep dive, he came up with five names of former employees that had left the company within a three year period and he began to track them down. Four days later, Gary had left three messages, he had one hang up, and he was unable to locate one of them. To his surprise, he had gotten a call back from, Leslie Camerotta, a former lobbyist and she agreed to meet with him in Manhattan where she was now residing.

The restaurant in Time Square was bustling as Leslie approached the table where Gary was seated. He had arrived forty minutes early to be sure he didn't miss her and he wanted to find a table in a remote section of the eating establishment.

"You must be Leslie," he said as he stood, putting forth his hand.

"Yes, nice to meet you, Mr. Mitchell." She took his hand with a firm business-like hand shake.

"Please call me, Gary."

She smiled and took a seat across the table with her back to the commotion. Gary thought her to be an attractive woman about thirty years old. She had fair skin and long, straight, blond hair. Her light blue eyes and bright teeth complimented a Scandinavian appearance. Standing nearly as tall he, Gary thought she could have moved into a modeling career.

"I'm surprised you were able to get a table in here so fast," she said as if she had dined there before.

"I arrived early and put my name in, and here we are," he said opening his hands toward the ceiling like a magician. "I have asked you here to discuss your former firm's dealings with Governor Bell's office relating to legislation enacted regarding Lyme disease." She didn't speak, she just watched him in action and she liked what she saw. He was extremely sexy to her and she briefly visualized a sexual encounter with him. "I have been investigating possible corruption in Connecticut, and how Governor Bell may be making legislative decisions based on corporate campaign contributions rather than public health. Why did you leave Barret & Melino?"

"I was fired," she blasted like a cannon.

"Fired, may I ask why?"

She swept back a strand of hair. "It's pretty simple really. My account was Reliance Health Group and I was lobbying with the governor's office to fight legislation proposed that would provide long term treatment of chronic Lyme disease and the administering of antibiotics to patients for lengthy periods of time." The server came over and took their order, they both chose salads. "I lost the fight and the lobbyists for the pharmaceutical companies won. With that loss, came the end of my employment."

"They terminated you for that?"

"This was a huge bill for us to lose."

"I'm familiar with Bill 5800, Act 01-027," he said.

She was impressed that he knew the designation of the bill. "Look, the pharmaceutical companies have deep pockets and probably struck a deal to throw tons of cash at the Governor and she went with them."

"I know. I've reviewed her campaign contribution documents." The server appeared with their drinks and was off as fast as she came.

"The insurance companies did not want that bill passed because it meant hundreds of millions of dollars in costs to them. A bill such as this requires insurance companies to pay for long term care for Lyme disease, including office visits, testing and medicines. Just think of the cost for a single chronic Lyme disease patient over a period of five years."

"Probably tens of thousands," he said.

"Yes, now multiply that by a hundred thousand. You catch my drift?"

"Yes, I do," Gary responded.

"Now think of the amount of money the pharmaceutical companies will make on this bill. The prices they charge for antibiotics are ridiculous."

"I know," Gary agreed. "The mark-up is astronomical in the United States."

"And the insurance companies absorb most of that cost." She took a long sip of her lemon water. "You have to understand that Pharmaceutical companies really don't want a cure or vaccine for Lyme disease."

"Why is that?" He already knew why, but he wanted to hear it from her.

"Lyme disease mimics so many diseases that all require prescription drugs. If we found a cure for Lyme, they would lose billions of dollars."

He concurred with a nod of his head.

"A person goes to a gastro intestinal specialist for acid reflux disease. It's really just the effects of chronic Lyme disease, but of course he tests negative like most people with the disease and he's treated with Nexium instead of Doxycycline." She drank from her glass. "A woman goes to an orthopedic surgeon for a knee problem and he convinces her to have surgery and she takes her doctor's advice. How much do you think the operation, follow-up visits, physical therapy, and pain killers amount to?"

"A lot," he said as he reached for his cup of green tea.

"Yes, and it was Lyme disease all along and it could have been cured with a heavy dose of antibiotics for a couple months. You see, doctors, pharmaceutical companies, and researchers really don't want a cure for this disease because they rake in tons of money from it."

"I see your point, Leslie."

"As you probably know, this disease can attack just about any part of our body, our eyesight, our joints, our stomach and intestines, our heart and organs."

"The nervous system," he added.

"Yes, and our muscular system too," she said with an arched eyebrow. "Think of all the specialized doctors involved in these treatments."

"And the drugs it takes to treat them," he added.

"There is way too much money involved to put an end to this cash cow called, Lyme disease," she said.

"So what you're saying is that many of these healthcare professionals and these corporations really don't care about the millions of people that are suffering every day of their lives."

"That's exactly what I'm saying. They only care about the money."

"I've said it a hundred times if I've said it once, greed is ruining this country."

"Amen," she followed. "Corporate greed. To be honest with you, I'm glad I got out of that business. I made a ton of money, but it's a dirty business. I can look in the mirror much easier these days."

"What are you doing *now*?"

"I work for a corporate law firm here in the city."

"I'm glad you've found something more suitable. You appear much to clean for the kind of work it takes to be a successful lobbyist."

"I do miss the paychecks, though." She smiled.

"Don't worry." He smirked. "Lunch is on me."

They shared a laugh and the server came over with their lunch. Gary left the meeting exhilarated knowing he was going to have one hell of a story to write.

At this point, Taylor was convinced Windows was not responsible for the murder of Dr. Brown, but she knew Preston would not be ready to go to the press with the story. She had to move fast to come up with some evidence that would prove another person was the culprit. After speaking with the lead investigator in Long Island that was assigned to the Lynch case, she was still at a dead end. The report deemed his death as a drowning accident, however, Yvonne Lynch and Taylor both figured it differently. Taylor thought that the person responsible was very good at killing because there were no traces of foul play and no witnesses that observed another boat near Dr. Lynch's vessel on the morning of the incident. The report also indicated that a retired CIO of an engineering firm in New York was having his morning coffee as he gazed out his window with a clear view of Dr. Lynch's boat. His statement was that he saw nothing out of the ordinary and that he was accustomed to seeing the boat in the sound around the same time nearly every morning. Dr. Lynch had sailed to his fishing location alone and there was no sign of a struggle on the boat, so how could he have been murdered? Taylor figured if someone was to swim out to the boat to kill Dr. Lynch they would have been noticed by someone, because it is very unusual for someone to swim in the sound that early in the morning and so far off shore.

The autopsy indicated that the cause of death was a drowning and there were no other signs of physical trauma, but how could this happen? If he fell off the boat, he was quite strong enough to swim to the stern and pull himself back up the ladder. Taylor was in agreement with Yvonne Lynch that both doctors were killed because they had knowledge of wrong-doing at the Plum Island facility, and she needed to find out what that was, and be able to provide some sort of proof. It also crossed her mind that whoever was responsible for killing the bio-scientists might not hesitate to go after her, if she got too close.

CHAPTER 19

Tara turned the key to her front door with Tanner following behind, lightly nudging her to get in. Pushing the door shut, she placed the shopping bag down on a table stand near the door. Her son darted to his room and she moved into the kitchen and switched on the light. Sitting on the counter was two empty beer cans and she became instantly bewildered on how they got there. They were the same brand that she kept in her refrigerator; however, she hadn't had a beer at home in over a week. Something told her to check the house, so she moved into the living room, and as she turned the corner, she saw the silhouette of a man sitting in the dark corner of the room.

"Hello Tara." The low voice was like a knife cutting through her skin. She slipped her hand into her jacket pocket and began caressing her cell phone buttons.

"Reggie, how did you get in here?" she asked with a tremor.

"The key hidden in the fake rock by the back door," he replied as he took to his feet. *How did he know about the hidden key? I've never used it in front of him.*

She thumbed the buttons and counted the rowed numbers. She pushed the number nine. "What do you want, Reggie?"

"You know what I want!" he stammered. She could tell he was drunk.

"Reggie, you can get into big trouble for being here." She pushed the numeral one, twice.

He moved closer and the light from the kitchen lined his face. "I don't care about no damn restraining order," he said in an elevated voice. "I gave you my heart and soul and I was kind to Tanner, and how do you repay me?"

"Reggie."

"Shut up!" he cut her off. "You repay me by throwing me to the curb like a piece of trash."

"It's not like that," she said as she found the send button.

"Isn't it?" he yelled.

She wanted to control the situation and keep him calm, but she saw how he was becoming agitated and working his self into a state of fury. The phone was dialing and she was afraid he would hear it, so she knew she had to drown out the ringing by talking louder.

"Reggie, can we sit down and calmly discuss this. I didn't throw you to the curb; I just needed some time alone to think. It's not that we can't have some kind of a relationship," she rambled. A woman's voice on the other line was sounding and she muffled the speaker with her palm, pushing it against her hip.

"Bullshit!" he yelled. "You're just saying that to save your ass."

"Mommy, are you alright?"

She turned to see Tanner standing in the doorway with a drooping lower lip. "Yes, honey I'm just talking to Reggie. Go back up to your room."

"Hey, buddy," Reggie slurred. "How's my Pal doing?"

"Go ahead, Tanner. Mommy will be right up." Tara knew the police would automatically dispatch a car because it was standard police policy on hang ups and situations like this. Her son did as he was told and she turned her focus back on Reggie. "Listen, we had a good time together, right?"

"Yeah," he said as he moved closer. "I say we continue having the good times right now."

Tara thought it might come to sex and she would have to play along for self preservation. "Let me check on my son and we can talk about that."

"Why, so you can call the cops again. I don't think so." He grabbed her by the arm and pulled her close. She could smell the liquor on his breath. Looking deep into his eyes, she became terrified realizing she never really knew Reggie, until now. She could hear the pounding inside her chest and her brow was growing damp.

"Alright, Reggie, let's have a drink together and get into the mood," she back peddled.

"I am in the mood," he said as he pulled her against him and started kissing her motionless lips. He pulled her to the couch and threw her down.

"Take it easy," she said.

"Forget easy," he said. "Tonight it's going to be rough." He grabbed her blouse and ripped it open. She began to struggle and he slapped her across the face with the back of his hand. Reaching under her skirt he latched onto her panties and began pulling them down. "No, Reggie!" she cried as tears began to develop in the corners of her terrified eyes.

Her words went unheard and he tore the panties from her body causing an abrasion on her thigh.

"Stop it," she cried out.

"Come on baby, just like old times," he said as he started to unbuckle his pants. His weight was pinning her down, but she found all her strength and began to struggle, pushing him off. A quick punch to the face slowed down her attempt, and the stinging blow knocked her senseless. As he began to pull up her skirt he heard the sound of car doors closing outside. He got up to look out the window, and as he pulled the shades back, he saw the police officers approaching.

"You bitch!" he said through gritting teeth. "You did it to me again."

He came toward her in a rage, and with all her energy, she screamed so loud the windows may have been in jeopardy. "This isn't over," he warned. "I'm going to kill you!"

As the police officers came in the front, Reggie went out the back and he was gone.

When Taylor's car pulled up in front of Tara's house, her heart rate began to increase. Three police cruisers parked at all angles sat empty, and she knew this was a serious situation.

Tara had called her, babbling in a frantic tone and not elaborating on what had occurred. Without hesitation, Taylor drove as fast as she could to the aid of her desperate friend.

"State Police," she said with her badge out as she entered the house. The two officers near the front door acknowledged her and she continued into the house searching for Tara. In the kitchen, Tara sat with glazed eyes and a sagging posture. When she saw her friend, she began to tear up and Taylor knelt down and embraced her. "It's alright, Tara, we're going to put an end to this." Taylor looked her in the eye. "Are you alright?"

"Yes, but I'm scared," she cried. "He said he was going to kill me, and I believe him."

"Okay, let's get up," she said. "Take a drink of water." She filled a glass with spring water and handed it to Tara and she drank.

"Let's get some fresh air and take a short walk."

"Alright," Tara agreed.

Outside, they began up the street in a moderate pace. "I want you to tell me what Reggie does in his spare time. Does he have any hobbies? What bars does he drink at? Who are his best friends and where do they live? Does he have any family that he visits around here?" She took out a pad and pen and began to take notes as Tara recollected all she could about the man she hardly knew. Taylor didn't write for very long.

CHAPTER 20

When the governor's aid handed her the morning newspaper, she had to sit down. The headline read: PROBE SOUGHT IN GOVERNORS DEALINGS WITH LOBBYISTS. The article went on to read that the states attorney was also looking into her two million dollar beach house that was built and financed at an extremely low cost by acquaintances of Governor Bell that she had awarded state contracts.

She placed the newspaper down on her desk with a hand that grew shakier since she first picked it up. Scooping up her phone, she told her secretary to hold all calls and cancel her appointments for the day, and then she called her attorney.

The same newspaper sat on Gary's desk with the headline staring him in the face. He felt good and bad at the same time. Even though he knew he was doing the right thing by exposing a corrupt politician, he also knew he was destroying a person's career and possibly her life, and this didn't offer him any intrinsic joy.

Gary thought about his life and the direction it was now heading, and he began to feel a slight surge of exhilaration. He was falling in love with Taylor and his career was giving him a certain sense of purpose and accomplishment. Looking up at the clock on the wall, he realized it was getting late as he scanned the room and noticed that most of his colleagues had left for the day. After logging off his desktop, he snatched the paper off his desk and headed for the exit.

In the parking garage across the street, Ben sat slumped behind the wheel of a black sedan that he boosted from the train station parking lot. He figured he had plenty of time to use the vehicle before its owner returned from his trip and reported it missing. Today, Ben was disguised as a woman wearing a blond shoulder length wig and red lipstick. He thought he actually looked better than most of the women he'd seen as he traveled through New Haven. If anyone was to notice him or catch his license plate number, he figured he would be covered, because the plate was from a stolen car and it was occupied by a woman; an attractive woman with a protruding Adams apple.

The garage was empty as Gary pushed open the heavy, metal, door that led to the parking area. He started down the ramp heading toward his car that was parked a distance from where he entered the garage. The sound of the vehicle turning the corner didn't mean anything to him, as he was complacent in the garage that he had been accustomed to for several years. As he continued down the ramp, the growing sound of the car accelerating behind him suddenly caught his attention. He quickly turned around, thinking the car was speeding way too fast for a parking garage, and he saw that it was heading in his direction. *What an asshole.* He looked deep through the windshield as it came closer and he noticed the face of a woman behind the wheel. Gary began to move to the side in order to let the car pass by him. In a split second, and at the same time he had taken his eyes off of the vehicle, the car made a quick turn in his direction. With the sedan traveling fifty-four miles an hour, it all happened in an instant, and once Gary noticed the car turning in his direction, it was too late. The impact was a sudden, painful, and stunning blow that knocked him eight feet into the air, and when he landed, he landed head first.

Ben looked into his mirror and saw that his target was lying on his side and not moving. Quickly scanning the parking garage, he thought it to be clear, so he shifted into reverse and was ready to back up over his target to make sure he was dead. He figured two times over the body would more than do the job to assure that Gary's investigative reporting days were finished. Just as he began to accelerate in reverse, he heard a loud voice yelling from the entranceway to the stairs.

"Hey!" Ben heard a man's voice and saw three people running toward his target. "Stop!" a young woman yelled. Ben thought that he might have enough time to get to the target before they reached him, but if he didn't, he might run them over as well and the whole thing would get complicated and messy and Ben didn't like to work messy. He prided himself on having a reputation with his employer as working very clean, and this was why they continued to retain his services, paying him top dollar. If he severely injured or killed innocent citizens, they would begin to look at him in a very different light because his employer did not believe in collateral damage outside of a battlefield. All this ran through his mind in a split second, as the three bystanders ran to the aid of his target. Hitting his brakes, Ben stopped the car for a brief moment and he saw a pool of blood beginning to grow around the head of his target. *He may very well be dead.*

"Wait right there!" one of the men yelled at him. Ben saw the second man on his cell phone and speaking to whom he thought would be a police dispatcher. Pulling the shift into gear, he stepped on the gas pedal and quickly drove off as the bystanders continued yelling at him to stop. Ben vanished into the city with the sound of sirens warning the evening air.

The next morning Taylor picked up the newspaper and started reading over a cup of coffee. As she scanned through the articles she stopped at a headline that read, *Reporter, victim of hit and run.* Her heart jumped a beat when she read that the victim was, Gary Mitchell, the man she had fallen deeply in love with over the past couple of months. She began to speed read looking for print that indicated how badly he was hurt. *Critical condition, he's still alive.* She read that he was taken to Yale Medical Center, and in record time, she dressed and darted to her car without bothering to shower. On the way to the hospital she prayed over and over asking God to keep him alive. With both hands clutched to the steering wheel, she drove as fast as she could, flashing her blue lights when she needed to get past a slow driver. When she removed a hand from the wheel, she felt a slight tremble, but she maintained her composure because she had to be strong for Gary.

Many thoughts began to race through her mind. *I hope he's not suffering, my darling Gary. I finally find real love and now this happens. What will I do if he dies? This is not an accident and I will find whoever did this. I promise you Gary, I will find them.*

In the waiting room, Taylor sat across from an elderly woman that was waiting for news on her husband of fifty years who had suffered a stroke. She sat with a rosary in her hand and was praying behind closed lips, as she slowly rocked back and forth, like a toddler trying to fall asleep. A father and mother also sat in wait with a few family members, and the man was pacing the floor, worried that he may never see his seventeen year old son alive again after running his car into a tree while traveling sixty miles an hour. This was the last place on earth Taylor wanted to be right now and it was the only place she could possibly be.

As Taylor sat in wait, the clock on the wall seemed to be moving in slow motion and she could find no complacency. A few hours later, a doctor came out and approached the parents of the boy that had the car accident and he escorted them into a private room that adjoined the waiting area. A couple minutes later, cries breached the walls and Taylor knew it was bad news for the family, and right then, she prayed that she would never see the inside of that room. The waiting room emptied, and she sat alone with the old woman, and for the first time since the death of her parents, she felt so very much alone. *Someone is killing people and now they attempted to take Gary's life because he was getting close to uncovering the truth. First, two reputable scientists are killed, and now Gary, a victim of some maniac assassin. Who is doing this and who is giving the orders? I think I know why they are doing it, but I need to find out who's responsible and put an end to it before another person dies. Am I next on his hit list?*

A young man dressed in a white smock with a stethoscope

draped over his shoulders came out and rapidly approached Taylor, he looked tired and hurried.

"Ms. Marshall?"

"Yes." She was hoping he didn't ask her into the private room, and he didn't.

He extended his hand and she stood up and firmly took it. "I'm Dr. Beatress." He gestured toward the chair and he sat down next to her. "Mr. Mitchell has sustained serious trauma to his brain and he has suffered a fractured skull and a concussion."

"Is he conscious?"

"No."

"Will he live?"

"Yes, I think he'll survive, but we're not sure of the extent of the damage to the brain. We had to drain fluid from his brain to reduce the swelling and repair damage to the skull. He also suffered a compound fracture to his right leg and a hairline fracture to his left, and his right wrist is broken."

"I understand." She felt relieved that he was going to live, but was he going to be a vegetable? "Can I see him?"

"Not right now. You should go home and get some rest. Leave your number with the nurse and when he wakes up we'll call you." He patted her on the arm, abruptly stood up and shuffled off.

On the way out, Taylor stopped by the gift shop and bought the biggest bouquet of flowers they had available and she had them delivered to his room. As she walked out the emergency room door, three of Gary's co-workers were coming in to visit. She didn't know who they were as she glanced at them in passing.

CHAPTER 21

Sullivan's shooting range was beginning to fill up and Taylor was glad she and Tara arrived early to avoid a cluster of gun toting cowboys. It was a rare occasion that she went to the outside range, but they were much less stringent regarding rules and this was the only reason she decided to take Tara there. Taylor figured the indoor range might ask to see Tara's gun permit before allowing her to shoot a weapon on the range, but at Sullivan's she flashed her badge and it was as though she owned the place. She had found a spot at the far left side of the firing range and set up the silhouettes of two burly bad guys pointing a handgun at them. Tara had a twenty-two caliber model forty-one Smith & Wesson automatic handgun clutched in her right hand. Taylor thought this was the best handgun for Tara to start with because it had minimal recoil and wouldn't intimidate her as much as the nine millimeter she would later familiarize her with.

"Keep both eyes open," Taylor instructed. Tara had one eye shut and she immediately did as she was instructed. Abruptly snapping her index finger back, the gun jerked up missing the target completely. "That's all right," Taylor said. "You need to slowly squeeze the trigger so that you won't even know when the round will go off. Focus on the center of the target, take in a deep breath, let it out and then slowly squeeze the trigger."

Tara did as she was told and the sound of the gun popping was a surprise as it resonated across the range. "Very nice," Taylor commended her and a smile erupted in Tara's face. "Now, do it again and again."

After popping off fifty rounds, Taylor thought she was ready to switch to the nine millimeter. The first shot startled her and she turned around with the gun pointing toward Taylor. "Slow down, Tara!" Taylor turned her gun hand back in the down range direction. "If you remember one thing here today, remember that all guns are considered loaded and you always keep them pointed down range, and never point a gun at anyone unless you're willing to shoot them."

Tara thoughtfully listened to her friend, understanding that this was serious business and what she said made complete sense. "I'll remember," she said, pointing the gun at the target and slowly squeezing the trigger.

Two hours later, they sat in a diner booth with a plate of eggs in front of Taylor and pancakes in Tara's reach. "You really did well today, but we need to get out to the range a couple more times."

"I appreciate the lessons," she said as she plunged a wedge of her food into a puddle of maple syrup.

"No problem. I would think you'll have your handgun permit within a few weeks."

"Good," she said as she poured more syrup over her flapjacks. "I think I'll buy a gun like yours."

"You mean the twenty-two?"

"Hell no," she said with a serious grin. "I want the big gun."

"The nine?" Taylor asked as she peeled off part of her toast and slowly folded it into her mouth.

"That's right. If someone comes at me they are going down, I'm not playing."

"I guess not," Taylor said. "Just remember what I said."

"I know. Never point a gun at someone unless you're planning to kill them."

"Well, unless you're planning to shoot them. We shoot to stop, not kill."

"You cops have too many rules." She smiled and carved off a chunk of pancake. "How's Gary doing?"

"He's awake and recovering."

"Now there's someone that should be shot, the bastard that

ran him over and kept going."

Taylor didn't comment, she cut into her egg whites and raised her fork. "So how's Tanner doing?"

"He's okay. He was shaken up by the whole incident, but he'll be fine."

"Good," Taylor said reaching for her drink. "You need to keep your eyes open in case this creep comes around again."

"Yeah, and if he does, hopefully I'll have a little friend he can meet."

"Hey, you can't just shoot him if he comes around; you need to feel as though your life is threatened."

"I know, or the life of my son, right?"

"That's right. If he ever sees your gun, he should be feeling the impact of a bullet in his chest."

"And how he will," she said. "How he will."

As Taylor followed Tara out of the restaurant, they passed by a mail carrier in uniform as he sat at the coffee bar sipping on a bottle of water and nibbling on fresh fruit. The uniform Ben had on was too baggy, he thought. Placing a ten dollar bill on the bar, he sprang to his feet and walked outside, tracing Taylor's steps from a distance.

Preston appeared outside Taylor's office, peering in to see her sitting behind her desk. She waved him in and he closed the door and took a chair. She was seeing a change in his attitude and she was glad, but she didn't trust his motives.

"How's the reporter doing?"

"Mr. Mitchell will live."

"Any word on who hit him?"

"No."

"Well, hopefully that will soon change." She didn't respond. "Where are we with the Brown case?"

"I'm following up on some leads."

"What kind of leads?" he asked dryly.

Taylor placed her pen on the desk. "I think that whoever killed Doctor Brown and Doctor Lynch is also responsible for running over Mr. Mitchell."

"Really, and what makes you think that?" he asked with a hint of sarcasm.

"He was getting too close and they wanted him out of the picture."

Preston rubbed his nose with the back of his hand. "Who are they?"

"I'm not sure, but it has to do with the Plum Island experiments. Someone doesn't want that information leaked."

"And you think they are killing people to hush it up?"

"That's exactly what I think," she replied earnestly.

"Come on Taylor, this is two thousand and one. People don't just go around killing citizens to cover up some biological experiments that were conducted by the federal government."

"They don't?"

"No, they don't."

"Well, Lieutenant, this is where you and I disagree."

"Alright, I'll give you ten more days and if you don't come up with something tangible, I'll have to pull you off the case."

"Thanks."

"Now, I want to talk to you about Bob Trombley." His voice seemed gentler.

"What about him?"

"Look, he's really sorry about what happened, and he's really worried about this complaint you filed against him."

"I guess he should have thought about that before he put his hands on me."

"I know, he was drinking and out of line, but he's really sorry about that. Can't you cut him a break, this one time?"

She looked at her boss with the puppy dog eyes and it crossed her mind that she might be able to use this as leverage to get additional time on the Brown case. "I'll think about it."

"Great!" He got up and moved toward the door. "I appreciate it, Taylor."

"Okay," she said feeling like the mouse that trapped the cat.

Gary was awake as she entered his hospital room. He had been moved from the intensive care unit and placed in a small room with no roommates or windows. A television hung overhead and it was on, but the volume was turned all the way down. The Yankees were on and he watched while his mind fought to concentrate.

"How are you feeling?" She asked as she rolled in with a plate of oatmeal raisin cookies and a smile.

"Great. I've been waiting for you to take me dancing," he said with a grin.

She laughed, but felt terrible as both his legs were in hard casts and one was elevated with a metal clamp pinned into it. His head was covered with a large bandage and his right arm was also in a cast. He looked awful, and she thought he must be in a lot of pain and had to force that joke out.

"We'll be dancing before you know it." She reached out and took his left hand and kissed him on the lips.

Gary looked down at the cast on his arm and smiled. "I see you've been here to visit." Her name was written in black marker.

"Of course I was." She squeezed his hand tighter. "I was really scared, Gary." Her eyes filled up and a single tear detached and rolled down her soft cheek.

"Well, I'm fine now and lying here helped me to realize something."

She swept the tear away with the back of her hand. "What's that?"

"How much I'm totally in love with you."

The tear almost came back. "Well, I'm totally in love with you, Mr. Mitchell." She kissed him again, ignoring his sour breath.

"Would you do me a huge favor?" he asked.

"Sure. Anything you need."

"Hand me that bottle of water." He gestured to a bottle on the table right next to her. She smiled and did as he asked and he drank through a straw.

"Are you in a lot of pain?"

"Not anymore," he said gazing into her eyes.

She squeezed his hand. "If there's anything I can do, just ask."

"Just stay with me for a while."

"That goes without saying," she said. "Gary we need to talk about what happened to you that night in the parking garage."

"Alright," he knew she would have questions; after all she was a cop.

"Did you get a look at the driver?"

"Yes, it was a woman with blond hair."

"Could it have been a man disguised as a woman?"

He thought about the perpetrators facial features and she did look a bit rugged. "Yes."

"Is there anything about the driver that stood out, anything at all?"

"Only that it was no accident," he said bitterly. "He was trying to kill me."

"Why do you say that?"

"I just knew." He coughed. "By the way he targeted me at such a high rate of speed in a parking garage."

"Well, you're right about that," she agreed. "Three witnesses stated that she appeared as though she wasn't finished after she hit you the first time and she began to back up, but they scared her off."

"I'm guessing they didn't get the plate."

"They did, but it was a stolen car. It was taken from the train station that afternoon."

"Okay, somebody stole a car and waited for me to get out of work so they could run me down," he slightly winced as he shifted his weight, "but why?"

"It has to be tied to the Plum Island case," she said with confidence. "Two people have been killed and we are getting close, too close."

"That has to be it, unless the Governor is really pissed off about my story."

"I bet she is, but I don't think she would go this far," Taylor said. "This is much bigger than that."

"Whoever did this must have been watching and listening to my conversations," he said thoughtfully.

"If the driver is the same person, or working in conjunction with the people that killed Doctor Brown and possibly Doctor Lynch, then they must have been listening to your conversations," she said as she rubbed his shoulder. "Otherwise it would just be guesswork on their part. I doubt they would attempt to commit murder over a hunch."

Gary looked up at the TV screen, but she knew he wasn't interested in the game. "Either my work phone is tapped or Mrs. Lynch's house phone is."

"Or both," she said thoughtfully.

"Taylor." He had a look of seriousness in his eyes that she hadn't seen before. "I'm worried about you."

"I'll be fine. You don't think they would try and kill a state police officer?"

"Yes, I do. I think they will kill anyone that tries to expose the truth."

"I'll be very careful, besides, I'm no slouch with a gun, you know."

"I know," he said, thinking she was no match for the killer. Whoever was doing this was a professional with no pity or remorse. He was like some sort of killing machine and she wasn't in that league. Gary knew it would do no good to try and talk her out of her involvement because she wouldn't listen, and he didn't want to drive a wedge in between them by pushing the issue. After she left, he said a prayer to the Virgin Mary asking her to keep Taylor safe.

CHAPTER 22

When her phone rang, Taylor was sitting at her desk absorbed in deep thought about the Brown case. "Trooper Marshall," she answered.

"Yes, Trooper Marshall, this is Yvonne Lynch calling."

"Yes Mrs. Lynch, how are you?"

"I'm doing alright," she responded less than convincing. "I'm calling because I've discovered documents belonging to my husband that I think you'll be interested in seeing."

She sat up straight in her chair. "What kind of documents, Mrs. Lynch?"

"Documents about the experiments conducted on Plum Island," she lowered her tone. "Secret government documents."

"Secret documents," Taylor muttered.

"Yes, Trooper Marshall."

"I can come to the island to meet with you on Saturday morning," she said.

"Alright, I'll see you in four days then."

"Thank you, Mrs. Lynch. Goodbye."

"Good bye."

Harbor Bay Park ran along the Charles River in a bustling Boston suburb. The sun was scorching hot which was typical for late July and people were wearing next to nothing as they sat reading under a tree or walking through the park with a dog attached to the end of a leash.

It was busy for a weekday, Ben thought as he stood waiting near the right corner of the information hut. He was glad it was crowded because he always felt more secure when there were many people moving about. Wearing a pair of light brown shorts and a white short-sleeve shirt and running shoes, he was a little warm and found a spot in the shade under a large maple where he stood in wait. His large, dark, sunglasses hid much of his face and his head was shaved bald. In his hand he held a map of the park and he toted a small camera which helped him to fit in with the rest of the park dwellers.

He had read the note the day before in a chat room on his computer. It was the same as always, just a simple set of numbers and letters that gave him a longitude and latitude reading for a particular location and a time and date for a meet. The locations selected were always parks, and this exact area was to the right of the information booth, exactly twenty paces from the designated location. His contact was never the same person, so every meeting was a first and last encounter for both parties. He always had a map in his right hand and a camera in his left and that was a descriptive method he used in order to be recognized by the courier.

In most cases, Ben saw the courier coming before they noticed him and today was no different. This time it was a woman that appeared to be in her mid-forties and she was dressed in a yellow blouse and a white skirt and Ben thought her to be in good shape for her age. The glasses she wore made her round face seem a tad narrower and her hair was jet black, resting just shy of her collar bone. Their eyes connected and Ben moved to take a seat on the park bench about fifty feet to the east. A few minutes later, she moved in and sat next to him, placing a manila envelope on the bench between them. After scanning the area, he thought it to be safe and he got up and walked away. Not a word was exchanged between them and they never made physical contact. Five minutes later, she got up and started back out of the park the way she came in, but without the envelope.

In his hotel room, Ben opened the envelope and he immediately became agitated as he noticed the five by seven photograph of his next target. He began reading the target profile, and when he was finished, he slammed the documents down onto the desk. At the top of the profile was a close-up photograph of Yvonne Lynch working in her garden.

Now wearing a brown toupee covered with a black baseball cap, blue jeans and a black t-shirt, Ben stood at a pay phone with a ringing receiver in his hand. The number he dialed had only been called once before, but it was stored in his memory like a file in a computer hard drive. The last time was four years earlier when a target turned out to be someone he knew. One of his conditions before taking a job was that he would not terminate a target that he knew, and the other was he wouldn't hurt a child under the age of sixteen. Ben hadn't indicated women as one of his conditions and he had terminated women in the past, but never an elderly citizen.

"Hello." The voice was low and subtle.

"Yes, this is Scorpion Corporation," Ben responded.

"Ten minutes." The line went dead.

Exactly ten minutes later the payphone rang and Ben picked up the line. "I have a problem," Ben said.

"What seems to be the trouble?"

"The product you sent is the wrong model."

"Elaborate."

"It's not what I requested, it's too old."

There was a brief hesitation on the other end. "Our records indicate otherwise, this is the model you requested."

"I strongly disagree," Ben said.

"I suggest that you take what was sent to you because the last item shipped you returned damaged, and that has jeopardized your standing with our company."

Ben knew he was referring to Gary Mitchell and his surviving the hit. His jaw tightened along with the grip on the phone as he thought of a response. "I'm not very happy with your line of products lately."

"You can always take your business elsewhere, but I doubt very much that you'll find such profitable bargains."

"This will be the last time," Ben said in a stormy voice. "Going forward, I demand more suitable products." Ben didn't wait for a response; he gently placed the receiver down and blended into the crowded flow of pedestrian traffic.

The next day Ben was on the last ferry that crossed over the Long Island sound. The docket he received in Harbor Bay Park had specific instructions that Yvonne Lynch was to die of natural causes. Ben figured he would make it appear as though she had a heart attack, after all, she was a grieving widow and that was a common occurrence at her age. This would be the end of his reign in Connecticut and Long Island, and he would take a long tropical vacation where he would ride the hard waves and soft women. This entire mission was out of the ordinary for him and he didn't like it at all. Having too many related targets is extremely dangerous and he didn't want to set a precedent for future contracts. In the beginning, he thought this would be a cut and dry assignment with the termination of Dr. Brown. All he needed to do was plant evidence on a patsy that had been given to him by his employer and he would be killing two birds with one stone. His target would be neutralized, and Windows, a career criminal, would take the fall. It was a perfect crime and it was carefully planned by his employer who wanted Windows to pay for his role in the stealing of government bonds.

As the sun was slowly falling toward the shiny glass-like water, Ben became lost in his past as he gazed out from the deck of the boat. He thought about his days in college and how his moral character had drifted so far away from where it once was. Thinking back to his graduation day from SEALS training, he remembered what Admiral Benson had said in a short speech he gave at the commencement of the ceremony. The words used to echo in the halls of his clean mind as he began his career in the Navy, but now, they somehow seemed stored away in some dusty corner of his cluttered thoughts. Digging deep, he pulled the words out, citing them in his head. As the Admiral stood tall at the podium in his dress whites, he belted out these words, *"Every morning when you look in the mirror to take a shave, ask yourself one simple question, am I proud of the man I have become today. Make sure your answer is an honest one, and if the answer is no, then you need to immediately chart a new course and stay true to your direction and your integrity. What we do matters, and our actions define who we are as men. Make yourself proud of who you are. Make us all proud."*

Conflict was pulling at his heart strings and he began to feel emotions that he hadn't felt in a very long time. *Maybe when this job is finished I should retire. I have plenty of money to live comfortable for the rest of my life and it's time that I find a good woman and start a family. I've had enough of this life and I should make a new one and live it in peace.*

An hour later, Ben was in his car and driving toward his destination. The daylight was fading and gray was defining the salty air as he passed the location where he decided to park his car. Whenever Ben executed a contract, he never parked his getaway vehicle near the target's location and he seldom parked it so far away that he couldn't make a quick escape. This was always carefully planned out because he considered it to be a crucial part of his strategy for success.

Once it was dark, he slowly pulled his car into a dirt road less than a quarter of a mile from the Lynch residence. He located a spot and turned the car around in the direction he would exit from once the contract was executed. Ben was not going to take the ferry out in the morning; he would close out the target, find any documents related to the case and make the drive out of Long Island, never returning there again. Once situated, Ben sat waiting for the perfect time to make his move. In the shadows, he was motionless and listening to the sounds of the night; the tree frogs, crickets, and an owl hooting in the distance performed a concert that would have rendered most men unconscious. Ben was wide awake as he glanced at his watch, deciding it was time to make his move. His target would be fast asleep, now, and he could move around her premises with impunity.

Opening the trunk, Ben quickly removed his shoes and

pulled on his black martial arts pants and replaced his shoes with black cross-training sneakers. With dull black tape, he began to circle his ankles just above the high-top athletic shoes, keeping his pant bottoms tight to his body. Nothing was going to be left behind and nothing was coming back attached to his regular wear, and all his outer clothing would be burned and buried, and his skin scrubbed clean. Once his bottom half was secure, he pulled a thin black sweatshirt tight over his torso and tucked it into his waistline. Placing a black knit hat over the top of his head in a way that made it simple to pull down covering his entire face, except his eyes and mouth, he was just about ready as he slipped on his dark latex gloves, completing the change. He briefly studied the blue automatic pistol in his view and he moved to the knife instead. The target was an old woman and he wouldn't need any firepower, but he thought he should bring a knife just in case he needed to quickly quell any alarming screams. After retrieving a small flashlight and his lock picking tools, he began making his way through the woods to his destination.

As he approached the house, Ben saw that all lights were expelled for the exception of what he surmised to be a bathroom nightlight. Having been at the residence before, Ben knew the layout of the premises and property. On his last visit, he had spent an entire night watching the slow moving targets as they paced from room to room. He knew that Yvonne Lynch had taken a bath every night before she retired to the soft comfort of her bed and that her husband George snored in a low rumbling pattern. Ben studied his targets and learned to know their routine and habits to the point where he felt as if he was part of the family. That was his gift - detailed observation.

As he crept to the back of the house, he could see a faint reflection of a weak moon off the sound where he terminated George Lynch just weeks earlier. A sudden wave of pride intercepted his emotions for a brief moment, as he thought it to be one of his best works of art.

To his surprise, the door to a walkout basement was left

open and he wouldn't need his burglary tool kit after all. With near silence and stealth, Ben moved through the house flashing on his tiny light as needed. As he forged ahead to the master bedroom on the first floor, he recalled his instructions to make it look like a natural death, so he decided to smother the target with a pillow as she slept. It would be a quick and painless death with only a minute or so of discomfort and then he could locate the documents his target had spoken of on the phone. He had not personally listened to the phone conversation between Yvonne and Taylor; his employer had agents that monitored the wiretaps and he was provided a copy of the transcripts.

The bedroom door was open and his eyes seared through the dark to see his target fast asleep in bed, and he peeled his ski mask up, so he could see clearer and breathe easier. Once he was finished in the house, he would pull his mask back down before heading back to his car. The lunar illumination was dim, but allowed just enough light for Ben to complete his operation without the use of his flashlight. He observed a cold pillow situated next to his target where her husband used to lay. Ben thought he was going to be wiping out an entire Lynch generation, and for a split second, he felt regret, until his analytical mind regained control. They were simply a minute measure in the scheme of life, and their deaths would make an insignificant impact on the world, but the negative government exposure could potentially be catastrophic, he rationalized.

The target was lying on her side with the covers shielding her face, as a cool breeze swept off the water through the open window. Picking up the pillow, Ben moved in to finish the job he was hired to do. He would use his hand to position her so that she was facing upright and then he'd place the pillow directly over her face firmly covering her passageways for air.

As he got closer, Ben noticed something odd about the target; her forehead seemed to be unusually shiny. After moving in and placing the pillow over her face, he immediately realized it wasn't going to go as smoothly as planned. Ben's instincts told him to turn and face the walk-in closet, and at that very moment, an abrupt flash instantly brightened up the room. The exploding impact to his chest was felt before he heard the crack of the firearm.

Standing in the doorway of the closet, Taylor stood with her handgun leveled at her target that was now lying motionless on the bedroom floor. The mannequin in the bed had been positioned there two days earlier with a wig the same color and style as Yvonne Lynch's hair.

Ben knew he was hurt badly, but thought he could survive the wound after neutralizing the threat that occupied the bedroom; so he played possum. As his adversary moved in to check his vital signs, Ben retrieved his knife from his waistline and before she could react, he plunged the blade into her side just above her left hip bone. A searing pain infiltrated her body and she immediately stepped back creating a distance from the perpetrator that surprised her so suddenly.

Lunging to his feet with the bloody knife in his hand, Ben quickly moved in to finish off his wounded foe that had now fallen down on the floor. A second flash brightened the dark room, and then a third, and for Ben everything went instantly black as the last bullet passed through his brain.

CHAPTER 23

When Taylor opened her eyes, she was lying in bed at Eastern Long Island hospital. The first thing she focused on was a huge bouquet of flowers on the table beside her cot, and as her vision cleared, she read the card: Get well Soon, Bob Trombley. She did a second take to make sure she wasn't hallucinating due to a loss of blood or effects from a pain killer. *Why would he send me flowers after I filed a complaint against him for sexual harassment? He must be getting scared and is trying to appeal to my emotions to get me to drop the complaint.*

Her thoughts slowly drifted and she began thinking about what happened the night she was stabbed. She knew she had killed the perpetrator, because in the muzzle flash she saw the bullet opening up his forehead. What Taylor didn't know was the identity of the man that tried to kill her and most likely killed the two elderly scientists. She also wondered who was calling the shots from the top and where she could find them.

Yvonne Lynch had vacated her house two days before the killer arrived and she was staying with a friend in the city. Taylor had brought a mannequin along the same day Yvonne left and she staged the bedroom and hid in wait, hoping the killer would take the bait. She was now sure that Windows was innocent, and she was going to do all she could to get him released from jail. A knock interrupted her train of thought and she looked toward the door as it slowly swung open and Preston came walking in. "How are you feeling?"

"I'll be alright," she said.

"I spoke with the doctor and he said you were lucky the knife didn't penetrate any vital organs." He placed a small vase of flowers down. "He said you lost a lot of blood, though."

"Thanks," she said admiring the flowers. "Why would Trombley send me flowers?"

"He didn't send them; he brought them in person."

"What?" She shifted in her bed.

"That's right. He was the first one here."

"And why is that?" she asked in a surprised tone.

"When we heard that you had shot and killed a home invader and was stabbed in the process, Trombley was concerned for your well being and he jumped on the next boat out," he said with a convincing nod of his head. "Hell, he was even bragging that you were once his partner."

"Really?"

"It's hard to believe, but it's true. He caught the first ferry out and placed them right here on this table while you were asleep."

Taylor focused on the arrangement of flowers. "I don't get it."

"I think it's a combination of things." He pulled up a chair and sat down. "I think he feels bad for what he did that night, and I also think he has always had a crush on you."

Taylor didn't respond; she just looked into the eyes of her boss. "He's outside in the waiting room and he'd like to say a few words."

She thought for a moment before responding. "I'll see him after you leave. Tell me about the scene; what do the New York people have?" she changed course.

"Well, not a whole lot I'm sorry to say. The perpetrator has no identification and no record has been located." He shook his head and frowned deeply. "It's like he never existed."

"That doesn't surprise me."

"We found his car located on a dirt road not far from the house. It was reported stolen from Hartford on Sunday," he said as he shifted in his chair. "This guy was a real pro."

"Yes, he was," she concurred. Not good enough, she thought.

"In the trunk of the car we found a handgun with a silencer, but not one single finger print."

"He must have worn gloves all the time," she said.

"Yes, it looks that way," he agreed. "We found a pair of black leather gloves in the car and he was wearing latex gloves at the scene. He also had three brand new holes when we found him." He smirked.

"So what now?" she asked.

He stood up. "Now I'll ask Trooper Trombley to come in."

As the door closed, she thought about Trombley's motives for doing and saying what he had after she was hospitalized. *Maybe Preston is right, maybe he does have a thing for me, but just went about it in the wrong way, or maybe he's just a jerk trying to cover his ass.*

When the door opened again, she didn't say anything as Trombley slowly crept toward her bed, like a child approaching a haunted house. "I just wanted to say that I'm really sorry for what I did to you."

His expression seemed sincere enough, she thought. "Are you, Bob?"

"Yes. I was totally out of line and I hope you'll forgive me." His lower lip began to quiver and his eyes welled up.

"Alright," she said, "I forgive you."

His expression changed and he looked relieved. "Taylor, we are all very proud of you."

His words made her feel good, but she didn't respond, she just smiled. As she turned to walk out, she spoke. "Bob." He turned around. "Thanks for the beautiful flowers."

"You're welcome," he said with a sigh of relief.

Taylor picked up the phone and dialed, and in three rings, Gary was on the other end. "Hello." His voice sounded faint, yet rough like a priest in a confessional.

"Hello, Gary."

"Taylor?" Her voice sparked enthusiasm and comfort.

"Yes, it's me."

"I just heard the news and was just getting ready to call you.

Are you alright?"

"I am now," she said.

"I miss you, Taylor."

"I miss you more than you will ever know," she followed.

"What happened?" he asked.

"It looks like it's all over now. I think we're safe."

"I heard." There was a hesitation, "Are you hurt badly?"

"I'll be fine," she said. "How are you doing?"

"I'm recovering and should be able to go home in a couple days."

"Look at the two of us, both lying in hospital beds," she said. "It's pitiful."

"It beats the alternative," he said.

"Yes, it does."

"I love you."

Along with her heart, her eyes filled. "I love you too, Gary."

CHAPTER 24

It was just after nine in the morning when Sergeant Cisner noticed the light on in Taylor's office. With coffee in hand, he immediately marched to Preston's office to notify him that Taylor was at her desk and appeared to be working. Surprised to hear the report, Preston put down his morning newspaper and went to see for himself.

Prior to knocking, Preston peeked in to confirm what his man had told him and there she was behind her desk with her head down and a pen in her hand.

Taylor looked up when she heard the knock and she saw that it was her boss, so she waved him in. He opened the door and entered half way through. "What the hell are you doing here?" he asked with a look of surprise.

"Working," she said in a serious manner. *What does it look like I'm doing, bowling?*

"You should be home resting," he said as if he truly cared. "Hell, you were nearly stabbed to death a few days ago!"

"It wasn't all that bad," she said. "Besides, I have a lot of work to do."

"Oh yeah, like what," he asked as he walked in and closed the door.

"I went to examine the body of the guy that did this." She gestured toward her wound. "He has no prints because they were removed." She put down her pen and engaged her boss with direct eye contact. "The medical examiner said it appears that he used some form of acid to eliminate all finger prints."

"But he still wore gloves at his crime scenes," he said opening his hands up in the air.

"Yes, he did," she said. "Even without prints his fingertips would leave a mark that would be unique to his fingers, but there wouldn't be a match on record anywhere." She paused for a moment and looked at the file on her desk marked - John Doe. "I think this was in case he didn't make it, we wouldn't be able to match his prints to existing records."

"That makes sense," he said as he took a seat opposite her desk. "No match found on his teeth either," he added.

"That would be too easy," she said. "He probably never allowed anyone to take x-rays. If he needed work done or a simple cleaning, he probably just had it done in a walk in clinic and paid cash."

"Sounds about right, or he may have made changes to his teeth as an adult to avoid a match from his military records," Preston said as he crossed his legs, seeming to relax a bit.

"I would say that all we have to go on is his face and the tattoo on his shoulder." She turned the folder toward her boss and he leaned in to take a look. "It's some sort of strange cross with the horizontal line going through the middle," she pointed, "but it's really four crosses at each of the four ends," she added.

"Making a total of five crosses if you include the one in the middle," Preston observed.

"Yes, I'll do some research and see if I can find out what this tattoo means, if anything," she said as she spun the folder back around to face her.

"Alright." Preston got up. "Let's get this guys face and his tattoo out to all local and federal agencies to see if anyone recognizes him or the tattoo."

"Okay, I'll do that today." She was already planning on

doing this, but she didn't want to say anything and spoil his moment.

"One more thing, now that John Doe is in the forefront, where does this leave us with Windows?"

"Good question." She swiveled in her chair and winced as a sharp pain in her side came to life. "I think we need to have a talk with the district attorney."

"Alright, you can handle that, and if you feel you need me to step in, let me know," he said. "And take care of that wound. I don't need one of my best investigators out of action long term."

"I will," she said with a half smile as he nodded his head and walked out. Taylor knew his change in attitude was because she had forgiven Trombley and dropped the sexual harassment complaint. Now, more than ever, she thought it was the right move.

In the New Haven public library, Taylor sat with a pile of books on ancient symbols and medieval Christian beliefs, folklore, and secret Christian societies. Her head was spinning with all the different Christian religions, sects and illuminati. After a couple hours she found a chapter in a book on Christian symbols and she began scanning. As she turned the fourth page, there it was. Her heart skipped a beat as she focused on the sketch of the symbol on the page that was exactly the same as the black ink embedded into the skin of the man she had killed. She began to read: *The character is a Rosicrucian symbol and is the keynote, as it were, of all Grecian architecture and art; which is all beauty, refinement, and elegance, with power at the highest. This is the foundation mark of the famous symbols-- Teutonic (Fourfold Mysticism.)*

Taylor began turning back pages to find the beginning of the chapter and once she found her place she began reading again: *Rosicrucianism is the theology of a secret society of mystics, allegedly formed in late medieval Germany, holding a doctrine "built on esoteric truths of the ancient past", which, "concealed from the average man, provide insight into nature, the physical universe and the spiritual realms.*

Between 1607 and 1616, two anonymous manifestos were published, first in Germany and later throughout Europe. These were *Fama Fraternitatis RC (The Fame of the Brotherhood of RC)* and *Confessio Fraternitatis (The Confession of the Brotherhood of RC)*. The influence of these documents, presenting a "most laudable Order" of mystic-philosopher-doctors and promoting a "Universal Reformation of Mankind", gave rise to an enthusiasm called by its historian Dame Frances Yates the "Rosicrucian Enlightenment".

Rosicrucianism was associated with Protestantism and in particular Lutheranism. It was also influential to Free-masonry as it was emerging in Scotland. In later centuries, many esoteric societies have claimed to derive their doctrines, in whole or in part, from the original Rosicrucian's. Several modern societies, which date the beginning of the Order to earlier centuries, have been formed for the study of Rosicrucianism and allied subjects.

Taylor selected two books and returned the others back to their resting place. The woman behind the desk was unusually young and beautiful for a librarian, she thought. Taylor had to open up an account and get a library card in order to take the books out and she used Gary's address. She didn't think he'd mind, and thought he may even like the idea. After checking out the books she decided to pay Gary a visit at his place and share the news on the man that had caused them both so much pain. Even though he was dead now, every time a sharp pain invaded her side, he came alive, if only for a brief second. In her mind, John Doe wouldn't be completely dead until she knew who he was and where he came from, and most importantly, who sent him.

The nurse answered the door wearing light green scrubs and a pink and green shirt flowered top. Taylor thought how nice and comfortable it would be if she could dress at work like that. The only problem would be the gun, how would she secure the gun to her hip? She would have to wear a shoulder holster and she wasn't having any part of that.

"Hello," the nurse said as she held open the door. "You must be Taylor?"

"Yes," Taylor replied extending her hand and they engaged. She was a bit relieved that the nurse was a round woman with a splatter of facial freckles on her cheeks, and that she didn't look like the beautiful young librarian she had just seen.

"I'm Justine," she said while beaming. "He just won't stop talking about you, you know." She closed the door and gestured toward the bedroom. "He's in there."

Taylor stopped her with a gentle tug of the arm. "How's he doing?

"He's coming along. He still has some pain, but won't take any pain medicine, just Tylenol," she added.

"He's tougher than I thought," Taylor said through a smirk. "We'll need some alone time together, you look like you might need a break," she said with a half smile.

"A break would be nice, but he's pretty easy, low maintenance compared to some of my other patients." She got the hint and headed toward the kitchen and Taylor the bedroom.

"I just got a fantastic report from your nurse," Taylor said while peaking around the corner.

"Hey!" Gary lit up like a Christmas tree. "If you told me you were coming I would have cleaned up and put on my finest attire," he said with his leg elevated in a hard cast and most of his body covered in white and looking like a mummy.

"No, I'd rather see you all natural." They shared a laugh and she moved in to kiss him. "I hear you're drug free now."

"Yeah, I had to get that monkey off my back," he groaned as he rolled his eyes around. "You're moving around pretty good for someone that took a blade in a belly." He squeezed her hand. "Shouldn't you be resting?"

"I'm fine," she lied. "I have too much to do."

"Like what?" he asked. "You shot the bad guy; I think you deserve a break."

"I'm still trying to figure out who he was." She pulled up a chair that was situated in the corner. "His finger prints were burned off and he has no dental records, but he has this strange tattoo of a cross on his shoulder."

"A tattoo." He tried scooting himself up, but was limited in his attempt.

"Yes, and I just came from the library." She picked up the hand bag with the long strap she had brought along and pulled out a hard-bound book. "Check this out," she said as she flipped the book open to a pre-marked page. "This is the same tattoo John Doe has." She pointed to one of many sketches on the page. "This one."

"That's a strange looking cross," he observed.

"That's exactly what I thought," she agreed. "It's actually five crosses and it's a Rosicrucian symbol that means, *The Order of the Rosy Cross.*"

Gary's ear's appeared to shift back as his forehead tightened. "What is a Rosicrucian?"

"It's some sort of secret society that dates back to the fifteenth century," she said while turning a page, "Originating in Germany."

"A secret society," he repeated.

"Yes, Rosicrucian Illuminati." She pointed to a paragraph in the book. "Kind of like the Free Masons."

"I never heard of this secret society," he said.

"Neither have I until today." She closed the book. "I think this guy was some kind of a modern day Rosicrucian," she wisped. "Why else would he even know about this type of symbol? It's not like it's painted on a subway wall somewhere."

"What next?" He placed his good hand on her knee.

"After I leave here, I'm going to enter his picture and this tattoo into the national database and see if anyone out there recognizes him."

"And what if someone does recognize him?" He was thinking he wanted to put all this behind them in order for them to move on and focus on their relationship.

"If we can find out who this guy was, then maybe we can find out why he killed Dr. Brown and Lynch, and who is behind it," she said with an unwavering look of determination that he knew he couldn't dilute.

"Alright," he said pulling her closer. "Let's talk about us now." Their lips met.

CHAPTER 25

Ryan Treemont pulled up a chair behind his desk at the FBI field training facility at Quantico Virginia. He had just showered after a six mile run with his new recruits in tow and he was conducting his morning ritual of checking his inbox and (NCIC) National Crime Information Center updates.

As he skimmed through the database, he saw that three prisoners had escaped from Folsom State Penitentiary in Represa California, and they were all felons with violent histories. As he continued on, he read that a bank in Reston Virginia had been robbed late yesterday afternoon and that a white male in his late twenties to mid-thirties was wanted in connection with the armed robbery. Ryan took a note of the particulars of the robbery because this was close to home and then he continued on. The next item made him halt in an instant, and he focused on a bulletin that came out of New London, Connecticut, where the state police were attempting to identify a deceased man possibly responsible for murdering an elderly man in New York and the attempted murder of a Connecticut State Trooper. What caught his attention was the symbol of a tattoo located on the perpetrator's left shoulder.

As he sat back in his chair, Special Agent Treemont's mind began to drift back in time. It was a time he would never forget; a time that carved him into the type of man he was and navigated him in a direction that would help him to become an FBI agent. The cross-shaped image he was examining he had only seen once many years ago, as he pushed his way through Navy SEAL training in San Diego California. He thought about his fellow SEAL trainee, remembering the first time he had noticed the small, funny looking cross on the oblate area of his shoulder.

"What's that?" he asked the lean SEAL as they quickly changed in the barracks.

"It's just something I did as a kid," he lied. It had been etched into his skin in his senior year at Yale.

"What does it symbolize?" Treemont asked, never forgetting his answer.

"A way of life," he coldly replied clearly wanting to end the conversation.

Treemont looked at the photo of the dead man and it didn't add up. Even though a corner of his forehead had been blown off and repaired, his features weren't as he recalled. The height and weight measurement in the bulletin seemed to be accurate, but his facial features were off. *If I could see his eyes, I would know. I would know for sure if he was in fact, Blake Fenton.*

When her phone started buzzing, Taylor was behind her desk going through the file on Alexander Windows. She was getting prepared for her visit with the DA to try and convince him to drop the charges against the man she knew was innocent, at least in the murder of Doctor Brown. She knew it wasn't going to be an easy task and she had to have her facts in order.

"Trooper Marshall," she answered as she put down the folder.

"Good morning, Trooper Marshall." He was surprised it was a woman. "This is Special Agent Ryan Treemont with the FBI. I have read your bulletin through NCIC regarding your, John Doe, and I'm calling because I think I may know who this man is."

The line was silent for a few seconds as Taylor processed what had just been said. "Well, Agent Treemont, that's the best news I've had in a while." The enthusiasm in her tone was apparent. "How do you think you may know him?"

"We may have been in Navy SEAL training together."

"SEAL training," she mumbled. "Did you graduate

together?" She knew a very small percentage of recruits in SEAL training actually made it through graduation.

"Yes, we both made it through," he said. "And I'll also add that Fenton graduated at the top of our class. He was a machine."

I certainly have no trouble believing that. "Are you sure it's him, this Fenton?" She glanced at the name she had written down when he had cited it.

"Well, not a hundred percent, but I'm pretty sure." He muffled the phone and sneezed. "Excuse me," he said. "It was the tattoo that caught my attention, not his photo."

"Yes, the tattoo is unusual."

"It is, and Fenton had the same tattoo in the same area of the shoulder. His face, however, looks different."

"How so?" she asked with her pen in the pole position.

"His features don't completely resemble Fenton," he said with conviction. "He had a longer nose and his jaw wasn't as square."

"Maybe it isn't the same man," she said. "Maybe he belonged to a group that embedded this tattoo on the same body part."

"That could be, but my gut tells me differently," he said. "He has the same build and capabilities."

"You mean the ability to kill?" she asked without hesitation.

"Yes." His finite answer echoed through the line.

"Agent Treemont, can I take down your information?" she asked. "There's something I need to do, but I'd like to continue this conversation later this afternoon."

"Sure, I'm out of the Quantico field office and my direct line is (703) 630-8860. What time should I expect your call?"

Taylor liked that he asked this question, it showed his interest. "I would say about one."

"That should be fine. I'll speak with you then."

"Thank you," she said and placed the receiver down, grabbed her jacket and headed out the door.

In the medical examiner's office, Taylor waited in the lobby for Doctor David Crimson. When she arrived, she was told he was busy working on a body and that he would be wrapping up in short order. Crimson was a grumpy man with retirement within an arm's reach, and he didn't like cops; he found them to be too pushy and he wasn't one that tolerated being pushed. Taylor had learned to handle him with kid gloves and she found that it paid off, because he was more receptive to her than others that carried a gun and badge. When she called to have him put a hold on the body of John Doe, he agreed without argument, even though he didn't like corpses rotting away in his facility.

"You're here bright and early," he said as the door swung open and he appeared looking as though he hadn't slept since the Carter administration.

"You know what they say, the early cop catches the bad guy," she said with a crispy grin.

He just looked at her without emotion as if he didn't get it or didn't find it amusing. "What do you need?"

"I think my, John Doe, may have altered his appearance and I was wondering if we could take a look and see if this is the case."

"I have ten minutes," he said as his eyes dropped to his wrist watch. *John Doe should be a pile of ashes and I'm still examining him a week and a half later.*

Pulling the drawer out, it slid open with little effort and sound. He unzipped the body bag and began examining the body with a magnified scope attached to his eye glasses. "If he had his appearance altered, whoever performed the procedure was very good."

"Anything noticeable?" she asked hoping for some reassurance.

"You see here." He pointed his pen to the area behind the ear. "There is a scar, a very tiny scar."

"That may indicate a facelift or something, right?"

He nodded his head. "I'll need to open him up to make any kind of concrete determination." He slammed the drawer shut.

"I don't have time for this now."

"I understand," she said with puppy dog eyes.

He looked at her standing there, like a child waiting for a treat on Halloween. "I'll cut him after lunch."

"Thanks Doc, I appreciate it." He examined her. "Really, I do. More than you know."

"Okay," he snarled. "Call me around one-thirty or two."

Taylor made sure she called Agent Treemont at one o'clock as agreed. She advised him she would get back to him after the medical examiner toured the body. Taylor picked up the phone again at two o'clock and dialed, and after seven rings, Crimson picked up. "Crimson," he growled like an old junkyard dog.

"Hi Doc. This is Taylor Marshall calling."

"I opened him up," he yelled out as if he was talking through a Dixie cup on a string. "He had work done alright."

"Really, what kind of work?" She picked up a pen.

"Rhinoplasty for sure," he said. "He had a ton of cartilage removed from his nose."

"Really, what else?" she asked gently.

"It looks like he had some work done on his jaw and he definitely had a facelift." He rumbled a cough. "This guy changed his entire look and the doctor that performed the surgery is very good."

Taylor felt an exhilarating chill run down her spine. "Doc, I am really grateful and I owe you one," she said with sincerity.

"I won't be around long enough to collect," he said. "Just find out who he is." The line went dead.

Without hesitation, Taylor pushed down the button and re-dialed. Before Treemont finished speaking, she cut him off. "He changed his face!"

"Are you sure?"

"Yes, the medical examiner said he altered his nose, his jaw, and he had a facelift." The excitement in her voice was obvious.

"I think he's our guy," Treemont said. "Blake Fenton."

"I need you to tell me all about Blake Fenton," she said as she prepared her recorder.

CHAPTER 26

Based on the information Taylor received from Treemont, she learned that Blake Fenton grew up in Red Creek, New York, a small town near the Canadian border. Holding a population of less than six hundred, Red Creek was a place known only to the local community and Salmon fisherman that would venture there for an outdoor getaway. It didn't take long for Taylor to find his parent's number as they were the only Fenton's listed in Red Creek, so she began dialing.

John Fenton was a soft spoken man that conversed with apprehension and suspect as Taylor probed him for information. After a couple minutes, she realized she was going to have to meet him in person in order to build rapport and gain ground on learning about his son and who his employer was.

John Fenton agreed to meet with Taylor and she made arrangements to meet him the following day. It was going to be a long drive, so she located a motel in Oswego and booked a room for the night. She decided to drive straight to the Fenton residence and check into the motel afterwards.

It was two in the afternoon when Taylor arrived at the Fenton house. She had started out at eight in the morning and stopped twice along the way for fuel, a restroom break, and a large cup of coffee. It was a peaceful drive and as she traveled north toward Canada, she wondered what people did for a living in such a desolate part of the country.

The long driveway that led to the house consisted of a marriage of dirt and gravel and was surrounded by thick brush. Taylor was certain it was not only home to the Fenton's, but also many forms of wildlife. Even though she was out of state, she kept a weapon in the car just in case she ran into a bear or some backwoods redneck like the characters in the movie, Deliverance. The house was a log cabin nestled in between tall oaks and evergreens, and as she exited her car, she could smell firewood lingering through the stagnant air. Carrying a small bag, Taylor walked past a wheel barrel filled with stone and a wood pile with an ax in the ready, wedged into a large stump. She thought he must be in decent physical shape to be able to labor to this degree. The man she shot to death had been in his mid to late thirties, so Taylor assumed his father would be in his early sixties. The cabin was fairly large and well kept, and as she ascended the front stairs, the second step cried out.

"I've been meaning to fix that damn squeaky step," a voice called out. Fenton stood inside the doorway to the side and out of her view. He would never fix the step; it was one of his alarms. Whenever Fenton heard the distinct crying of the wood, he knew someone was coming and he knew where they were standing, exactly.

"Mr. Fenton," she called out as his silhouette came into view. His large frame filled much of the doorway, and with thick soles and a baseball cap, he appeared even taller.

"I thought we'd sit outside," he said in a low, rough voice. "Are you thirsty?"

"Yes, thank you," she said wondering if he would open the door and greet her as a gentleman.

"Have a seat on the porch and I'll be right back."

She listened to the sound of his boots as he moved through the house and she moved to a pair of rocking chairs on the porch and sat. It was a quiet and peaceful place, yet she could see how one could easily become lonely absent regular company. A few minutes later, the door swung open and he appeared carrying two glasses of what appeared to be lemonade. He was older than she thought he would be; which impressed her even more. *He has to be in his late sixties or seventy, but he's solid as a rock.*

"I don't get much company these days," he said as he

handed her the glass and took a seat in the chair next to her.

"You're wife isn't here?" she asked with apprehension thinking it may be a mistake.

"Kathleen died two years ago," he moaned. "Cancer."

"I'm so sorry."

He looked deep into her eyes and saw that she was sincere. "Yeah, so am I." He broke the stare and peered out to the wood line. "People have said there's a mountain lion out here," he said changing the subject. "Some say they've seen it perched on a large rock or bedding in the tall grass, but I've never seen it." He took a long drink from his glass and placed it on the floor to his left. "I've seen questionable tracks, though."

"Sometimes things aren't what they appear," she said, thinking about his dead son and softening the mat for his fall. "Maybe these people saw something else, a deer or a bobcat."

He grunted and reached down for his glass. "This lemonade is very good," she complimented.

"You said on the phone, you wanted to talk about Blake." He dismissed her compliment.

Taylor looked at the handsome man next to her, wondering if he ever smiled. "Yes." She thought about how to begin. "When was the last time you saw him?"

"About a year before he died," he said without looking at her. "He surprised his mother and me on Christmas."

Taylor put her glass down. *This doesn't make sense; he died a couple weeks ago.* "How long ago was that?"

"Ten years ago, last Christmas," he said. "His mother was very grateful she was able to spend that Christmas with him before he died."

"Ten years ago," she mimicked. "How did he die?"

"I don't know for sure," he said in a tone of disappointment. "They said it was in the line of duty."

"In the line of duty," she repeated.

"The CIA never provides any detail, not even to the parents," he spurted. "Everything is classified, top secret."

"You had no indication of where he was or what he was

doing?"

"No, just that he died abroad serving our country," he said in a crumbled tone. "Did you know Blake was adopted?"

"No, I didn't." *That explains the disparity in age between father and son.* "We couldn't have children of our own, so we decided to adopt."

"That's a noble thing to do."

He didn't respond. "We were so proud of him when he graduated from Yale."

"I bet you were," she said. "And when he graduated from the SEALS, you must have been ecstatic."

"Yes, we were." The small talk was wearing thin and he was now ready to ask why she had paid him the visit. On the phone Taylor was slippery and evasive regarding her inquiry; simply stating she would prefer to speak with him in person. "Why have you come here today?"

His question was like a ninety mile an hour fast ball targeting her head. She wanted to say she was doing research on CIA operatives that died serving our country with no explanation from our government as to how, where and why they died, but she couldn't. He was Blake Fenton's father, a man that adopted him so many years ago, hoping he would grow up to become a productive member of society, never imagining he would turn out to be a government assassin. Nevertheless, Taylor figured he deserved to know the truth and offer his son a decent burial. "Mr. Fenton." She cleared her throat and he could sense it wasn't good news by the change in the shade of her face. "Your son didn't die when you were told, or how."

His frame became rigid in his chair. "What do you mean?" he asked with hard, fixed eyes.

"He died a couple weeks ago in New York," she said in a certain but cracked tone of voice. "We believe he was still working for the government in a covert capacity, and they had you and everyone else that knew him believe he was deceased."

Fenton seemed to shrink before her eyes as if he was slowly

deflating like a balloon with a tiny puncture. "Are you sure this man is, Blake?"

"We are pretty sure," she said unconvincingly. "He had a peculiar tattoo of a cross behind his left shoulder." Taylor reached into her bag and retrieved a piece of paper with a copy of the symbol she had taken off the library book and she handed it to him. The look on his face confirmed that his son had such a tattoo.

He nodded his head. "How did he die?"

His question came sudden, but not unexpected. "He was shot by a police officer while attempting to take someone's life." She cleared her throat again. "We believe he was a government assassin."

Fenton rose to his feet without speaking and walked to the edge of the porch, gazing out at the vibrant vegetation. "It's a beautiful country this time of year," he said in a near whisper.

Taylor thought about what he might be going through in his mind. How he may be processing the reality that this beautiful country he loves so much is cluttered with bureaucratic debris and unscrupulous men. "Yes, summer is a beautiful time of year out here," she clarified.

"I'll be right back," he said as he slowly shuffled off the porch and into the house, like a defeated boxer back to his corner. A minute later, he reappeared with a flag tightly wrapped in the shape of a triangle in one hand and a letter in the other. "This is what they sent us," he grumbled. "His mother never understood why they were so impersonal." Taylor took the paper with the letterhead, Central Intelligence Agency, and began reading. When she was finished with the short notification, she handed it back. "They wouldn't say where he died or what happened, just that he died in an explosion and there were no remains," he said. "Now, maybe I understand why." He handed her back the letter. "I suppose you're here to find out what they did to my son, and why," he said as if his son was a victim. "You may need this letter to find out who lied to us," he said. "You keep it."

"Thank you, Mr. Fenton." She touched his shoulder. "Someone will be in touch to make arrangements for you to identify your son and take him home," she compassionately said. "His appearance had been altered with plastic surgery, so he'll look different."

"If its Blake, I'll know it," he said in a confident voice. Taylor folded the letter and placed it in her bag and started back toward her car. Before she reached the car his voice rang out. "Trooper Marshall!" She turned to see the man standing on the porch holding the American flag. "You were the officer that killed my son?"

The question or statement, she wasn't sure which it was, came like a punch in the gut. The man on the porch carried a look of torment, but she knew he deserved to know the truth. "Mr. Fenton, I had no choice." As the words came out, she felt a weakness in her legs and an awkward depleted feeling in her core. Those were the last words exchanged between them. She looked in her rearview mirror and saw Fenton where she had left him standing on the porch and holding the flag; her car kicked up a cloud of road dust and it faded into the country.

CHAPTER 27

In her office, Taylor was going through the crime scene report from the Lynch residence. Leaning back in her chair, she scratched the scar where Blake Fenton had plunged his blade into her a few weeks earlier. The stitches had been removed and the healing was progressing, but was causing an itching sensation. Every time she looked in the mirror at the centipede looking scar on her side, she thought of the look on Fenton's face when she told him the truth about his son. It didn't make sense to her that a Yale graduate turned Navy SEAL and a combat veteran would all of a sudden become a cold blooded killer. *Maybe he was fed a bunch of lies by the CIA about his victims and he thought it was in the best interest of national security to exterminate them.*

As she flipped a page and continued studying the forensic report, something caught her attention and she stopped to focus. *A hair fiber from a Korat felis catus was removed from the ski hat worn by Blake Fenton.* Opening her desk drawer, she removed her Webster and began turning pages, and when she found what she was looking for, she began reading. Closing the book shut, she returned the dictionary back to its resting place, fetched the phone number for Linda Kasinski and began dialing.

"Hello."

"Mrs. Kasinski?"

"Yes."

"Hi, this is Taylor Marshall. How are you?"

"I'm doing okay." Her voice was withdrawn.

"I'm sorry to disturb you, but I have a couple of questions to ask."

"Sure."

"When I was at your father's house, I saw a scratching post in the basement and I thought it was odd because your father didn't have a cat. I notice these things because I own a cat myself."

"Yes, he did have a cat and it died just a few weeks before he did."

Taylor felt a tingle down her spine. "What kind of cat?"

"It was a rare breed from Thailand," she said.

"Was it a Korat?"

"Yes, how did you know that?"

"I'll keep you informed, but I must go now. Thanks for your time." The line went dead.

To her surprise, the District Attorney took Taylor right in without delay. She had arrived ten minutes early and didn't have to wait. He came out and opened the door for her as a gentleman would and it was pleasing to her because chivalry seemed to be a dying concept in the courthouse.

"Please come in and make yourself comfortable." He gestured toward the chairs in front of his desk and she sat down. "I read about your injury and the unfortunate incident that occurred in New York," he said as he took the chair next to her. Taylor liked that he didn't sit behind his desk like a king on his thrown casting down judgments. He crossed his legs and folded his hands and she thought he was comfortable with her and why she had come. "Are you healing well?" he asked in a manner of concern.

"Yes, thanks for asking." Taylor had met him on one occasion a year earlier at a fundraiser and since he had taken the office she had heard good things about him; that he was a fair man with high integrity. Thomas Morrici had been elected to the office after many years of running a successful criminal defense law firm. He was voted in by a wide margin, ousting the incumbent with a campaign promise of integrity, honesty and justice, which had been compromised in the past several years.

"You wanted to see me regarding, Alexander Windows."

"Yes, I'm here to ask you to drop the charges against Mister Windows."

A curious look befell him. "This is unusual to say the least," he said. "You are the arresting officer and he gave a full confession. It's pretty cut and dry, isn't it?"

"No," she said reaching into her briefcase. "Mr. Windows confessed only because he was promised relocation out of Stonington. He had been attacked and nearly killed, and he would have said anything to get out of there," she said. "He has since recanted his confession." She handed him a signed statement where Windows admitted he didn't murder Dr. Brown and he confessed to the murder in order to be moved to a safer facility.

"You believe him?" He stared her down as he waited for a response. His dark brown eyes were piercing, yet they contained a look of reason and fairness.

"Yes. And here's why." She straightened up in her seat. "Mr. Windows is a career criminal, but he has no history of violent offenses, never mind murder."

"Maybe he felt threatened by the victim and reacted without thinking," he shot back.

"I don't think so."

"What about all the evidence that put him at the scene?"

I believe it was planted by this man." She handed him the file on Blake Fenton. "This is the man I shot and killed in New York. His name is, Blake Fenton, and he is a former CIA agent that had been documented as killed in action a decade ago." Morrici had a strange look on his face and she knew she had one chance to clear Windows and she had to cover all her bases. "We believe he was a government assassin sent to kill Doctor Brown because he was about to blow the whistle on a government conspiracy involving, Plum Island, New York, where he had been employed as a scientist."

He drew his shoulders back a bit. "Go on."

A couple weeks later, another scientist, Doctor Lynch, who

was a good friend of Doctor Brown and had also worked on Plum Island, also turned up dead."

"How?"

"He drowned in the sound within an eye's view of his house. The same house that I shot Blake Fenton in." Morrici could sense the conviction in her voice. "He had come back to kill Doctor Lynch's wife because she knew too much, but I was there waiting for him."

"Let me get this straight," he said. "This Blake character killed Doctor Brown and planted evidence to implicate Mister Windows, and then he went on to kill Doctor Lynch and subsequently he tried to kill Mrs. Lynch but he ran into your bullet instead."

"Yes, that's right."

"Why go through the trouble of framing Windows if he was a rogue killer?"

"I don't think he went rogue," she said. "In the beginning I think they thought by getting rid of Doctor Brown that would be the end of it, but they had run wiretaps and learned Doctor Lynch and his wife were also a threat." She put her hands together, placing her fingertips on her chin as she thought about how she could clearly state the chain of events. "They tried to make the Lynch death look like an accidental drowning, but it doesn't add up because Doctor Lynch was in good shape and a good swimmer. When Blake Fenton came to kill Mrs. Lynch, he was going to suffocate her with a pillow and make it look like a heart attack." She stood up and walked to the corner of his desk. "He had been following me and tried to kill a reporter in New Haven by running him over." She choked up and he knew this was disturbing to her. "He almost succeeded," she added.

"What did the reporter have to do with this?"

"He was working with me and he'd been covering Lyme disease and corruption at the state and local level," she declared. "We got too close."

"This all sounds so incredible."

"I know it does," she agreed, "Windows had nothing to do with the death of Doctor Brown and something stinks at the federal level and I'm going to find out what it is and who's responsible."

He was thinking that she was over her head and it was apparent by his demeanor. "Look, both doctors worked at Plum Island Animal Disease Research Center for decades and they were best friends," she said. "It's pretty clear that the person responsible for killing Doctor Brown had killed Doctor Lynch and was shot by me while attempting to kill Mrs. Lynch." She walked over and sat back down and engaged him in a direct stare. "He thought that killing Brown was going to be the end of it, but it wasn't, and he was ordered to take out all the threats." She reached into her case and pulled out a report. "A cat hair from a rare breed of cat called a Korat, was removed from the ski cap Blake Fenton wore the night I shot him. Doctor Brown had a Korat." She handed him the report. "This links Blake Fenton to the Brown murder," she offered in an elevated tone. "He was in that house."

Morrici sat still, absorbing the information he had just heard. He had gotten bits and pieces through his channels and the media, but Taylor had put it all together, and he knew he didn't want to put an innocent man in prison for life; he didn't want that on his conscience. "I need time to digest this," he said as he took to his feet. "I think I'll pay a visit to Mister Windows myself." Morrici looked her in the eye. "If he's telling the truth about his innocence in the Brown case, I'll see it in his eyes."

Taylor stood and picked up her briefcase. "Mr. Morrici, I appreciate your time today and I know you'll do the right thing." She extended her hand and he took it. "It was a pleasure meeting with you and I'm grateful for all that you do."

He walked her to the door. "I'll be in touch soon," he said as he opened the door. She walked out and he closed the door and sat down to process what he had just heard.

Two days later, Taylor sat in her car in front of Victor's tavern. It was nearly ten at night and she had been waiting since eight-thirty. Reggie had managed to slip through the cracks and she knew she had to find him quickly before he decided to pay Tara another visit. This bar was one of three that Tara had mentioned during their walk the night she was attacked. This was Taylor's third time sitting in front of a bar with a keen eye spying the entrance. The first two times had proven fruitless and she was hoping for a change. Watching as a yellow taxi pulled up and stopped near the front door, Taylor slid down in her seat to avoid detection. A few seconds later, out popped a head that began immediately scanning the area. Reggie had surfaced for a night of drinking and Taylor wasn't surprised that he arrived in a cab because his car was at the police impound. Taylor waited for five minutes, allowing him time to get comfortable in a warm bar stool, with a cold drink, before she made her move. This time she was going to make sure he didn't get away.

Slowly, Taylor pushed open the door to the tavern, and she saw him sitting at the bar staring into his glass as if all his answers were contained there. He didn't see her as she approached like she owned the place, gliding across the floor. When she was five feet away, an inner rage took hold of her as she thought about what he had done to her best friend. She glanced around the bar and saw that there was only four people in the bar, including a female bartender and two drunks at the far end. A tweak of pain in her side reminded her that she was still healing and she should not be rolling around with Reggie, and she knew there was a good chance he wouldn't go easy.

"Reggie Cummings!" She called out, as she stood two feet from him and to his right rear quarter. Turning his head, Reggie scanned her over, instantly realizing she was a cop and he concluded he wasn't going to jail today. Without speaking, he swung his right hand in a backward motion, attempting to strike Taylor in the face. With her left forearm she blocked his strike, and firmly situated in her right hand was her taser, and in a split second, she jammed it into his neck. Reggie immediately hit the floor with three hundred thousand volts running through his body, totally incapacitating him. With her right foot she kicked him over onto his stomach, as he continued to twitch and jolt about. Without hesitation, she twisted his arms behind his back and slapped on the cuffs. "It's alright," she yelled. "State police. This man is under arrest!"

Taylor called the local police for assistance, and she waited with Reggie recovering in the back seat of her car. Ignoring his threats and cursing, she stood outside the car knowing he would soon be back out in the street. She could only hope that he would stay away from Tara. Watching the police cruiser as it turned the corner, she raised her hand to draw attention. As it rolled in closer, she looked into the back seat with little optimism that this was going to be the end of the Reggie Cummings saga.

CHAPTER 28

It was approaching mid-august and the breeze was sweeping across the sound against many boat sails. Taylor and Yvonne sat on the back porch sipping hot, green tea. They had learned they had much in common, but it was never mentioned. Taylor saw an unwavering strength in Yvonne that she admired and a sense of optimism that seemed contagious.

"Since he retired, my husband drove into the city every Thanksgiving and fed the homeless at the soup kitchen. I had asked him if I could come along, but he always said he wanted to do it alone. I think this was one of those times that he was able to reflect on his life and all the blessings he had, while helping others at the same time."

"That is a selfless and noble thing to do," Taylor said.

"Yes, it is."

Taylor could feel Yvonne's sense of pride when she spoke of her husband. Her eyes lit up as if the stories brought him back to life, and to her in many ways, they did. "He was a lucky man to have you."

"No, I'm the lucky one," she said looking out to the open water where he perished. "Well, I must say we certainly out-smarted the bad guy this time, didn't we?"

"Yes we did," Taylor agreed. "You did a great job playing along on the phone, and because of that, he fell for it."

"It was your idea, sweetie. How did you know my phone was tapped anyway?"

"I didn't know for sure, but I had a hunch that many phones were being tapped, including yours, so I took a gamble."

"Well, your hunch paid off," she said raising her cup in a

toasting gesture. "It's hard to believe that something like this could happen here in America." Taylor stared into the eyes of her old friend and she could tell that her sense of security had been shaken. "It is scary that there are others involved and we may never know who they are, and who knows how many more they will murder."

"Yes. It's a complicated world we live in," Taylor said while looking deep into Yvonne's eyes, wishing she could have seen all that her eyes had seen over the years.

The mist grew heavy and the tea cup had lightened, so they moved inside. Taylor thought about how a person's home told a story of who they are, as she walked through the house as if it were a museum, with her hands clutched behind her back. Along a window line, she found herself staring at a five foot long model of a seventeenth century sailing ship that was on display. The detail was amazing, she thought. Running her fingers along the mast, she traced it down to the deck. Everything was perfect, from the smooth wooden hull to the rope ladders. She wondered how long it took him to complete such a work of art, as she found her fingers drawn to a three inch treasure chest that sat in the center of the deck. Like a child, Taylor felt a surge of curiosity consuming her thoughts, and using her fingernail, she lifted up the latch and opened the cover, and what she found inside created a tingle that ran down her spine.

Yvonne walked into the room with more hot tea. "Have you seen this?" Taylor asked.

She took her place next to the detective and they both stared into the open chest that contained a single key. "No, I haven't," she answered with a look of surprise.

"What do you think it's for?" Taylor asked

Yvonne reached into the miniature chest and extracted the key from its resting place. Turning it over and over again, she wondered why her husband had never mentioned the heavy gold key to her.

"May I see it?"

She handed the key to Taylor who examined it for several

seconds, and then she looked at the old woman that she had grown so fond of. "I think it may be a safety deposit box key." Taylor remembered as a young girl the few times her father had taken her along to the bank where he kept a rare stamp and coin collection. Once she had asked him about his safety deposit box and he handed her the key. She remembered the heavy gold key with the crown-shaped end and it was similar to the key she now held in her hand.

"George never mentioned that he had a safety deposit box."

"What bank did he belong to?"

"The Island Federal Credit Union, in Hauppauge."

"I think we should take a drive," Taylor suggested.

"Yes, I think we should," Yvonne concurred.

The two ladies stood in line at the bank, and when the teller smiled, they took a step forward. Yvonne handed her the key and she immediately dismissed the notion that it belonged to their branch, advising her that they didn't have safety deposit boxes and that she might try a larger bank.

Outside the bank, the pair stood thinking about other possibilities. "What is the largest bank in the area?" Taylor asked.

Yvonne thought for a moment. "I don't know, maybe the Bank of New York."

"Let's go," Taylor said with a look of determination."

This time they were seated in two comfortable green leather chairs, where they had been directed by a teller. A thin man with glasses and a balding head came strutting over. His dark blue suit was wrinkled and hanging off his boney shoulders, like a wide wire hanger.

"Good afternoon ladies. I'm the bank manager, Mr. Starks," he said as he shook their hands in a fast and detached manner, as if they had leprosy. "Please come this way." He gestured to an office and they followed him in. "Please take a seat."

Once they were both seated, he took a seat behind his large wooden desk. "How may I help you ladies?"

"I have this key," Yvonne said as she handed it to him.

"Yes, this is for our deposit box," he said at a glance.

Taylor felt a slight rush inside and Yvonne's curiosity took hold. "My late husband had an account here and I'd like to view the contents."

"May I please see some identification?" She handed him her license and he examined it.

"Please wait here." With a slight bow of his head he was off and a few minutes later he returned. "Yes, Mrs. Lynch, your name is also on the account. You can come this way, but your friend must stay here." Yvonne placed her hand over Taylor's indicating that she wouldn't be long.

When Yvonne came out she had an uneasy look on her face. She thanked the bank manager and walked straight for the door. When they got outside, she turned to Taylor appearing nervous and speaking through shaky lips "I have found documents that may endanger both of us." One look at her and Taylor knew she had discovered something probably involving the federal government and most likely top secret.

"Let's go back to your place," Taylor wisped.

There were no curtains to draw and no way to cover up the windows facing the back of the house. Yvonne had wanted it that way to allow the sunlight through, brightening up the inside of the house. At this very moment, she wished she would have made a different decision so many years ago. Looking out the window, she scanned her property to its edges wondering who was out there watching them. It wasn't long ago that a killer was shot in her bedroom, and prior to that, her husband's lifeless body emerging to the surface of the sound. They must have been watching her every move and why would they stop now? Now that she and Taylor held in their possession documents that would expose the truth about despicable experiments that had gone out of control and the tragic negligence that followed. The worst part, she thought, was how far the government had gone to cover it up. Had they come forward and admitted their mistakes, eventually it would have been forgotten by most people, and some other scandal would have taken precedence.

"Have a seat here," Yvonne said as she placed the thick folders on the table and pulled out a chair for Taylor. She took her place next to Taylor and opened the first docket and began scanning through it. "George had been adding notes over the years as new information was discovered."

"Yes," Taylor agreed. "It looks that way."

"Look here," Yvonne said as she pointed to a document that appeared to be very old. "Project Paperclip." She cleared her throat and began reading the document and Taylor quietly read along in amazement. "April 19th 1950 at the artillery range at Fort Terry, Doctor Erich Traub released the vector to infect the animal population," Yvonne said in a voice of disbelief. "Fort Terry is what they called Plum Island before the CDC became involved," Yvonne added, "back then it was under the control of the U.S. army."

Taylor continued reading. "The vector consisted of the Cayenne and Lone Star species." She looked at Yvonne appearing confused.

"Ticks," Yvonne surmised. "Look here, at the notes from George," Yvonne continued. "He noted that the ticks examined were infected with several diseases including: Bartonella, Ehrlichia, Babesia, Mycoplasma and Borrelia." She looked at the young detective sitting next to her. "Borrelia is the bacteria in Lyme disease. This would explain why so many people living around Plum Island have become infected with Lyme disease. The infected animals must have migrated to the mainland."

"Look at the date of this footnote," Taylor said. "It was just a few years ago."

Yvonne kept reading. "The ticks removed from the Island were consistent with the ticks examined by the CDC that were found on the mainland, in that they were also infected with associated diseases. They are not contained to Plum Island; they have spread throughout the United States." Yvonne stopped to gather her thoughts before continuing on. "The probability that a single tick would host so many different types of disease is remote to impossible. The vector were inoculated."

Taylor looked at Yvonne with uncertain eyes, like that of an abused child. "Why would anyone inoculate a tick with a number of diseases?" she asked. "I can understand a scientist infecting a lab rat in order to conduct studies, but a tick the size of a poppy seed." She shook her head. "It just doesn't make any sense."

"You're right. It doesn't make sense," Yvonne agreed, "unless their intention was not for studying the diseases, but to develop them as a weapon."

"A weapon," Taylor repeated.

"Think about it, my dear," Yvonne said as she placed her hand over Taylor's. "Other than the mosquito, what other blood sucking insect would be the perfect weapon for infecting a population?"

"A tick," Taylor replied under her breath.

The old woman kept reading. "Studies in lab 257 concluded that Borrelia is a spirochete that burrs itself into the cell and releases a toxic element inside the cell called (reactive oxygen species) that are essentially free radicals that destroy the DNA by destroying the cell membrane." She took a deep breath before continuing. "The spirochete attacks all areas of the body, including the heart and brain, and in many cases, can go undetected. It is a smart bug that hides itself and mimics many other illnesses. There is no known cure."

"This could be a perfect weapon," Taylor said. "It may not kill the victim right away, but it incapacitates them and the people that are providing care, not to mention the financial burden to the country affected."

Yvonne nodded her head and turned the page. "Look at this note!" The volume of her voice increased. "The vector had been inoculated with, Mycoplasma, a bacteria first patented by the U.S. Army on June 18th 1986, patent number 875, 535. The same bacteria responsible for the gulf war syndrome."

"Oh my God." Taylor sighed as she read Dr. Lynch's notes. "Our government essentially invented a deadly strain of bacteria that was used to kill our troops during the gulf war."

Yvonne looked at her comrade and continued reading. "How did over one hundred thousand military personnel and their families become ill and several thousand die from a disease that was discovered and patented by the U.S. Army?"

"Let me get this straight," Taylor said. "What your husband was saying is that this disease, Mycoplasma, was discovered and patented by our government and they had inoculated ticks with it to be used as a biological warfare agent?"

"That and many other types of disease," Yvonne said, "but these ticks must have been inoculated many years ago because the diseases found in these ticks go way back."

"And this disease, Mycoplasma, is the cause of our troops and their families becoming sick and in many cases dying during Desert Storm?"

"Yes, that is what he's saying." Taylor noticed she was speaking in present tense as if her husband was still alive.

"It must have been in the artillery rounds," Taylor said thoughtfully."

"Yes, the question is whose artillery rounds?" Yvonne asked.

"It must have been ours, unless Iraq had Mycoplasma as well," Taylor said as she stood up and walked toward the large window facing the sound. "If they did, they must have gotten it from us during the war between Iraq and Iran." She pushed a strand of hair out of her face and turned toward Yvonne who was sitting like a statue. "This is incomprehensible."

"Yes, and my husband and Harold were killed by our government to prevent the public from learning the truth." Her eyes began to well up. "The people need to know the truth."

Taylor engaged the old woman and she could almost feel her pain by the look in her eyes. "The people will know what happened. I promise you, they will know," Taylor assured her.

CHAPTER 29

Gary sat on the couch with his leg in a soft cast elevated by two large throw pillows. Taylor sat next to him thumbing though the original department of defense documents that Yvonne had brought home from the bank. Each time she found something important, she brought it to Gary's attention and they marked it with a bright orange page tab.

"This Erich Traub was one reckless bastard," he said.

"I'm sure he wasn't the only one," Taylor added. "I still can't believe our government would hire Nazis to conduct biological warfare experiments on Plum Island right after the Second World War." She shook her head in disgust. "Just a few years after they were killing our soldiers and millions of innocent Jews, we have them over for dinner."

"Dr. Lynch was really troubled by these experiments," Gary said. "For him to get his hands on some of the original experimental results documents and hide them all these years is amazing."

"Yeah, and he even added his own notes to clarify and elaborate on what some of the findings meant," she said as she thumbed through the thick folder.

"Taylor, I'm so proud of you and what you have uncovered here." He leaned in to kiss her. "We need to expose these bastards and get it out in the open."

Taylor reached over and took his hand and gave it a quick squeeze. "You understand how dangerous it is having these documents?" she asked.

"Yes, but once this is public knowledge, the danger to us will diminish. At that point the government will be focused on putting out the fire, not adding gasoline to it."

"I guess you're right," she agreed. "How will we do it?"

"I'll bring it to my editor with the condition that I write the story in its entirety."

"Will he go for it?"

"Why wouldn't he?"

"There's only one reason I can think of," she said. "Politics."

Victor Harris, the editor of the New Haven Register sat in his office with a brief in front of him on the information he received from Gary. He had been optimistic that their paper would be the media to break the story about the Army's development and negligence in the spreading of Lyme disease. His optimism was killed a few minutes earlier when the Register's editor, Jim Wright, came into his office regurgitating the bad news. Wright told him that he was advised by United States Senator Lebner, that it would be detrimental to national security and the New Haven Register, if the story were to be printed, and that it would be a grave mistake to the future of the newspaper. He went on to say that any documents relating to this matter are classified and property of the Federal Government and anyone in possession of such material is committing a federal crime. Wright ordered his editor to call Gary and convince him to turn the documents over immediately, and then Wright would personally hand them over to the Senator. Harris picked up the phone and dialed without delay.

"Hello," Gary answered in a monotone voice.

"Gary, this is Victor. Are you alright?"

"Yes."

"You sound like shit."

"I was just napping, what's up?"

"Gary, I have bad news."

He thought for a second as his mind cleared. "The paper isn't going to run the story, right?"

"That's right. Gary, it's a great story and I commend you on it, but Jim is not on board with it."

He sat up in bed. "Why not?"

"It's political."

"Since when does our paper bend over for politicians?" he asked with a pinch of anger.

"This is not a story about some senator cheating on his wife or a governor taking dirty money; this is about national security."

"National security, that's an oxymoron if I ever heard one," Gary replied sarcastically. "Have you read the brief?"

"Of course I read it and I'm with you on this, but shit rolls down hill, and I just got a mouthful," he said contemptuously. "Gary, I need you to turn in the documents and any copies you have, right away." The line went silent. "Gary, are you there?"

"Are you kidding me?"

"No, Gary. I'm very serious, and so is Jim. We need to turn the documents over to the feds."

"Victor."

"What?"

"Kiss my ass!" The line went dead.

A few minutes later, Gary picked up the phone and called Jim Bolten, an old friend from college who was a reporter for the New York Times. After a brief conversation, Jim agreed to meet with Gary. After placing the receiver down, Gary crutched his way to the door and checked the deadbolt and then he drew the curtains, closing out the world.

CHAPTER 30

Taylor decided it was time to drive down to Washington and she thought it would be best to do it while on vacation. She had contacted Ryan Treemont and told him about her meeting with Mr. Fenton about the a letter he received from Blake's CIA supervisor stating that his son had died a decade earlier, and that his son was killed in an explosion and there were no remains. Treemont responded by saying it all sounded suspicious and that he had a friend who was a retired CIA agent that he would contact to gain some insight. They agreed to meet in the city for lunch at the Hilton hotel where she would be checking in.

Taylor had advised Preston about her meeting with Fenton and he agreed that something smelled funny. She also advised him about her meeting with Morrici and that he was going to think about the Windows case and make a decision on dropping the charges. Taylor asked Preston if he would make a call to Morrici supporting her request to have the case dismissed and he agreed to do so. Preston was alright with granting Taylor vacation time; he actually suggested she take two weeks instead of one and she told him she would think about it. She decided not to tell him about her plan to drive to the District of Columbia and meet with Treemont because she thought Preston might frown on her looking into possible wrong-doing by certain CIA officials. Although her relationship with Preston was improving significantly, she knew he would do whatever it takes to cover his own ass, so she decided to keep her trip a secret for now.

When Taylor checked into the Hilton, she was informed

that Ryan Treemont was waiting for her in the lobby. From a brown leather couch in the corner, Treemont sat with a newspaper shielding his face. He had watched as Taylor headed toward the front desk and he thought she looked much more attractive than the photograph that was attached to her file.

As Taylor approached, Treemont stood up to receive her and she was surprised by his appearance. Through the phone line, she had created an image of a nerdy man with glasses and a rounding waistline, but what she saw was the complete opposite. *It's funny how we imagine what a person looks like by the sound of their voice and the content of their dialog, and we are seldom right.* "Agent Treemont." She approached with an extended hand and a smile. Ryan took her hand and she immediately noticed his finely manicured fingernails, and soft, yet strong hands. "Please call me, Ryan," he said with a brief handshake and a half smile. He was wearing a black pinstriped suit and black Italian made shoes. His white collar was pressed and spotless under a dull red tie that was held snug with a gold yin and yang tie clip. "I reserved a table for three in a secluded area of the restaurant."

"Three," she said with a curious gaze.

"Yes, the retired agent we spoke of on the phone, remember?"

"Yes, I do," she said with a look of approval. "Thanks for setting that up."

Treemont nodded his head and looked toward the exit. "Shall we head to the restaurant?"

"I'll follow you," she said motioning for him to lead the way.

They were immediately seated in an area off the main dining floor and nestled in a cove that seemed to be made for the round table and four chairs. Taylor thought that Treemont had probably been there before and sat at the same table. He took the chair with his back to the wall as he always tried to do to avoid being compromised and having a clear view of anyone approaching. Taylor could tell that he was very fit and exercised regularly and he carried himself with unwavering confidence.

"So, you were a Navy SEAL," she asked.

"I still am," he said in a confident manner.

She knew what he meant. Once a SEAL, always a SEAL. "I've read the training is brutal," she said as she examined him with intrigue.

"You have no idea." He frowned.

"I suppose I don't." Through her peripheral vision Taylor observed someone approaching and quickly determined it was the waiter. Dressed in a maroon vest and white shirt, the young waiter handed them menus and took their drink order. "Will your third party still be joining you?" he asked in a British accent.

"Yes," Treemont said. "He should be arriving shortly."

The waiter placed a menu on the table. "Yes, Sir." He took their drink order and he was off.

"I'd like you to understand something about Blake Fenton," Treemont started. "Many of the men during our SEAL training looked up to him as their role model, including me," he finished in a lower tone. It was apparent it troubled him that Blake had turned out the way he did. "There wasn't a stronger man in the academy and I'm not just talking about physically," he said. "His mental strength was beyond compare."

"It's unfortunate that his integrity wasn't quite as strong," she said bitterly.

Treemont didn't respond because he knew she was right in that regard. "Eric, good to see you," Treemont said as he stood to greet the approaching man. Taylor stood and swiveled in place to see the man they were waiting for, as he approached from behind her like a tiger in the hunt.

"Hello, Ryan." He reached out his hand and then he turned to face Taylor.

"This is Taylor Marshall." Treemont introduced them and they shook hands. "Have a seat." The waiter came over with two drinks and took Eric's order, and once again, he vanished toward the kitchen.

"How long have you been with the Connecticut State

Police?" He asked through a neatly trimmed beard that was fading from light brown to gray around the chin.

"Almost twelve years," she said realizing how quickly time had passed.

"Do you know Lieutenant LeBlanc out of the Stamford barracks?"

"No, I don't."

"He's a good man and an old friend." He looked at Taylor and then back to Treemont. "How can I help you?"

"Two weeks ago I shot and killed a man that worked for the CIA," she said, expecting some sort of reaction from the former CIA operative, and finding none. "Well, I think he may have worked for the CIA," she back peddled, "I'm not sure he was still employed there at the time of his death."

"What makes you think he may have worked for Central Intelligence?" he asked cautiously.

"I met with his father." She reached into her bag and handed him the letter. "He gave me this." Eric took the letter and read it in a glance. "I see."

Taylor thought he must be a speed reader. "What do you make of this?" she asked.

"The letter is signed by Jake Marley," he said with a peculiar grin. "It was an ongoing joke with the firm," he said. "If someone received a letter signed by Jake Marley, the firm was hiding something."

"Who's Jake Marley?" she asked.

"There is no Jake Marley." He smirked. "Jake Marley is a ghost, he doesn't exist."

"Jacob Marley." Treemont smiled. "The ghost that was Ebenezer Scrooge's partner.

"A Christmas Carol," Taylor mumbled.

"That's right." Eric looked at her with hard eyes. "This man is a ghost." He pointed to the signature on the letter.

"Who would have the authority to send such a bogus letter?" she asked. "Why would someone send such a letter?"

"Someone wanted his family, and everyone else for that

matter, to think he was dead." He cracked his knuckles. "From what you told me on the phone," he looked at Treemont, "this guy was killing people and someone didn't want him caught. And if he was caught, they didn't want him to be identified."

"Who are these people?" Taylor asked with a look of disgust.

"This had to come from the top," Eric said.

"The Director?" Treemont asked.

"If not him, then someone very close to him," he said. "An order like this had to come from someone high up the food chain."

"I think it's time to start looking into the background of some of these people," Taylor said as she folded the letter up and placed it back into her bag.

"I'd be very careful if I were you," Eric said. "These are very powerful men and a person meddling where they shouldn't be could easily disappear." He stood up and shook Treemont's hand. "Even a Connecticut State trooper," he said looking Taylor in the eye, and then he walked away.

The waiter came strolling over with a drink in hand. "Is your other party in the restroom?" he asked.

"No, he won't be joining us after all," Treemont said. "You can take our order now." The waiter did his job and was off with Eric's undisturbed drink in hand.

"Your friend Eric is a peculiar man," Taylor concluded.

"Yes, he is at that," Treemont concurred.

Taylor examined the special agent. "His real name isn't Eric, is it?" Treemont didn't answer; he just glanced at his watch and drank from his glass.

Taylor sat in the District of Columbia Library located on G Street. She began by researching the background of CIA Director Robert Carol. The man had an interesting background, she thought. Carol had graduated from Annapolis Naval Academy with a degree in Physical Science and he went on to complete law school at Columbia University after giving the Navy five years for his education. Carol practiced law for eight years in Virginia as an assistant district attorney, prosecuting murder cases and serious assaults. After completing a full term in congress, he became Chairman of the National Intelligence Council and was later appointed as a Deputy Director of the Central Intelligence Agency. When the Director seat opened up, he was first in line for the position and he was appointed by the President.

Something told Taylor that Carol was not the type to be involved in murder. He was just too clean and he'd been a prosecuting attorney with a reputation for relentlessly hammering the bad guys. She switched gears and began looking into Thomas Garrison, the Executive Director.

As she began looking into his background, she thought he was possibly the type that could be involved in this case. Garrison had graduated from Yale with a degree in international relations and a minor in languages. While attending Yale, he was on the swim team and he had taken the Connecticut golden gloves middleweight championship. Garrison went on to earn a master's degree in international affairs from Princeton University. During his final semester at Princeton, he had been recruited on campus and this had started his career in the agency. Garrison had started out as a field agent and methodically worked his way up the ranks to eventually find himself in charge of five centers that effectively enable the CIA to carry out its missions. *This guy is a career agency man that speaks three languages, English, Russian and French. For the first twelve years he was working covert operations abroad and there is no documentation as to where he was and what he was doing. He is a classic spook.*

There was something about this man that bothered Taylor and she decided to look deeper into his past. It took some digging as she spent hours looking through newspaper archives and magazine articles. Information on the internet was limited, but she kept searching, looking for something that might shine some light on the man known as the Executive Director of the CIA.

Taylor read that Garrison had played high school football and she began to trace the history of the former high school linebacker. She lightly tapped her pencil on the notebook sitting on the desk to her right. *He played football for Greenport High School in Long Island, New York. That's ironic; it's not very far from the Lynch residence.*

It was time for a coffee break and a phone call, so Taylor walked outside and found a diner just up the block. She ordered a coffee to go, found a seat on a park bench and began dialing. The woman on the other end answered. "Greenport High."

"Hello, I was calling to verify a former student's attendance at your school."

"Please hold."

Taylor took a sip from her cup as she waited. "Records," the woman on the other end screeched.

"Hello, my name is Taylor Marshall, and I was wondering if you would verify that a former student of your school had graduated."

"What's the student's name?"

"His name is, Thomas Garrison."

The line was dead silent for three seconds. "You mean the CIA guy?" she asked.

"Yes, that's correct," Taylor replied figuring that it made sense she would know who he was.

"Yes, he was a graduate of our school, but not as, Thomas Garrison."

A strange feeling took hold. "What do you mean not as, Thomas Garrison?"

"When he attended school here his name was Thomas Connell," she said in a lower tone as if it was a secret. "He changed his name after graduation."

Taylor held onto the phone without speaking. "Is there anything else I can help you with?"

"No, thank you." She pushed the button on her cell phone and the line went dead.

CHAPTER 31

Taylor leaned against the long wall looking out at the endless names carved into the stone of the men and women that paid the ultimate sacrifice in Vietnam. She searched for, John Habbot, a neighborhood boy she knew was killed during the Tet Offensive. John was a neighborhood legend, and murky stories of him charging the enemy with a fixed bayonet, covered with green and black war paint, while delivering a deafening death call had resonated throughout her community for years. After fifteen minutes she exhausted her efforts, as the names had no defining order and there were over fifty-eight thousand. She noticed there had been a book that displayed the names of the diseased in order, but it had been vandalized and was no longer legible.

It was a long walk through the National Park and this was just what Taylor needed in order to think about the chain of events that had occurred and figure out what her next steps would be. She walked past the Vietnam memorial of the three soldiers and then stopped at the statue of the wartime nurses and took a picture. She was glad there was national acknowledgment of the female sacrifice and contribution to the Vietnam War. After observing the Lincoln Memorial, she used the restroom and decided to head back to the hotel. On the way back she paced the white house property, taking a few more photographs along the way. This was not her first trip to the area, she and Dave had traveled to DC right after they first started dating and she had an entire scrap book dedicated to the sites in the District of Columbia.

In her hotel room, Taylor sat on the bed with a phone in her hand thinking about what she would say to Gary when he picked up. A minute later, he was on the other end.

"Hello." He sounded as if he had just woken up from a nap.

"Hi Gary, how are you feeling?"

"Well, I'm not ready to run a marathon, but I'm coming along. How's it going in DC?" He pushed himself upright in the bed.

"It's going well. I took a long walk through the national park today - it was a beautiful day."

"That sounds nice. I wish I was there with you and you could have given me a tour in a wheel chair." He laughed and she followed. "How's it going on the other front?"

"I had an interesting meeting with a CIA guy, and I think I may be on to something."

"Really, what's that?"

"The signature on the letter to Mister Fenton is a phantom. There is no Jake Marley at the CIA."

"Someone sent the letter," he said in a defeated tone.

"Yes, someone did, but who is the question. I did some digging and I found out that, Thomas Garrison, the Executive Director of the CIA had changed his name from Connell to Garrison, and guess what?"

"What?"

"He grew up in Long Island, not far from the Lynch residence."

"That's ironic."

"Yes it is. I'm going to head to the library and see what I can learn about Mister Connell and his family tree."

"Let me see what I can dig up on my end as well," Gary said.

"Sounds good, I'll call you in the morning."

"I love you, Taylor."

"And I love you."

"Bye."

"Goodbye," she said in a whisper and place down the receiver.

After a light dinner, Taylor headed to the library and began her research into the Connell family. She was on the internet reading about, Robert Connell, Thomas's father who was a retired electrician that worked for the electrical union for nearly forty years. There was limited information on Robert, except an article in the Suffolk Times regarding an incident where he had been zapped early in his career while climbing a pole, and was lucky to have survived. Taylor had also located an article from the Times that read about Robert's accomplishments while working as a General Foreman and directing renovations at the Suffolk County Community College.

As Taylor continued her search, she began to look back into the forties and fifties searching for information on Robert Connell's father. Looking for anything under the name Connell, she immediately spotted an article in the Times and the date was 1948. The headline completely took her by surprise and caused a chill to travel from the base of her skull, down her spine and settling in her toes. An overwhelming feeling of exhilaration swept through her, like an overdose of adrenaline as she scanned the article that was titled, JOHN CONNELL APPOINTED AS DIRECTOR OF PLUM ISLAND. Once she finished reading the article she knew her hunch on Thomas Connell turned out to be real. His grandfather ran Plum Island for nine years and he was in charge of the facility during operation paper clip; when Erich Traub was conducting his bio-weapons experiments on the island. *What is so important to keep quiet that he would commit murder?*

Taylor decided she needed a drink. She wasn't sure if it was to calm her nerves or celebrate, but she was jonesing for alcohol, so she printed out a copy of the article and headed to the nearest bar.

When her cell phone rang it was just after eleven in the morning. Taylor had worked out at the hotel gym before eating a light breakfast in the restaurant. As usual, she was appalled at the prices the hotel charged for breakfast and she thought they should be ashamed for taking advantage in such an extreme way; nearly twenty dollars for breakfast.

"Hi Honey," Taylor answered as she saw Gary's name light up on her cell phone.

"Hey, Babe. How are you this morning?"

"I'm doing great. I was just going to call you." He could hear the excitement in her voice. "I did some digging last night and I found out that our Executive Director of the CIAs grandfather, John Connell, was the director in charge of Plum Island during operation paper clip; when they were conducting the biological weapons experiments."

"Yes, I know," he said.

"You know?" Taylor was surprised that he had uncovered the same information so quickly.

"Yes, I did some digging myself and I also learned why Thomas Connell changed his name."

Taylor was impressed with Gary's investigative capability. "You did, why did he change his name?"

Thomas Connell never got along with his father and was ashamed that he was just a construction worker." He cleared his throat. "So after college, he changed his last name to Garrison."

"Where did you get all this information?" she asked in an excited tone.

"A very close friend of mine has a brother that's been a member of local 25 for most of his adult life." The line went silent for a few seconds. "That's the electrical union in Long Island where Garrison's father, Robert Connell, was a member," he finished.

"I see," Taylor said.

"I also found out that Garrison was very close to his grandfather and that he was practically raised by him."

"Do you think Thomas Garrison would commit murder to preserve the reputation of his dead grandfather?"

"I think he might have ordered the killings for both that reason and to keep the dirty secrets of the government out of the public eye."

"Two birds with one stone," she mumbled.

"Yes. What do we do now?"

"Now, I take a ride to Langley and pay Mr. Garrison a visit."

"Do you think that's wise?" She could hear the concern in his voice.

"Probably not, but I need to look into his eyes when I divulge what we know."

"And what do you think that will accomplish? I doubt you'll crack this guy."

"I don't know. It's just something I need to do."

"Just be careful what you say and how you say it. This is a very powerful and dangerous man."

"I'll choose my words carefully," was all she said.

CHAPTER 32

To Taylor's surprise, CIA headquarters located at, 2430 E Street NW, Mclean, VA was situated right off the main highway. In her mind, she pictured it being compounded in a rural, wooded, area secluded from the public eye. She had known the place as being located in Langley, but when she looked at a map, Langley wasn't listed. It didn't exist. This was another one of those CIA mysteries that was well hidden from the public along with countless others that wouldn't be uncovered unless otherwise dug up. When she called to make an appointment, she was told by Garrison's assistant that he did not take appointments from the public and for her to send any inquiries in the form of a letter. It wasn't until she asked Garrison's assistant to tell him it was about Blake Fenton and the deaths of two Plum Island scientists that she was put on a security clearance list to visit the building so very few had entered.

As she drove her car past the tall, iron, gate that sealed the compound, Taylor watched as an armed guard diligently approached from a small security shack he had been spying her from. With an automatic weapon at his ready, he stopped her automobile as it rolled up parallel with the hut.

"May I help you, Mam?" he asked in a firm, yet polite tone.

Taylor wondered if he had a rocket launcher in the hut, or grenades at the very least. "I'm here to see Mister Garrison."

He walked back to the hut and retrieved a clipboard. After a quick glance at the sheet of paper attached to the board, he asked her for identification and she produced a license. Matching the name on her license to that on his list, he handed her back the document. "May I see another form of identification, Mam?"

She hesitated and thought. *It is the CIA headquarters after all.* Taylor took out her badge wallet and handed him the entire leather wallet containing her gold shield and police identification. After a quick examination, he offered her a half smile and a nod of approval. "Please proceed ahead."

"Thank you." She tucked her wallet into her handbag and drove through.

After parking her car, Taylor walked up the walkway to the main building that was an aging brick structure that appeared well maintained. An older black man knelt outside the front entrance applying mortar to the wounded dwelling. *Now I see why this place is so well maintained. They probably have someone working on it around the clock.* As she passed by the maintenance man, she noticed the identification card clipped to his shirt pocket. He didn't look up, even though it was obvious to him that she was passing by.

Upon entering the lobby, the first thing Taylor noticed was a wall with many stars flanked by two flags, the stars and stripes on the left and what appeared to be the colors and seal of the CIA on the right. Walking straight to the thick window, she was attended to by a young man that sat on the other side of the bulletproof glass.

"May I help you?" he asked through an intercom.

"Yes, my name is Taylor Marshall, and I'm here to see, Executive Director Garrison."

"Please take a seat." He glanced at a bench situated directly across the lobby from where the wall of stars was located.

"Thank you," she said and proceeded toward the intriguing wall that she had read about many years earlier. Taylor scanned the perfectly rowed stars that were carved into white marble and she didn't count them, but figured there were close to a hundred. She knew each star represented a CIA employee that was killed in the line of duty. Above the display of stars in gold block letters was the inscription, IN HONOR OF THOSE MEMBERS OF THE CENTRAL INTELLIGENCE AGENCY

WHO GAVE THEIR LIVES IN THE SERVICE OF THEIR COUNTRY.

Under the display of stars, Taylor's eyes were fixed on a black goat-skinned bound book called the "Book of Honor," that sat in a slender case jutting out from the wall and was framed in stainless steel and topped by an inch-thick plate of glass. Inside it displayed the stars, arranged by year of death and, when possible, listed the names of employees who died in CIA service alongside them. The identities of the unnamed stars remain secret, even in death. As she scanned the book, she found herself fixed on the year 2001 and the single star listed for that year didn't have a name designated for it.

A steel door to the left of the lobby window opened and an attractive blonde lady dressed in a light gray pant suit with black heels appeared packing a clipboard. As she walked toward Taylor, the door closed shut behind her with a loud bang. Right away, Taylor knew this was not a good sign.

"Ms. Marshall." She reached out her hand before she closed the gap.

"Yes." Taylor took her soft, clammy hand.

"I'm Barbara Candle, Mr. Garrison's assistant. Can we take a seat on the bench?" She gestured toward the bench and Taylor moved to sit down. "Mr. Garrison had an urgent meeting and will not be able to meet with you today. However, he has asked me to meet with you on his behalf and address your concerns." Her smile appeared as if it were forced and was pasted on her face, like a smiling lap-dummy.

"Well that's unfortunate," Taylor said. "I drove all the way down here from Connecticut because I had an appointment with Mister Garrison. "I can wait until his meeting is over. I really need to speak with him in person,"

"I'm sorry, Ms. Marshall, he will be tied up all day."

"Alright, I'll just come back tomorrow."

Her smile began to waver. "He won't be able to see you then, either." She moved her pen into position, gently touching the pad. "Mister Garrison asked that I help you with your concerns. I can assure you that he will receive the information from me exactly how you present it."

Taylor took to her feet, standing over the puppet. "You can tell Mister Garrison, what I have to say to him must be said directly to him." She secured her pocketbook strap onto her shoulder. "Thank you for your time." Taylor didn't offer her hand, she was not in a courteous mood, and she turned and walked out.

As she began back down the walkway leading away from the main building, she glanced at the maintenance man as he worked on the building. Then abruptly, she stopped and stood looking at him as he continued in his effort to repair the aging wall. "Excuse me, Sir." She moved toward him and he stopped and turned to face her without speaking. "I was wondering if you would help me."

He glanced at the camera that was attached to the building and pointing in his direction. "Yes."

"I was admiring the wall in the lobby with the stars and I was wondering if you were the craftsman that added a star when we lose an agent?"

"No, Mam." He cleared his throat. "That is done by Tim Johnston, a professional stone carver."

"I see," she said. "I also noticed that there is one star inscribed for this year. Do you know when that was done?"

"Why, Mam, that was just done last week."

"Last week huh." She smiled. "Thank you."

"You're welcome," he said and turned back to his task at hand.

The diner where Taylor rested was so busy she had to sit at the counter between several construction workers that ate as if it were their last meal. She sipped a coffee while she thought about Thomas Garrison and his background. *How am I going to confront him if he won't see me? Maybe I can find out where his favorite restaurant is located and catch him with his mouth full.* One of the construction workers sitting across from her caught her eye and gave her a wink and a smile. Taylor smiled back and reached into her purse and dropped two dollars on the counter and left the diner.

While walking down the street, Taylor glanced in the windows of the retail shops, not looking for anything in particular. As she passed by a sports-wear store she spotted a poster of Olympic gold medalist, Ian Thorpe, doing the crawl during the 2000 Olympics games in Sydney Australia. At that very moment, it hit her, and she stopped to gather her thoughts. Taylor remembered reading an article about Garrison having been on the swim team in college and how he continued his daily swim routine to keep in shape. She immediately changed direction and headed to the library.

It took less than a half hour of scanning articles before Taylor located the information she needed. Every morning before heading off to the office, Garrison did a mile long swim at a private health club located in, Mclean. Taylor immediately picked up the phone and called the club and made an appointment with a sales representative that afternoon.

CHAPTER 33

Tyson's sport & health club was offering a three day pass for prospective members to come and try out the facility and Taylor was happy to take advantage of such a generous offer. She had met with a club representative the day before, and after receiving her free pass, she headed to the sporting goods store where she had seen the poster of, Ian Thorpe. Taylor figured the least she could do was give the business to the store that displayed the poster that resurrected the information hidden in the rear closet of her brain regarding Garrison's daily exercise routine. After purchasing a red one piece bathing suit and a swim cap she went back to the hotel to give Gary a call and hit the hotel gym for a hard cardiovascular workout.

In the pool area, Taylor sat in a chair waiting for Garrison to arrive. She had gotten there ten minutes after the doors opened at five in the morning because she wanted to be sure she didn't miss him. It was exactly six-fifty-two when Garrison came walking through the door with another man that was clearly his swimming buddy. They were chatting as they headed to the shower to rinse off before heading to an open lane to begin their regimen of laps. Taylor was about to approach him, but something told her to wait for a better time, so she just sat in her chair as if she was resting after a long swim. The two men slipped on their goggles to protect their eyes from the bite of the chlorine and they began their swim.

Taylor's mind began to drift back to the day when she had arrived at the scene of the murder of Doctor Brown. As she watched Garrison glide through the water, she thought about her visit to the Lynch residence and her short conversation with

Doctor Lynch just before he had been killed. She was almost inclined to jump into the pool and hold Garrison's head under the water until the bubbles disappeared, just like the death Doctor Lynch had suffered on his order. The thought of Gary being run down in a parking garage and nearly killed made her angry at the core, and finally, the knife that cut deep onto her flesh still tingled when she twisted her torso in a certain way.

The swim was over and the two men walked up the steps and out of the pool to find their towels that hung on a hook on the wall near the sauna. Taylor thought she would have to make her move and approach him, because he would soon be in the men's locker room and she would lose contact with him. As she stood up to begin her journey to the other side of the pool room, she watched as the two men went into the sauna room. *Perfect, I have him in a secluded place where he will be sitting in a quiet area.*

Taylor pushed open the sauna door and entered the co-ed room. It was a small sauna occupied only by Garrison and his friend. She placed her towel on the bench and took a seat with Garrison's friend in between them. Both men watched as the young woman with the smoking body entered their space, but neither greeted her or offered a friendly smile.

"It's a shame you wouldn't see me yesterday, Mr. Garrison." Her heart began to race as he looked at her comprehending who she probably was. "I had to wait here for two hours this morning in order to have a word with you."

"Do I know you?" He asked in a condescending manner.

"No, but you do know Blake Fenton, don't you?"

"That name doesn't ring a bell," he lied.

"Let me refresh your memory, Executive Director. He is the CIA operative that murdered two elderly men and tried to kill an old woman before I shot him."

With the completion of that remark, Garrison's swimming pal got up and walked out of the sauna.

"I'm afraid I don't know what you're talking about." He wiped the sweat that was accumulating on his forehead. "There is no CIA operative named, Fenton."

"Enough of the bullshit, Director," she barked. "I read the letter his father had received from the agency that read he had been killed in action ten years earlier, a letter that was signed by Jake Marley. Nice touch, Director." His expression appeared to be depleting. "The funny thing is that there aren't any stars listed in the "book of honor" for that year, and that's probably because I killed him this year."

"This certainly sounds like an entertaining story," he said with a smirk, "And maybe a good one for a fiction writer."

"I think not, Director. This story is non-fiction, and is actually a good piece for a journalist."

Garrison didn't like her comment. "You are overstepping your boundaries, Trooper Marshall!"

"Maybe so, Director," she fired back. "What I couldn't grasp is why the agency would kill a couple of old scientists over fear that they might blow the whistle on our government's involvement in the spreading of Lyme disease." He scanned her body to make sure that she wasn't wired and he knew there was no place she could hide a wire with only a tight bathing suit on. "Then after I looked into your family history, I found out why. You were protecting the reputation of John Connell, your grandfather that ran Plum Island, who was ultimately responsible for inoculating ticks with Lyme disease that eventually spread to the general population."

"I think I've heard about enough of this nonsense," he roared, "you have nothing but a few crumbs that won't amount to a satisfying morsel."

"I also found out that an anonymous star was listed in the Book of Honors just last week," she said as she took to her feet. "Was that the star for Blake Fenton?"

He didn't answer, but even in the dim light, Taylor saw the look in his eyes that she hoped for. As she opened the sauna door the light came through illuminating the room and right there on his left calve was a tattoo of a five cross symbol, exactly the same as the one on Blake Fenton's shoulder. "By the way," she said with a smile. "Nice tattoo."

As Taylor walked out of the sauna and through the pool area, she could feel the blood rush through her veins. Garrison stayed in the sauna and wouldn't move from that spot for several minutes.

As usual it was busy at the Soup to Nuts restaurant and Tara was glad she was able to retain a table for her luncheon with Taylor. She sat holding a copy of the New York Times with a bold front page headline that read, FEDERAL GOVERNMENT RESPONSIBLE FOR LYME DISEASE?

Glancing over the top of her paper, she saw Taylor approaching. "A gift for you," she said as she handed Taylor the paper.

"I already have three, but thanks anyway." She smiled and took a seat.

"This is unbelievable," she said tapping her index finger on the headline.

"Yes it is, and two people died because of it, but I can't prove it."

"Well, this headline is certainly going to cause a ruckus."

"Rumor has it there are a half dozen law firms already contemplating a class action lawsuit against the U.S. Army," Taylor said with glee.

"What about Gary, how's he doing?"

"He's doing alright, should be getting his soft cast off next week. Those spineless bastards at the Register fired him, so he's out of a job. They didn't like the fact that he didn't roll over when they demanded him to turn over the documents."

"And now they're probably kicking themselves in the ass that they weren't the paper to break the story," Tara said.

"You're probably right."

The server came over and took their order. "How are you feeling? Tara asked.

"A little soar when I twist the wrong way, but it's almost completely better?"

"Can I ask you something?" she asked while sitting tilted.

"Sure."

"What does it feel like to kill someone?"

Taylor thought for a moment, remembering the look of surprise and horror in Fenton's eyes as the bullet passed through his body. "It feels like you have committed the worst sin possible and you question if there can be divine forgiveness for such an offense." She looked out the window at the people bustling in the street. "It's like you lose a part of your own soul."

"Even though he tried to kill you, it still feels that way?" In her mind, Tara thought she would have a clear conscience after pulling the trigger.

"Yes. Probably less than if he were innocent," she said wonderingly, "I suppose it depends on the individual and their conscience."

Tara looked at her friend not completely understanding her feelings. It wouldn't bother me one bit to kill a guy that tried to stab me to death, she thought. "When is the hearing on the sexual harassment case?"

"There's not going to be a hearing."

"What?" Tara looked puzzled.

"I decided to drop the case."

"Why would you do that?"

"I already took one life this year. Some people deserve to be forgiven and I think he's one of them."

"You have changed," Tara said.

"No, not really. I just grew up."

"I suppose you did."

"So, word is that Reggie is going to take a plea bargain with the DA," Taylor said.

Tara's eyebrows elevated. "Really, what does that mean?"

"It means he won't go to trial and he'll do a year in jail, maybe less."

"That's it, huh?"

"That's our justice system," Taylor said through a disappointing grin.

"Well, I'm a pretty good shot *now*, you know?"

"Yeah, I know," Taylor said. "Let's hope you never have to prove that."

"Yeah, let's hope so. I want my soul intact."

"Yes you do," Taylor said as they both peered out the window in silence.

"The summer flew by this year and here we are, September already," Tara said.

"Maybe for you, but for me this was the longest summer I've ever had."

"Where are you going with the case now?"

Taylor thought about her question and then a sinister look appeared on her face. "I can't exactly say right now, but let's just put it like this. Soon, a follow –up story will hit the news media and it will be on the front page of every newspaper in the country, and with that, certain government officials will be exposed and heads will roll."

"And the last thing they will see is, Taylor Marshall, standing before them with her hand on the guillotine lever," Tara said.

Taylor laughed. "You're crazy, you know that?"

"Yeah, but it's a crazy world."

"Yes it is," Taylor said. "Yes it is."

CHAPTER 34

The doorman held open the door to the New York Hotel in Manhattan as Gary and Taylor walked on through. Gary was walking with the aid of a crutch and Taylor was holding his other arm close to her bosom. His idea was to take her to the big apple for a fine dining experience now that he was out of his cast, and she was excited about the pending evening.

They located the restaurant in the hotel and were immediately ushered to an intimate corner table that Gary had requested five days earlier. The waiter took their drink orders and was off in a flash. Taylor reached over and took his hand. "Thank you for taking me to this magnificent place tonight."

"You're welcome." He leaned in and gently kissed her.

"How can you afford this place without a job?" she asked.

"Well, that's part of the reason I wanted to take you here is to celebrate my new job."

"Don't tell me you got the job?" she gleefully asked.

"Yes I did." He smiled. "I got the call yesterday. I'm now working for the Hartford Courant."

"Gary, that's great. Congratulations!" Her face was beaming as she took his hand into hers.

"It is exciting, isn't it?" His eyes bore into hers.

"Yes. I think we are going to need some champagne."

"Only the best for you, Taylor," he said as he kissed her again. She wanted more. They had been seeing each other for months and hadn't made love, and they were both feeling like it was time.

"We have been through quite a bit together in the last few months, haven't we?"

"It certainly hasn't been boring," he said.

The waiter appeared with their drinks and Gary ordered a bottle of Dom Perignon champagne, as well.

"Well, your story has certainly caused quite a stir around the country," Taylor said.

"Yeah, I know. The protesters are growing by the day," he said. "When the story breaks on Garrison and the CIA, it's really going to get ugly."

She sipped her wine. "I read that twenty-three people were arrested in Seattle yesterday."

"It seems to be moving around the country," he said. "Last week it was New Jersey."

"I suppose Lyme disease has no borders," she said coyly.

"It's just too bad that it has taken violent protests and class action law suits to get the government to start doing the right thing regarding this disease."

Taylor thought carefully about what he said, and for a split second, she felt ashamed to be American. "I read that the government has now allocated fifty million dollars in funding for research and development."

"Yeah, a little too late, don't you think?"

"Yes, a little too late," she mimicked.

"Well, here's to your efforts." She raised her glass.

"And your accomplishments." He touched glasses with hers. "Oh by the way, I saw that the DA is dropping the charges against Windows."

"Yes, he did the right thing. Even though Windows is a bad guy, he doesn't deserve to be tried for a crime he didn't commit," she said. "I read that Governor Bell has finally decided to resign."

"Yeah, it all came a tumbling down on her."

"Another notch for your belt." She smiled.

"Hey, she made her bed; I just pointed out the dirty sheets."

"Well said." She stood up. "I must powder my nose."

"Do women really powder their noses *anymore*?"

"Mostly the coke heads."

He laughed. "I don't have to worry about that, do I officer?"

"No chance." She was off with a smile in tow.

Dinner and champagne followed, and when their table was cleared, Gary began to feel anxious.

"Taylor, there's something I want to tell you."

"What is it?" She saw the serious look on his face and she was concerned.

"I am totally head over heels in love with you."

Her heart began to beat faster. "I'm in love with you, Gary."

He got up and went down on one knee and produced a black velvet box. He opened it up and she was looking at a full carat diamond with two onyx stones flanking it. "Will you marry me?" His eyes began to water and his hand was trembling.

Taylor didn't notice the tears creeping out of her eyes because she was mesmerized by the question and the beauty of the ring. "I would love to be your wife," she said without hesitation.

He took the ring out of the box and slipped it on her finger, and it fit perfectly. He had measured her finger with a piece of string as she napped a week earlier. Taylor stood up and took his hand and guided him off his knee and she moved in to embrace him. He could feel her breasts pressing against his chest as she kissed him and Taylor could tell he was becoming aroused.

She reached into her purse and handed him something that felt like a credit card. "You're not paying for dinner," he said, looking down and immediately noticing that it wasn't a credit card.

"I know, but I paid for the room," she said.

A huge smile formed on his face. "When did you do that?"

"When I went to powder my nose."

Gary chuckled and pulled her in tight. "You just made my night – no, my year." His words resonated as they looked into each other's eyes. "My decade," he said.

In the room, they lay naked in the king sized bed, both

thinking how great the other performed. Gary remembered the many times he had sex for the first time and how awkward it felt, but not this time. Waiting for months had been a good idea, painful, but good, he thought. Her body was soft and tight at the same time, and her kisses delivered a sensation that spread throughout his entire being. He wanted to consume her whole and make her one with himself.

Taylor loved everything about her man. The way he undressed her so very slow and delicately, as if he was a young boy opening a special gift on Christmas morning. Taylor quivered as he ran his fingers along her entire body, like she was a precious artifact. She loved how he whispered in her ear as he made love with her. His words of love brought fulfillment, contentment and security.

"That was amazing," she said as she looked deep into his eyes.

"Yes, and worth the wait, I might add."

"Definitely worth the wait," she agreed. "I want you again," she said through a sexy grin.

"Give me a minute," he said youthfully.

"Tell me, now that you have exposed a government secret regarding the development and spreading of Lyme disease and the CIA's involvement in the murder of Doctor's Brown and Lynch, what are you going to do *now*?"

He took her hand into his. "You've heard of the West Nile virus, right?"

"Of course I have," she said.

"Did you know that on April 26th, 1985, the U.S. Army sold the West Nile virus to Iraq?"

Taylor smiled and shook her head. "It looks like you're ready for round two."

"Yes I am," he said. "In more ways than one."

CHAPTER 35

There was nothing unusual about this Tuesday morning. People were frantically scrambling around cities to make it to work on time. Some sat at their kitchen table with a cup of coffee and the morning paper. Country folk moved about at a slower pace starting their day off in a crawl that usually ended in one as well. It was just a normal day in America, except, every notable newspaper in the country had the same story written on the front page, CIA IMPLICATED IN MURDER.

It was eight-twenty in the morning when Garrison arrived at his office. As he passed by, Kathy, his secretary, she just looked at him with concerning eyes and neither of them offered the ritualistic morning greeting. The morning paper sat on her desk in front of her and she had read the lengthy article twice before Garrison arrived.

Three minutes later, Garrison's phone beeped. "Yes."

"Director Carol would like to see you in his office immediately."

After a brief silence, he responded. "Thank you." The news came to him like a defendant expecting a guilty verdict.

When he knocked on the door, he wondered if it would be the last time his knuckles would make contact with the Director's mahogany door. "Come in," Carol announced. Garrison entered as if he had been summoned to the principal's office for misbehaving during class. "Take a seat," Carol ordered, as he sat with three different newspapers spread out on his desk. "You have really fucked up this time, haven't you?"

"It doesn't look good," Garrison responded.

"Doesn't look good," he scolded. "It could not possibly ever look this bad." He stood up and walked around his desk. "Our operative, Blake Fenton was shot and killed by a police officer as he attempted to terminate an old lady, just after he shoved a knife into the ensuing police officers stomach, who happens by the way, to be a woman."

"It all went completely wrong," Garrison said in a crumbling manner.

"Did you see the newspaper?" Carol stormed.

"Yes, of course I did."

"They have a photograph of a tattoo that both you and the killer have engraved into your skin," his voice boomed. "Some sort of secret society that you and Fenton belong to." He shot both his hands into the air. "What the hell is that all about?" Garrison didn't respond. "You do have this tattoo on your leg, right?" He pointed to a photograph in the paper.

"Yes."

"Fenton had the same tattoo on his shoulder and the police had taken a photo of it at the crime scene."

"What does that prove?" Garrison asked snidely.

"Well, let me spell it out for you. In itself, *nothing*, but when you add on the false letter of notification regarding the death of Blake Fenton, that his father received on agency letterhead, and the fact that this was all related to the experiments conducted on Plum Island that your grandfather happened to run back in the fifties. It begins to add up to a conspiracy."

"Bob, you knew about this problem and the potential that these experiments on Plum Island could be exposed. You asked me to handle it, and I did,"

Carol moved in closer and leaned over Garrison. "I asked you to handle it. I never asked you to terminate two retired scientists."

"How else was I going to handle it?" He asked as if murder was the only option.

"I'm not sure, but not like that." He walked back behind his desk and took a seat. "The press has been hounding me all morning and the President called for a briefing in two hours. This is going to be the worst scandal this agency has ever had, and it's on my watch!"

"What can I do, Bob?"

Carol looked at him with burning eyes. "I'll expect a letter of resignation on my desk by the close of business today."

Instantly, Garrison felt light headed and dizziness took hold as he processes what was happening. He cleared his throat. "What about you?"

"What the hell do you think?" he snarled. "The President is probably going to ask for my resignation as well. You killed us, Tom." He clenched his right fist. "Can you comprehend the magnitude of this? Not only will we lose our careers, we will most likely be brought up on criminal charges and sued by the families of the victims. We will be lucky to get out of this mess with the shirts on our backs."

Garrison took to his feet; his legs could barely hold him up. "I'm sorry, Bob."

"Yeah, so am I, Tom." Garrison slowly moved toward the exit. "Tom."

Garrison turned around. "Yes."

"What the hell happened to you?"

Garrison didn't answer. He just turned his back and walked out.

In his office, Garrison sat behind his desk wondering how everything could have gone so terribly wrong. He had such a good life and promising career and he began thinking about how this tragedy would affect his family. How could he possibly face them again? He picked up the gold pen that was a gift to him from the President of the United States and he began writing. The letter he was writing wasn't the letter of resignation his boss had requested; it was a suicide note to his family. Once the letter was finished, he glanced up at the clock on the wall and saw that it was 8:45 AM. Peering down at the paper on his desk with the headline that would ultimately seal his doom, he looked at the date on the paper thinking how this would be his last day on earth. *September eleventh, two-thousand and one.*

For a brief moment in time, the world stood still. The first airplane crashed into the north tower of the world trade center. Five minutes later, Kathy, came bursting into his office without knocking. "Turn on the TV!"

"Why?" he asked in a beaten tone.

"Tom, just do it."

Garrison's eyes were glued to the television as the second plane crashed into the south tower. Kathy sat next to him watching in horror. "Oh my God!" she said.

"We are being attacked," he said.

Kathy looked at her boss. "For you, this is a blessing," she said as she pointed to the paper on his desk. "This mess is already forgotten."

Garrison just looked at her without speaking as he processed what she had just said. "Thanks, Kathy. Please give me some time alone."

As the door closed behind her, Garrison picked up the letter he had just written, he glanced it over once, turned on the paper shredder and fed it through. He fixed his eyes back on the television screen and watched as the people of New York City ran through the streets as the first tower collapsed and billowing dust consumed Manhattan. He saw the cameras capturing the tears flowing from people as they cried out in anguish and fear. And with all this, he had a smile forming on his face, as he thought about how glorious terrorists could be.

TRUE LYME DISEASE TESTIMONIALS

My Lyme Story

"I'm not sure when I contracted Lyme disease. What I am sure of, is when it began to take control over my body. I was bitten as a teenager while pushing through the bush in Rhode Island, but I never noticed any symptoms after pulling a wood tick out of my shoulder. It was thirty-two years later when I began to suffer the consequences of the spirochete, Borrelia Burgdorferi. I truly believe the bug can lay dormant for months or years and surface and take control once our immune system has been severely compromised.

In August of 2006, I was sleep deprived and coming down with a cold, so I did what any red blooded American might do, I tried to drink it out of me. Less than a week later, all hell broke loose. I was weak and tired, had heart palpitations, my lower back went out and I could hardly walk, my neck was stiff and sore, numbness set into my hands and I had a shock-like tingling in my left upper back area.

Now, keep in mind, I'm very active including: running, weight training, martial arts, golf, and basketball. All of this came to a dead stop. At this point I didn't know what was wrong with me, so I went on the internet and began to research my symptoms. What kept popping up was Lyme disease. Also, my mother in law had just gotten over Lyme and she had similar symptoms. I went to the clinic (it was Sunday) and I tested negative for Lyme. I insisted that the doctor give me antibiotics, and he did, but only 10 days worth. In 3 days I began to feel better, but the shock-like tingling never went away. In February of 2007, it happened again, and this time, it came back even harder. All the symptoms I had before and I could hardly get out of bed. I also had blurry vision and the left side of my face was numb. My left foot had a burning sensation and my right wrist was so soar I couldn't pick up a glass. I went to my primary care physician and he tested me for Lyme (negative) again. I told him I was pretty sure I had Lyme and he said I didn't because it wasn't showing in my blood. I told him I had done research and that it's been estimated that 65% of people with Lyme test negative. He blew off my concerns and agreed to give me 14 days of light antibiotics. I asked for 30 days and he refused stating he was reluctant to give me any. Again, I felt better until October and it hit me even harder this time. I quit using my PCP and found a doctor that had been recommended by a friend that had Lyme and was treated for 90 days and it worked for him.

A new era in my treatment began. My new PCP tested me and I came up positive for Bartonella (Cat scratch fever) an associated tick born bacteria. Even though I didn't test positive for Lyme, my doctor indicated that many times patients will have more than one associated disease. He started me on a cocktail of strong antibiotics. Keep in mind, at this point I was a walking mess and I felt like I was going to die. I began to get better and continued treatment by switching every 30 days to different drugs. I continued this treatment for nine months and was feeling better, but the symptoms were not completely gone (especially the shock-like tingling in my back) this is a tell tale sign for me. At this point, I decided to stop antibiotics and see what would happen, (Mistake). The symptoms began to get worse, so I decided to find a (LLMD) Lyme Literate Medical Doctor. I found one in Orange CT, and he wanted $1,200 cash to see me, (didn't accept insurance). I wasn't about to buy a greedy doctor a new large flat screen TV, so I kept looking. Randy Sykes, a Lyme patient and advocate, gave me the name of a doctor in Longmeadow Massachusetts and I made an appointment. It took me 5 months to get in to see her (this is how many people are suffering from Lyme) and I have been seeing her ever since. On my first visit, she spent over an hour with me, getting to know my history and explaining the disease and how it affects our immune system. She asked me which antibiotic (out of several I had taken) made me feel the best. I told her Doxycycline worked the best for me. She offered a FIVE tier approach with me: A long term regimen of Doxycycline, an array of supplements and Chiropractic care to build up my immune system, a low sugar, high protein diet (Lyme hates protein, loves sugar) regular exercise, and meditation or a stress relieving exercise.

It has been two years since my first visit with her and I am feeling 90% better, and I've been off antibiotics for 3 months. I still feel the disease is somewhere inside my body, but not strong enough that my immune system can't control it, for now. I am still doing all the other methods she recommended, except the antibiotics.

This disease is the absolute worst thing that has ever happened to me and I feel for the millions of people out there that are suffering and dying every day. This is why I decided to write, *The Lyme Conspiracy.*"

—Joe

"Dear friends and partners, it has been a few weeks since I have talked to most of you. I am writing to give you an update on why you have not heard from me, and to tell you that I just got out of the hospital and I'm in much better shape than when I went in. You see the light at the end of the tunnel is not always a train.

Nevertheless, it was one of the most gruesome experiences that I have ever known. After 20 horrific days of fighting an unknown enemy that had severely impacted my body, we finally discovered that it was the dreaded Lyme disease that seemed to have given me a meningitis type of effect. Who could have figured as my first thought went back to the previous operations on my neck four years ago? After weeks of deliberating, emergency room and doctor visits, I was finally admitted to the hospital. It was about this time that I developed Bells Palsy, and they found that my spine was swelling. The diagnosis was that it had all been due to Lyme disease and now we have the pain and swelling under control. The next steps are: I will have to take intravenous antibiotics for the next 28 days to try and kill the disease.

This is why I need to take it slow and listen to the doctor. With that said, my hope is to follow up with just a few critical matters at work and leave the rest until I'm better. Of course all this is up in the air until I know if I have beaten the bacteria. Hopefully, I'll be on the mend and I look forward to seeing you all again soon!"

—Paul

"I don't know when I was first infected; I never had a rash, fever, malaise, or any symptoms after being bitten by a tick. I now have Chronic Lyme Disease (CLD) and here's my story.

All my life my health has been excellent and I've considered myself blessed with good fortune as it has allowed me to remain active and participate in many athletic events including: running marathons. Nothing could have prepared me for the disabling, debilitating sickness of CLD.

While this story may be long and detailed, it is important to see how chronic Lyme disease can engulf an otherwise healthy life to one of humility and desperation. This story begins with the 2008 Christmas Holiday when I developed a very different ache and burn in my left hamstring. I was treadmill running, and assumed this ailment was another athletic overuse injury and that my body was just getting old. This strange feeling seemed to gradually worsen over time, even though I backed off from running.

Over the spring, my hamstring became more painful. Driving became a problem and it felt as though my hamstring was burning from the inside out. The stiffness was more pronounced in both legs now, from the hips down to my knees. My love of yard work was no longer fun. I caught poison ivy in late May and needed steroids to help get rid the allergic reaction. After I finished the three week prescription, something very frightening happened;

one Saturday morning in June I could not get out of bed. My legs, back and arms were so painfully stiff and there was joint pain in my hip and knee. My arms were tingling and felt partially numb and the burning in both hamstrings was so intense like something I've never experienced before. Once upright, the muscles in my legs felt as though they were tearing apart. The worst problem I had was with my arms. They burned, had numbness, tingling, electrical shock sensations and a feeling of heaviness. At times I wished I could cut my arms off. There is no exaggeration when I say this would go on for days without relief. The pain was continuous from the moment I woke until falling asleep. This continued for the next few days and I began to suspecting Lyme disease, so I went to my doctor to explain the symptoms. He ordered a Lyme test but did not prescribe anything for me. The results of my Lyme test were negative, but my (CRT) was off the charts indicating an inflammation was going on, which was causing my muscle and joint pain. The doctor diagnosed me with Polymyalgia Rhuematica (PMR), prescribed 20 mg of Prednisone a day and I was told I should see a positive response and improvement in three days. The only change was some relief of pain but the symptoms continued. After researching my symptoms, I wasn't so sure that PMR was my condition and thought it could be more of a MS or Lyme disease diagnosis.

Over time, I realized it was difficult for me to concentrate on simple tasks and found myself getting easily confused. There were several instances where I drove in the wrong direction while driving on roads I was familiar with; causing a couple of anxiety attacks. Also, I had a few very intense fits of rage and felt completely out of control. I was unexplainably exhausted, which was not like me. My other symptoms seemed to migrate. I never knew which joint or muscle would be troublesome next. I began to worry I might never learn what was wrong and it would plague me for the rest of my life.

In July, I was tested again for Lyme and the results were negative. My generalist referred me to a specialist, a Rheumatologist at Hartford Hospital. Many tests were run and the results concluded there was no rheumatoid or osteoarthritis involved, nor did I have Fibromyalgia. When I brought up Lyme, the doctor didn't want to talk about it. Sobbing, I wanted answers to why I had pain, muscle weakness, and exhaustion? He agreed to order another Lyme test which again was normal. The Rheumatologist stuck by my generalists' original PMR diagnosis, but further refined the diagnosis as an 'a-typical' form of PMR, and he doubled the dosage of steroids to 40 mg / day. This was so wrong, so as I left the office I requested copies of all my tests and files and I never filled the prescription.

The next step was to I contact a neurologist to determine if I had a neurological condition such as MS or MD. My mother died at age fifty-four from MD and wondered if I might be developing some form of MD; after all, I had three false negative Lyme tests.

The Neurologist gave me a thorough exam and ruled out all myopathic and neuromuscular conditions such as MS, MD, Fibromyalgia, Chronic Fatigue, and PMR. After eliminating these diseases, she ordered another Lyme test and it was negative. My Neurologist felt there was a strong possibility of Lyme but was reluctant start antibiotics without a positive test and prescribed me Vicotin, which didn't help anymore than the OTC pain relievers. Vicotin only took the edge off for a couple hours and then right back to pain, so after three days I discontinued the drug.

Over the next couple of weeks I was making calls daily to seek out Lyme Literate Medical Doctors. I contacted some of the most well known LLMD's in New England, speaking with doctors from Massachusetts, New York, Long Island, and here in Connecticut. No Lyme Specialist was able to see me for at least three months and I needed immediate attention. Monitoring my own prognosis, I predicted within three months I'd be partially paralyzed and bedridden, unable to work or care for myself. I was not sleeping well and losing weight. I was more depressed than ever, stopped smiling and laughing altogether as became disengaged with life. I wasn't sure I would live to see my 15 year old daughter graduate from High School. It was difficult for me to shower and dress myself, never mind driving and walking. I began to feel helpless, hopeless and so alone, and depression overcame me. I began conjuring ways to end my life. My faith in God would be what kept me alive.

During my worst flare in early October, my brother in law, also afflicted with chronic Lyme disease, came down from New Hampshire to check on my condition. He felt strongly his Lyme literate MD could clinically diagnose me based on my symptoms and he insisted I send my blood work to IGenX. Desperate; I had my blood tested for the 5th time and waited nearly two agonizing weeks for the results. The diagnostics was positive for Lyme disease, so began my treatment with the same LLMD that was treating my brother in law in New Hampshire.

During my first visit, I learned that all the steroids I had taken, weakened my immune system and allowed the Lyme bacteria to grow and invade my body at a faster rate. This would negatively impact the length of time for my treatment plan. I was prescribed multiple antibiotics which ultimately saved my life. Also, I was prescribed a sedative to help with the pain and to help me sleep.

I am now almost four months into treatment. According to my LLMD, the fourth month is a key marker, and he expects to see a change in my condition and I'm heading in that direction. I will be starting a new drug therapy this week designed to go after the cysts, after which I should see more improvement. In retrospect, I can say some of my symptoms had begun in 2007 as minor, short lived interferences, but came into full bloom after the first round of steroids for the poison ivy. The steroids were the trigger in my case. I look forward to the day when the CDC and IDSA will recognize this debilitating disease as treatable with long term antibiotics, and I hope and pray this will happen soon. My heart goes out to all those before me and those yet to be diagnosed with this terrible disease."

—Susan

"My name is Joshua and I have had Lyme disease since the summer of 2000 when my mother pulled two ticks from my body, one behind my left knee and the other behind my right ear. I never got a bull's-eye rash and I started having joint pain in the fall, and was told by my pediatrician I was having growing pains and fatigue due to my intense karate training. I got physically worse and worse as time progressed. I had extreme fatigue that was unrelieved by rest and sleep. My joints ached and I lost small patches of hair the size of quarters all over my head. I had headaches, could not concentrate in school, lost my short-term memory, and could not play sports or take karate. I was dizzy and had chest pain and neck stiffness and for a short time I couldn't walk. With my mother's persistence, the doctor tested me for Lyme disease in the spring of 2001. I tested positive for Lyme and received three weeks of Doxycycline. My symptoms improved and I thought I was better. In October 2001, I had a relapse and I felt like I had the flu with extreme fatigue and severe joint pain to the point I could hardly walk. I came home from school one day and was in the worst pain of my life and I was unable to stand on my own two feet. My mom rushed me to the emergency room and the doctors at the hospital diagnosed me with joint complications due to the flu. They fit me for crutches at the hospital and told me I would be better in about three days. Three days passed and I was not better, but much worse. My mom sent me to school on crutches and I couldn't finish my school work or play with my friends. I was in extreme pain day and night and even though I was on several pain pills it didn't relieve my pain but only made me feel worse and gave me stomachaches.

At this point, I looked as sick as I felt and many classmates asked me what was wrong and if I had cancer. Our pediatrician told my mom that I could not have Lyme because I was already treated for it. I had more blood tests that showed positive for Lyme disease and I was sent to a rheumatologist at the Children's Hospital. He looked at me for about 60 seconds and sent me for x-rays. Ignoring my positive Lyme test, he diagnosed me with arthritis and told my mom it would be a long time before I would walk without my crutches. He told my mom to call the office and schedule an appointment to have an operation in two weeks to have my hips drained. My mother ignored the rheumatologist's suggestion to pursue surgery and I went to see an infectious disease specialist. He told me that my symptoms were all in my head and he told me to tell my mom the truth that I was making it up so I didn't have to go to school. I was in the worst physical health I had ever been in, it even hurt for me to talk and he told me to stop pretending. He told my mom I did not have Lyme disease and that antibiotics wouldn't work. I was misdiagnosed again and my positive Lyme test was overlooked.

My parents could not find a doctor to treat me for Lyme that would be covered by insurance, so they took me to Dr. Charles Ray Jones, a Lyme literate doctor. My parents paid out of pocket for my treatment and Dr. Jones took the time to listen to me and cared enough to diagnose me properly. I was given Amoxicillin and Zithromax and was walking without crutches after three weeks. I continued my treatment for nine months and had significant improvement in my health.

I have been off all medication now for over a year and a half. I am taking karate classes again and I'm studying for my black belt. I am thankful to God for my health and thankful for the responsible physicians who take the time to listen to their patients even if the patient is a kid."

—Joshua

"My name is Elise and I have chronic Lyme disease. Three years ago I was misdiagnosed with rheumatoid arthritis by my primary care physician because I had migrating joint pain. I never saw the tick and I did not have a bull's eye rash. Luckily, as my own health advocate, I did more research and I obtained a second opinion.

Two and a half years ago, I was given a clinical diagnosis of Lyme disease from a doctor who understands tick-borne diseases and who uses a lab that is proficient in identifying the antibodies created by the Lyme bacteria. I was treated with seven months of oral antibiotics before I decided it was safe to try and conceive a second child.

At this point I had been hosting the disease for over three years. We had intentionally postponed having a second child until we felt we had done our best to rid my body of the dangerous bacteria. I conceived our second child in March 2002 and I entered the pregnancy feeling confident that we would have a healthy child. The 15-week ultrasound showed a healthy baby with a strong heart and all its organs were functioning normally. At 16 weeks, the remaining test results were all perfect. At 18 weeks, I sensed something was wrong and my instinct was correct. When the time came to deliver our child, the baby boy was dead.

Soon after I began wondering if Lyme disease had caused this tragedy. I had read that Lyme disease could cause miscarriage, but there was no evidence to prove it. I called my Lyme doctor and a lab skilled in detecting the bacteria so I could determine how to test the fetus and the placenta for the bacteria. I needed an answer and I received that answer the next Monday when the OB called me to report that the fetus and the placenta were PCR-positive for the Lyme bacteria. He concluded that the Lyme bacterial infection had caused the fetal demise.

We grieved all over again. How had these small bacteria survived seven months of antibiotics and continued to destroy our lives. We thought that the Lyme disease had been killed after seven months of antibiotics, but we were wrong.

If the insurance company would have paid the four hundred dollars for a detailed band blood test and not just the basic blood test they cover, we would have known the disease still invaded my body and we would have been spared the tragedy of losing a child and the cost would have been much less for the insurance company in the end. These insurance companies are blinded by greed."

—Elise

"It pains me today when I think of how many people really have Lyme disease but are being treated for Multiple Sclerosis. Think about it: Nobody knows what causes MS, so why treat it with steroids and not antibiotics? In 1987, when I was pregnant with my daughter, I had a rash on my stomach. The doctor said it looked like some form of shingles, but it didn't hurt. Jacqueline was born a beautiful, healthy girl. During the next two and a half months, we noticed her eyes did not seem to focus. Her legs would turn purplish in color and one time her leg swelled three times its normal size. On June 6, 1988, she passed away from Sudden Infant Death Syndrome. When I was pregnant with my son, I started having debilitating fatigue. But I was told this was because I was pregnant. After he was born, the fatigue was still there. But now my doctor said it was due to depression because of the loss of my daughter. In 1990, I went to the emergency room because I was vomiting, lightheaded and had pains in my stomach. I was told I had a viral infection. I started having nausea, pain in my left ear and the fatigue was still present.

On October 31, 1992, I had to leave work because I was vomiting, had lightheadedness and I was off-balance with my walking. My mother brought me to the emergency room. When we got there, the nurse replied, "She looks like she's having a stroke." The physicians did blood work and checked me

out. I was lying on a stretcher when they told me I should go home and
sleep. After my symptoms became worse, I had a CAT scan and an
MRI and I saw a neurologist. I was admitted to the hospital on November 4
and had blood work drawn and was started on steroids. My PCP came in and
told me he had news. He said, "You had Lyme disease at one time, but you
don't have it any more." He proceeded to tell me that I had Multiple
Sclerosis and life as I knew it would forever be changed. I thought about
what my doctor had just told me, but I was never treated for Lyme disease,
so how did it go away all by itself? When I got out of the hospital, I asked
my PCP if I might still have Lyme and he said no. Over the next month, I
had profuse vomiting, Diarrhea and debilitating fatigue. My PCP now stated
I had the flu because of my immune system was weak from the MS. Over
the years, I would question if Lyme disease was a possibility because I was
always so sick. There were so many different symptoms and I was so
debilitated that I could not function. My life was a miserable existence. Over
the years, I have had steroids intravenously eight times and had been
prescribed over fifty different medications for my so many different
ailments. Eventually I had been treated with chemotherapy for a legion on
the brain. I started experiencing pain throughout my entire body. My nausea
was so bad I wanted to die. The light hurt my eyes and if someone hugged
me, my whole body would hurt. Clothes bothered my skin and my skin felt
like I had bugs crawling in it. With little hope left, my husband and I
decided to research my medical records from the hospital I had received
care at so many years earlier and we found a positive test for Lyme disease.
I brought it to my PCP and he said, "Yes. The blood test was positive, and
that's why we did the spinal tap." All those years I was told nothing showed
positive for Lyme disease and now my doctor tells me that a test did show
Lyme, but that it was gone now and that maybe I could have Fibromyalgia
now on top of my MS. I told him that I wanted to see an infectious disease
doctor but he said, "No, because he will say you have Lyme disease and put
you on medication that you do not need. Finally, out of desperation, I
brought my records to a doctor in New Jersey. He looked at my records, did
blood work, and he was the first doctor to say, "You have chronic Lyme
disease and you have had it for years. He immediately put me on an
aggressive treatment of antibiotics and over the next couple of months my
family and I would notice considerable improvement. I got a lawyer and he
would subpoena my records from all the doctors and hospitals I saw over the
years. I have improved tremendously from where I was two years ago and to
think that all of this could have been avoided if I had a competent doctor
that didn't dismiss Lyme disease so easily because he was ignorant about the
disease."

—Tammy

Joseph J. Bradley is a former metropolitan police officer with a Masters Degree in Criminology. He is the author of several mystery thrillers, including, Ticket To Paradise. Joseph lives in Connecticut with his wife and three children. He has been fighting chronic Lyme disease since 2006.